To my Darling Mizuki...

My Sunshine on
The cold Days.

Thank you for supporting
Local Art and Thank
you for being my
friend.

WL Bush
03/15/06
#013

Kill Switch

WL Bush

WingSpan Press

Author's Note: Several instances occur where British grammar and Afrikaans are used to enhance the atmosphere of this narrative, such as in the news article that begins it. Also, the intent of this novel is not to glorify violence or promote criminal activity in any form.

Printed in the United States of America

Published by WingSpan Press, Livermore, CA
www.wingspanpress.com

The WingSpan name, logo and colophon are the trademarks of WingSpan Publishing.

ISBN 978-1-59594-144-2

First edition 2007

Library of Congress Control Number 2007923052

"Time is a river, a violent current of events, glimpsed once and already carried past us. Another follows and is gone." – Marcus Aurelius

Dedicated with love to: MH Bush, G Bush, S Robinson, J Hanna, JA Dougherty, V Sonandzi, N Luhabe, F Kahlo, D Fairclough, D Greer, U Newkirk, C McCray, and the Republic of South Africa.

PROLOGUE

CAPE TIMES

MONDAY FEBRUARY 7, 2005

TULANIVILLE RESIDENTS PICK UP THE PIECES

1,700 homeless in blaze, 2 dead

PHILDA ASSOP and SAPA

PEOPLE LIVING in the Tulaniville informal settlement will start to rebuild their lives today after a devastating fire ravaged their densely populated settlement, leaving about 1 700 homeless.

The skeletal remains of an adult were found, one infant died from smoke inhalation, and seven people, including two children, were seriously injured as the flames destroyed hundreds of homes late Sunday night.

One of the residents claimed a man who had left a paraffin stove unattended as he took a nap started the fire.

Spokesman for Cape Town Disaster Management Johan Minnie said the fire had affected 442 families. "If you want to know how many individuals were left homeless you can multiply that figure by four," said Minnie.

He said the fire had been under control since early this morning as firefighters in 17 vehicles and aided by a helicopter battled the flames. This had been the first instance where a helicopter was deployed to fight a shack fire.

As the smoke cleared amidst the mangled remains of corrugated iron that would be recycled for new homes, several scavengers and scrap metal vendors quickly cleared what could be carried off. It was during this scavenger hunt that the charred skeletal remains of an adult person were found chained to a makeshift braii. SAPS were called in to investigate.

Nomalibongwe Mkwhe is unemployed and lived in Tulaniville with her two young children. Her story is not dissimilar to those of many victims of the blaze. She said she lost everything. “All our clothes got burnt in the fire and I don’t have any family to call upon in Cape Town after I broke off the relationship with the father of my children,” she said.

Most families left homeless by the fire were housed and fed in several marquee tents set up at the nearby Joe Slovo informal settlement, which had itself been razed by a shack fire on January 15. It costs the government R300 000 to house the people in the tents.

Minnie believes arsonists are to blame for many of the Peninsula fires over the past four days. “Yesterday there were seven fires: three in Hout Bay and on Red Hill, next to Ocean View, one at Tulaniville and at Strandfontein,” he said.

Though authorities do not believe the fires were connected, one thing is certain: on Sunday, there were several fires, including this devastating blaze at the Tulaniville informal settlement in Langa that appears to have left at least two people dead.

CHAPTER 1

WITHOUT DEVIATION, fifty-six-year-old Owen Nelson slept soundly between the hours of nine p.m. and five a.m. This was a habit he'd picked up from his father, Arthur Nelson. And – had he ever spent time with them – a habit he might have passed down to his own children. But Nelson belonged to that fading generation of American workers who were unapologetically married to their professions. The ones who wrote of martini lunches, golf outings, and lap dances as business expenses. The ones that took working vacations, dispensed fatherly advice via telephone, and only came home on holidays or for a quick change of laundry before the next flight to Denver.

But woe unto those who cross paths with Nelson the morning after his sleep has been disturbed. Tales of the irritable CEO firing underlings for being "too damn cheerful" were standard company lore. Yet it was with no regard for such unfortunate souls that Chuck Garland, Board Chairman of Global Media, made the late night call to Nelson's scrambled satellite phone. A groggy Nelson answered the phone on the fifth ring.

"Hello?"

"It's Chuck. There's just been another entry posted to the blog."

"So? Why wake the whole goddamn world? It's three in the fuckin' morning!"

"Owen, you need to start taking this more seriously. His entries have just jumped five years."

"So?"

"So our techs say the timeline is linear but the entries are random; there's no predicting him. He could start running his mouth any time."

"No shit," said Nelson, lighting a *Merit* cigarette in spite of his doctor's direct warning. A few months earlier, Nelson had undergone triple-bypass surgery so involved that his heart was moved two centimeters to the right.

"I've spoken with other members of the Board, my friend. We...

just don't think you have a handle on the situation. It's escalating. The number of hits to his website, the unfavorable e-mails we're getting, the internal questions…and now there's coverage in online news blogs. We just can't discount their influence. All we need is one national news source to pick up the story and we'll be fucked like a Saigon whore."

"Chuck, I've-"

"We'll lose billions in contracts, and our political connections will run for cover at the first sign of scandal. There'll be a run on our stock; afterwards our shares won't be worth using to line a birdcage and you're bothered by a wake-up call? You *need* a wake-up call!"

"I've got a plan," said Nelson, exhaling thick clouds of smoke into the darkness.

"So far, your plan has involved letting your prodigal son continue his blog, meaning continued publicity for us. We want you to pay him his money and be done with it."

"Now wait just a goddamn minute!" Nelson bellowed, sitting up in bed. "My father, God rest him, built this company, while you were still pickin' your ass and callin' it candy! He died at his desk, breathin' his last breath for this company! And you have the balls to dictate to me this company's best interest?"

Nelson's startled wife crossed the hall from her room and flung open his bedroom door. Peering in, she saw Nelson in bed smoking. She shook her head disapprovingly and stomped back down the hall while the two men held their phones in silence, realizing they may have both gone too far.

"Out of respect for your father," said Garland, "we elected you as our CEO. And while you may be the largest individual stockholder, it's our money and influence that's keeping you in silk pajamas. We paved the way for GM's global expansion, domestic surveillance, and military applications – things your father never imagined. So while you're doing all your planning, bear this in mind: you're *not* John Wayne. You're the CEO of a multi-billion dollar global corporation who needs to stay focused on business. Don't make it personal."

Nelson poured a glass of water from the stainless steel pitcher on his nightstand. "So what do you distinguished gentlemen of the Board want me to do?"

"We want you to pay him his money and close the issue. But…

keep him on the payroll. If the AIDS research pans out, we can take credit for it; if it doesn't, it's a tax write-off."

"And if he decides to keep the money…can we write *him* off?"

"I'm not sure what you mean, my friend, but certainly we know from experience that such things shouldn't be discussed on the phone, regardless of the level of security."

Nelson rubbed the scarred chest that held his rapidly beating heart and contemptuously curled his lip. "If we pay, that means I pay! My bonuses, my bottom line!"

"Owen, we don't give a damn about the money. It's *nothing* to us. You gave him the keys to the kingdom so you're right; it is your bottom that's on the line! The Board is not happy. There are enough votes against you now to convene and force you out!"

Nelson ran his fingers through his disheveled white pompadour, dropping ashes onto his silk pajamas. He thought about his father, GM's founder. He realized he was being blackmailed into spending more money than Art Nelson had made his entire life. He took two aspirin from an almost empty bottle of *Bayer* and washed them down.

"Okay...I'll make the arrangements to pay him. But I'm sure this is gonna come back to haunt us. Hell, Chuck, I know Joe better than he knows himself. I made him! He's already made it personal."

"Well congratulations; you made him too well. We'll expect to hear from you within the next -"

"I believe him, by the way," Nelson interjected. "I believe he really *is* gonna give it away. He's got no kids, no responsibilities, and he was crazy as a loon from the get-go. Now you wanna make him crazy and wealthy."

"It's better than him making all of us *un*-wealthy. Just do what the Board wants. Get over your pride."

"Damn it, somethin' just don't sit right. Chuck ol' boy, I'm callin' in a favor."

"What favor?"

"What is it, Tuesday morning? Just give me seven more days – seven days to resolve this shit my way. If I can't, I'll do things the Board's way."

"What do you have in mind?"

"I'd better keep you in the dark 'til it's over."

"And why should we believe this will work?"

"Oh, it'll work. I'm calling in Mr. K."

Garland fell silent while he considered this new development. "Okay Nelson, I'll talk to the Board. You've got your week; 'til Tuesday, February first. Otherwise, you'd better learn to swallow your pride, or take up gardening."

"Fine. We have ourselves a deal."

"Sure. A deal. Only, we've scoured half that continent in the past month and turned up nothing; how in hell do you expect to find him?"

"With bait, ol' boy. Carefully selected bait."

"Bait?"

"You gotta use honey to catch flies."

"What honey?" Garland asked perplexedly.

"His."

Chapter 2

I WAS not sure why Global Media had flown me from Michigan to its headquarters in Manhattan with such urgency. My daily numbers as of this morning were a respectable eighty-three and eighty-eight percent. Neither could it have been my weeklies; it was still only Thursday. Three hours later, after meeting with senior level management, I was *still* unsure.

I sat through that meeting dumbfounded, listening to Global Media's CEO and my Area Supervisor delicately hedge around their recent invasions of my personal privacy. They seemed to be telling me that my personal background qualified me for a confidential assignment but they would not say exactly how. Since they were also sketchy on the assignment itself, the Rosatti in me guessed it involved something unethical, if not illegal. But since they repeatedly tossed out the phrase "all expense paid," I decided it could be my long awaited chance to travel abroad. I sat up straight, presented my best corporate grin, and agreed to their top-secret assignment.

"Ms. Rosatti," Nelson said, "how do you feel about visiting Africa? The...*Dark Continent*?"

"I guess I'd be excited," I said smiling. "Any place is better than Michigan in January."

I began to loosen up, unclenching my hands and placing them on the marble conference table.

"Good," said Nelson, nodding his head.

Owen Nelson was our CEO and the name on the bottom line of our paychecks. He sat alone, atop an information database worth billions. Knowing everyone's secrets kept him the lone tap on that keg of information and also protected him from anti-trust legislation.

Nelson was old but wore age like an obvious disguise, like a wolf hurriedly dressed in sheep's clothing. Staring at me, Nelson kept nodding his slick pompadour of peppered white hair in agreement. It suddenly felt more like he was staring *into* me and knew everything about me, even intimate things.

"Good. Real good," Nelson said. "Because, if you accepted our offer to be our confidential emissary in South Africa, your per diem would be three times that of any state-to-state assignment. In addition, we'll increase your AMEX business account to…what is that Dave, twenty thousand?"

"No, ten thousand's the max," said Green.

"…Ten thousand for things above and beyond," said Nelson, exaggerating quotation marks in the air with wrinkled fingers. "You'll be staying at the Metropole Hotel in Cape Town. Strictly four star. Discreet but still near everything. You'll also have a driver – all expensed."

"I don't mind staying at a chain hotel, I'm not real-"

"No, you'll stay at *that* hotel!" Sensing his severity, Nelson forced an iron smile and switched gears. "Lisa, we don't mind spendin' a lil' extra money because…your performance in the field has been exemplary the past year, and-"

"Six months," Green added. "She's only been with us for six months."

"Is that all? Well she performs like a goddamned seasoned vet!" Nelson said, glaring at Green who averted his eyes to the manila folder in front of him. "The point is you've done a great job for us and you deserve ol' GM to spend a few extra bucks on you, right Dave? Ha-ha! This ol' girl has proven her commitment to us, time and time again."

I smiled and tried to look appreciative but was surprised that Nelson had taken the time to notice my work in the field. It did not seem like something a CEO with over five thousand employees would naturally do. In fact, that was the first time I had seen him in the six months I worked there.

On the other hand, everyone knew our ubiquitous company president, Susan White. She had shaken my hand last August when she spoke at our training school in Florida. She was sweet and mannerly, kind of like my mother, so I guess I always knew there had to be someone like Nelson in the background. There's no way White could have been the one steering GM, a multi-billion dollar info industry, bound in blood to the highest levels of the federal government. That was as unlikely as Mom running the Rosatti family business, since our family business was crime.

Green leaned forward, clearing his throat to speak, and slid a manila file folder across the green marble table. "We're budgeting this assignment for five days. So if you find Joe early, you can hang out there on our tab. Go to the beach, get a tan…whatever."

If Green was being humorous, I didn't know him well enough to tell. Although Green was my Area Supervisor, I knew nothing more than I had heard gossiped about him. He was a company man from balls to bones. He was recruited directly out of college and had spent the last seventeen years at GM, rising steadily in its ranks. As a result, he is the divorced father of two and has a full head of gray hair at age thirty-nine.

I spoke to Green by phone once every few days and saw him perhaps once a month. GM has the type of management structure that most workers want: never seen and seldom heard. Green was just a Monday morning conference call; a name on sticky labels I use to forward hard copies of reports. He and Nelson were both faceless names; faceless gray-haired names that were suddenly throwing money at me but had not told me why.

"Dave," I said, "I guess I'm still not sure what you want me to do. Could you be a bit more specific or-"

"Stop the tape," Nelson said, tapping a button on his intercom. "And Lila, honey, no interruptions."

Green stood up and crossed the floor, closing the conference room's privacy blinds. He returned to his seat opposite me and looked at Nelson. Nelson, who was sitting at the head of the conference table, leaned closer to me – close enough for me to see his blue eyes were rimmed with gray – and began speaking to me slowly in a patronizing Southern twang, like he was a tourist who had just stopped me on the streets of Tijuana and was asking for directions.

"I'm talkin' to you confidentially now, Lisa," he said as he grabbed my shoulder. "What I say can't ever leave this room. Otherwise, it would violate your confidentiality agreement with Global Media and we'd have no choice but to prosecute you under State and Federal law. You understand that, sweetheart?"

"I understand," I said. But he was the one that should have feared prosecution; between calling me *sweetheart* and massaging my shoulder, he was certainly breaking some kind of law. He might as well have slapped me on the ass and sent me for coffee.

He would not have cared even if he realized what he was doing; men like Nelson never got so much as a parking ticket. The world worships power, and information – the breadcrumbs we all leave from the cradle to the grave – is the last true power. Since GM warehouses and controls that information, GM is the world's new god.

Global Media was a pioneer industry when Arthur Nelson started it in 1954, coinciding with the advent of television. Since then, GM had patented all viable media ratings systems. By using their surveys as benign springboards into people's homes, GM had spent the last fifty-one years quietly collecting seemingly trivial information on every household in America. The result has been a media and data gold mine.

Hospitals call us before admitting patients who are not conscious or cannot verify insurance coverage. An auto policy is rarely written in America without a call to GM to rate the type of driver an applicant is likely to be. And while we do not actually *score* credit, we do provide a probability index that major creditors use in predicting an applicant's likelihood of debt repayment.

I did not know how much information we warehoused for sure but I knew GM maintained an extensive file on every American born since 1955. When Art Nelson died in his office in 1986, all that power and wealth ceremoniously passed to his only son, Owen – along with all its privileges and perks.

Although GM maintains a veil of secrecy, it's well known within the company that during the nineties, the Democratic National Convention became captivated with GM's unpublicized ability to correctly predict the outcome of presidential elections (three *consecutive* presidential elections) state-by-state. The odd thing was that on each occasion, GM had correctly predicted the outcome the night *before* voting booths were open. It was done with a proprietary formula involving phone surveys and absentee ballots.

GM also advised the Clintons that middleclass voters cared less about sex scandals than the economy. After sweeping into power, The Clinton White House showed their gratitude by signing off on legislation allowing GM to go global. In a joint effort with the Pentagon, the CIA, and the NSA, the White House granted GM the security clearance and funding enabling them to track world figures and so-called Enemies of the State by satellite.

It's strange how much the media focused on all those space shuttle trips during the nineties, but never focused on the unmanned satellites we shot into space. There were six but one fell. The biggest one, Wormwood, has infrared/heat imaging like the others, but it also has a telescope bigger than NASA's Hubbell. It can zoom in on a man watering his front lawn and tell you if his nozzle is brass or plastic.

We have always been connected by consent to the phone lines of millions of Americans, but few people know we *randomly* download phone calls to "test the integrity of the line" used for TV data transmission. Such practices are otherwise known as domestic surveillance–something the NSA and the Pentagon are Constitutionally barred from doing. When the Bush Administration came into power, they found this to be GM's most impressive credential. The Republican-controlled Congress rammed through legislation giving GM even more discretionary authority, and that is how GM chooses to remain: discreet. Controlling things remotely. Observing from the shadows. Even our stock trades under an assumed acronym.

With government help, GM went global, financially exploiting the worldwide implications of our probability formulas and near infinite database. Information is power, and that power makes GM virtually immune to prosecution. In fact, if I did try and sue, GM could screw up my identity so bad, I wouldn't be able to get a job serving *Happy Meals*.

Bearing all that in mind, I adjusted my chair and reached for a glass of water, diplomatically freeing my shoulder from Nelson's clutch while he prattled on.

"Lisa, you have been quite impressive in your time here. I'll tell ya, I'm proud as a poppa possum to have you on my team. One of Nelson's Angels, ha-ha! With our African expansion, excitin' opportunities are opening up for Field Reps like yourself. Reps who want to have a bright future here at GM! But there are other employees…greedy little pissant, blackmailing scum, who actually want to-"

Green coughed, signaling Nelson to catch himself. Nelson adjusted his chair, positioning it even closer to mine, and continued.

"Now, we have a *huge* pot of gold at the end of the rainbow, for those who've proven they will put the company first. Dave here will tell you this job has its rewards, but you need to treat it with love and respect; the way you would your own family. 'Cause, at the end of the day, that's *all* we are here – a big ol' happy family. Ha-ha!"

Nelson chortled at his own perceived eloquence. I smiled supportively but was still clueless. All I could hear was "all expense paid."

"Lisa," Nelson continued, "It saddens me to say that one of our key family members has gone off the range. He's run off into the bush down there and gotten jungle fever. He's completely lost his fuckin' mind and…I just can't believe I'm saying this, he has…son of a bitch! Dave, help me out?"

"Joseph Bosco Junior," Green said.

"Sorry?" I said.

"Do you remember Joe Bosco?"

"No. Should I?"

"He was a Field Rep, like you. Worked in Michigan for a while, then New York and Florida…have you ever met him? Open that folder, there's a picture of him in it."

I looked at Nelson, whose face was now beet red. He dabbed at it with a handkerchief, sneering his displeasure at the sound of Bosco's name. I opened the folder to a sudden flood of emotions and fought to keep my complexion from flushing.

"I never saw him before. What's this about?"

"Joe was appointed Special Project Director for our African Expansion Project," Dave said. "He went down there, worked for eight months, and hasn't been seen since. He's been our man there since last April. For over eight months he posted record target numbers, getting us more data and demographic penetration than we ever expected. Then, last December twenty-ninth, he just vanished. Now we can't get to any of the data his team collected; we think he locked us out of our own mainframe."

"The issue here is money!" said Nelson slamming his fist on the table. "This expansion took five years to coordinate and hundreds of millions to set up. Our investors and business partners are pissed! The Board convened an emergency session two days ago; we have five days to clean this shit up or I'm gonna fire people left and right! Y'all get the picture? Heads are gonna roll!"

Nelson popped a few pills in his mouth, downed a glass of water and continued his path toward coronary thrombosis. "Do you know what a blog is, Lisa?"

"Yes. It's like an online personal journal, right?"

"It's a diary made for cyber-pervs to confess how they like butt-fuckin' little boys. Three billion dollars to set up the information highway and most of the world uses it for masturbation.

"As you know, our Internet Division is dedicated to tracking online activity. Part of that involves keeping tabs on the use of our brand name and logo. Since Joe vanished, online activity referring to GM has risen over three hundred percent. In one month, there've been over a million references to us online. That's damn high for a company whose existence is unknown to ninety percent of world.

"Most of the online chatter involves a blog – *Head167*. It went online within hours of Bosco's disappearance. Our files suggest the blog exactly mirrors Joe Bosco's life. It's linear but it's updated at random. Our concern is that...private company business will be made available online when he posts dates that coincide with his employment here. Actually, we think that's his ultimate goal." Nelson ran his fingers through his hair, looking flustered.

"What does that mean, the blog's name?" I asked them.

"We don't know yet," said Green, "but we're working on it."

"Mr. Nelson, why...why don't we just get some kind of legal order, shutting the website down?" I asked.

"Dave?" said Nelson.

"No, that wouldn't work," said Green. "We had legal look at it as soon as ID discovered it. The blog's internationally and constitutionally protected. We can't get a cease and desist if we can't prove who's making it. It could be some guy in China. We can't even use the standard employee agreement to legally attach the blog as GM work product. How could we prove when he wrote it? His laptop was recovered in his hotel room, with the hard drive wiped clean."

"And what about the police over there or the FBI?" I asked. "He *is* a missing American citizen, right?"

"No. Absolutely no police," Green said. "This is a confidential assignment. Doing things like declaring him missing or contesting his website would only lend it credibility and create a media frenzy that could spill over onto our confidential partners and shareholders."

"Forgive me for asking obvious questions but can't we just trace the IP addresses that correspond with the entries?" I asked.

Nelson looked at his watch visibly annoyed and slapped his hand flat on the table, needing something to hold to keep from rising up in a rage.

"I'll field this one Dave. And we'll have to make this the last question; I've got a board meeting. The blog is legally protected and has an encrypted password. We don't know anything until the pages appear online. Right now, we're working on cracking the password but he must be changing it every other second. We're also negotiating with its web host for access but we're not holding our breath; they're First Amendment freaks. All we could get out of them was that the account was paid in advance through this year but they won't say by whom. We're puttin' the screws to them though. Don't worry; we know everybody's got some skeletons in their closet. Right Lisa?

"But what are we really talkin' here? I could make one phone call and buy the site's entire domain. Hell, I could even buy his IP. But who's to say his blog wouldn't pop up an hour later under another domain? What if he overreacts and rashly publishes things that are… not only lies, but also not his right to publish? No. We got to run this thing to ground. Chop it all down from root to fruit."

"Lisa," said Green, "I've known Joe since he joined GM. I was his trainer. He's been to my house and played with my kids. I know what he's like and some of this blog is word-for-word things he's told me about his personal life. Based on that, probability dictates it's either Joe or someone directed by Joe. Plus, if anyone has the brains and nerve to cripple our mainframe, it would be Joe.

"Even so, when you find him, tell him we don't want to prosecute. We don't even want to terminate him. We just want our AEP database back online and all's forgiven. We'd try and restore it ourselves but we don't want to end up with twenty million dollars worth of scrap metal."

"Maybe the mainframe malfunctioned because of user error," I said defensively, "or just…just broke down on the same day he quit. That's possible, right? I mean, if you have no proof, this could all be a coincidence, right?"

"Coincidence?" Nelson sneered, "Honey, when you get more than six months under your skirt, you'll find there *are* no real coincidences, only probabilities; most of them controlled by us. Oh, there's no doubt he did it, just like there's no doubt that you *will* find him."

"We've polygraphed everyone else down there," said Dave, "Joe just seems the most probable suspect at this point, especially with that blog. It looks like he used his supervisor access to remotely disable the mainframe but we can't prove it until the mainframe's back up. It would be pretty much near impossible for most people to even think of it. You'll see when you get there; our AEP headquarters runs with the precision of an atomic clock and is locked down tighter than Fort Knox. It's heavily secured but as the Director of the AEP, Joe would've had two-way access to the mainframe, twenty-four hours a day – even from his field laptop.

"This past December twenty-ninth at eight a.m., the AEP mainframe simply ceased to function. Since then, the only data we can get out the mainframe is the error prompt: **System Failure: No One Should Own Information**. Around the same time, Joe Bosco effectively vanished from the face of the Earth."

"Look, we need that data!" roared Nelson. "Joe was a master at suckin' up to the tribes and cultures down there – especially the indigents. Our chances of recollectin' the same data in the field are less than five percent, and every day we can't manipulate that data costs us millions in projected revenue. But we can't risk losin' it all by monkeyin' around with the mainframe! We need his goddamn anti-virus program!" Nelson was standing now, leaning over the table in front of Green. He was blood red, shaking and pointing. "We are hemorrhagin' millions of dollars per day! You trained that cocksucker *and* recommended him for the AEP! I won't *ever* forget that!"

Nelson sat down. His white shirt sticky with perspiration and breath heavy, like an out of shape boxer in the late rounds. His hand trembled noticeably as he clutched for the water pitcher.

"Dave...Lisa...I apologize," Nelson said with a veneer of contrition. "My daddy and I – God rest his soul – built this company from the ground up. We have survived corporate takeovers, allegations of monopoly, of wire-tapping...we didn't do all that to watch it die in scandal on the evening news.

"I personally don't give a damn if Joe never comes back. He can marry a goddamn gorilla over there and spend the rest of his life knee-deep in ape shit. He never has to hear from GM again and you tell him that. Tell him we won't prosecute. We'll pay out all his accrued benefits, and put up another…million in cash. All we want is our data and for him to shut down that damn blog!" Nelson stabbed the table demonstratively with his finger while he spoke.

"Now I could be wrong," he continued. "It could all be a *coincidence*, like you say. He could be dead from…malaria or AIDS or whatever else; who knows what he's stuck his pecker into down there. But if he's alive, we want you to find him, make contact, and burn up the phone lines contactin' us!"

"And what do I do if he's…dead?" I asked.

"You buy a shovel!" said Nelson.

"And a camera," said Green.

Nelson massaged his forehead apprehensively before continuing. "He wanted this assignment and used up every favor owed him to get it. He lobbied for the job like a goddamn Washington insider. So in all fairness, I shouldn't be blamin' just Dave. I had the final say and interviewed him *twice* before promoting him! I had the usual battery of psych reports, background checks…I knew more about Joe than he knew about himself. He was a crazy son of a bitch; but the way he was able to gather our data and get folks to cooperate made him…invaluable. Though unsound, he personified our formula."

Nelson stood up again and walked over to the wall-sized safety glass window. He looked out on the evening skyline, watching life roll by on a river of clouds. "He was on the edge but never went completely over it. We could control him," he said. "It was somethin' down there that changed him; somethin' down there in the asshole of the world.

"You tell him it ain't about the money. I can have the full hundred million wired in five minutes and not even break a sweat. But we can't bend to blackmail at *any* price. Hell, if it were that easy, any fool could do it. Why bother workin'? Just hit up ol' GM! You tell him our offer. He can stay down there pissin' his life away, tryin' to save those monkey molesters! But I want two things: I want our AEP database back online and I want that damn blog shut down!"

"Basically," Green said, "All we want you to do is locate him, contact him, and call us for further instructions. Get it?"

"I got it. But…is there any danger?"

Green looked down at the table. Nelson ignored the question

completely and gestured toward the file in front of me. "If you'll open that folder again please, Lisa?"

I opened the folder. Inside it was an up-to-date printout of www.head167.blogspot.com, a personnel photograph of Joseph Bosco Junior, a grainy CCTV printout of him, and a USB flash drive. There was also a contact list of those he'd seen on company business before he disappeared. Maybe the blog's title is some kind of map, like heading 167 paces in one direction.

"Like Dave said, he was Joe's trainer and friend, so he knows a little about him," said Nelson. "Based on his own observations, and on Joe's and your employee profile/psych work-ups, Dave recommended you for this assignment. Frankly, I don't care if we sent Jesse Jackson over there, as long as he got the job done in the next five days.

"You and Joe are both from Michigan, both lived at one time in Royal Oak, both graduated from U of M, and both scored in the top percentile of your GM training classes. And your personal lives exhibit some of the same…conflicts. So we expect you'll be able to think like him. And if you knew our boy, you'd know it doesn't hurt that you're an…attractive woman."

"To recap," said Green, "we have a key employee who's left his area of responsibility and broken all ties with the company. He also hasn't touched his bank accounts, his credit cards, or contacted a single relative. No ransom demands have been made. No corpse even generally fitting his description has turned up down there and all our attempts to find him have been unsuccessful. So, because of your… similarities and your loyalty to the company, we're offering you three times your normal salary to find him. Are you with us?"

Nelson's hand was on my shoulder again, as tight as a hangman's noose.

"Okay," I said. "I'm in."

I was anxious to get back to Michigan, even though GM had flown me first class for once. I won't land until after ten tonight, so I plan to wait until tomorrow morning to tell the family about my trip to Africa. I wished Nelson had given me more time to break it to them.

"When can you be ready to fly?" Nelson asked me earlier. "We want you in the air as soon as possible."

"Well, I'll need to make some arrangements. Today is Thursday; um…how is Sunday?"

"Friday? Great call! Friday night it is then. Time is critical!"

I looked around at everyone on the plane dressed for winter and then thought of exotic sandy beaches and a lovers' reunion. Then I remembered Nelson's grin and his icy clutch on my shoulder, and how I had to hold my breath until he released me. Could anyone really be released from GM? They say the only ways out are a gold watch or a pine box.

Joey had found a way out though. He had found a way to leave on his own terms and management was pissed.

I did not understand what they expected me to accomplish in such a short time. Nelson wanted Joey found by next Tuesday, February 1st. My twenty-two hour flight is Friday night so it will already be Saturday night when I get there. Assuming the media affiliates are closed on Sunday, I only have Monday and Tuesday to interview them all and try to find Joey. Just two days! I should have asked to be paid upfront.

The clean-cut man next to me busied himself with his laptop the entire thirty minutes of pre-flight. Something was odd; he seemed determined not to make eye contact with me. I turned on the overhead light and opened Joey's file. It was weird seeing the word "CONFIDENTIAL" in red block letters. I felt like I was in a movie or playing spies again with my brothers. Lisa Rosatti, code name: Luna.

What had Nelson said as I was walking out of the conference room? "An encrypted flash drive is in that folder; wear it at all times. Someone from GM will contact you and advise you what to do with it."

I picked up the flash drive and placed its yellow lanyard around my neck. They believed they had roped me in so brilliantly but they had no idea I only applied to the company to be near Joey in the first place. I would have found him for free.

Joey and I met just over a year ago at a club in Royal Oak – one of those meetings that lasted all night. He left for New York about a week after that and we somehow just lost contact. That night had been extremely special, though I think neither one of us appreciated it at the time. Now I feel like we have a second chance.

I did not tell Green and Nelson because it would have ended up in the files back at Global Media. I do not think one-night stands should be part of company background checks.

I stared at Joey's company photo – it was a work of art compared to the mug shot GM had taken of me; a friend of mine had accidentally kneed me in the eye a few days earlier and it still showed. Plus I am much too pale. I can take another one after I tan a few shades on the beaches in South Africa.

I looked over the last known photograph of Joey, taken December 26, 2004 – three days before he vanished. It was a CCTV shot of him entering the doors at E-TV's Cape Town station. I stared at the video printout that had been blown up to provide facial detail. He was darker and thinner than I remembered and had grown a thick goatee. He was almost unrecognizable except for his smile, directed at the camera as if he knew GM would be watching the tape. There was something about that sarcastic half smile of his…something about the detail of it that had always attracted me. A soft flat line, turned up sharply at the left corner of his mouth – that was his smile! And he wore it for the camera in an obvious show of defiance.

Once in flight, I ordered *Belvedere* vodka with a splash of dry vermouth in Joey's memory, but had to settle for *Absolut* on the rocks. Mr. Clean-cut neither passed me my drink nor responded to the flight attendant when she leaned over him to do so. I was sure I had seen him somewhere before, which was quite probable if he was a frequent flier. As a GM Field Rep, I did a lot of traveling. I flipped through the file to the up-to-date printout of the blog and began to read:

***

She lay there in the hospital bed
Refusing to push so they clamped my head
And pulled me from her pool of red.
From her breasts I never fed;
Sometimes I'm sure she wished me dead.

20June1968: Spit Baby: *n. Informal* 1. A perfect likeness: *He's the spit and image of his father.* [Alteration of *spit and image* from *spit* an exact likeness as in *the very spit of*].

That is what I was born as: the spitting image of my father. So much so, that when he showed up intoxicated an hour later, he named me "Joseph Bosco Junior". My mother named me "Get-It-Away-From-Me". I wanted to be named "Not-Theirs" but no one asked me.

20June1969: Today is my first birthday. Joe had to work so Mother Mary took me to Belle Isle with my sister, Marisa.

I was strapped in the straightjacket of my baby chair and crying my eyes out because no one had the sense to shield me from the sun. Tears filled up the hole on my face where I stabbed myself while playing with a pencil the day before. Soon, a black halo of blowflies circled my head, looking for a place to lay larvae. They melted my scar with their saliva and blew worms into it.

People think babies cannot feel anything except teeth coming in or the pleasure of a good shit but they're wrong. I felt what it was like to have worms crawling inside my face, leaving a circle scar I will see in my reflection for the rest of my life.

20June1970: Today is my second birthday. We drove to London, Kentucky to leave me with Granny Lonetree (she was never married to Grandfather Bosco) while Joe and Mary "work things out."

As we walked in Granny's house, Joe's older sister said: "My word! Let me get a look at him! Oh, my Lord! Joe, you done spit this boy out!" Before long, everyone had nicknamed me *Spit* but no one asked me.

20June1971: Today I am three. Mary's mother photographed Marisa and me in the vacant lot next to our house off Tireman Avenue. It is the oldest photo that exists with just the two of us; we are rarely living in the same place at once.

In the photo, I'm wearing boxing gloves Joe had just given me for my birthday. Mary did not get me anything; maybe because of something I did wrong like knock over a houseplant or wet my bed. It never took much to set her off, especially if Joe stayed out too long.

I had trouble pronouncing names. As a result, Grandma became Nani, Marisa became Maris, and our new baby brother – Jackson

- became Jack. We all lived together, unhappily, in our pink dollhouse next to the vacant lot.

Our house was painted pink because it had a child-bride for a decorator. Mother Mary wanted to become a Broadway showgirl but deferred her dream at the age of sixteen when her doctor knocked her up. That was my father, my father the doctor. These days, Mary's just a go-go dancer around Detroit. It's amazing what some women will do for money. If I had been born with a few bucks, she probably would have breast-fed me.

20June1972: Today is my fourth birthday. Mother Mary has just beaten the hell out of me with a white extension cord. "Pick up your toys," she yelled to Jack and me from the kitchen. Jack mocked her and she came running to see who said it. Maris was coming down the stairs and said, "Spit said it!" So did Jack.

"No Momma, it wasn't me! It was Jack," I pleaded, but it was too late. She held me up in the air by one arm and dragged me into the living room. Ripping the extension cord from the wall, she beat the hell out of me while jerking me around in the air like a one-armed swing. She beat me until blood spritzed the pine floor. I wanted to call out for someone but...who do you call when your own mother is the one hurting you?

I cried for hours in my room, even missing dinner. Later, Mary came in and rubbed a stick of *Johnson & Johnson's* cocoa butter on me to make the welts go away. It smelled sweet and rich, like candy from a psychopath. But the welts were internal and would never go away. If I had been older, or even just two feet taller, I would have shoved that stick of cocoa butter up her ass and hitchhiked to California.

20June1973: Today is my fifth birthday. Mother Mary bought me some Dr. Seuss books, a coloring book, and a *Crayola 64 Pack*. Her brother got me a *Dick Tracy* badge and cap gun. The best gift, though, came from Joe, who was now living with two of his friends. Mary called them, "Two whores hooked on heroin." But I digress...

Joe had a swing set/teeter-totter delivered to our dollhouse; Maris and I divided it up before it was even erected. She got the swings and I got the teeter-totter. We learned the division of assets from watching our parents. There was nothing left for poor Jack to claim, except that he was related to us but we knew that was only half true. I was the spitting image of Joe, while Maris was a lighter and thinner version of Mary. Jack, however, had the look of someone who'd done time for Grand Theft Auto.

It was Jack's lack of biological resemblance to Joe that precipitated the divorce. It turned out that Jack's real father was a member of a motorcycle gang - The Outlaws - and had knocked up Mary in the backroom of an East Side go-go club.

23June1973: Today I swung in my teeter-totter until the sun went down. I swung so long that the whole damn thing wrenched out of the ground and fell down on me. I thought I could swing up and touch the stars. The next thing I knew I was flat on my ass, seeing stars.

I lay crumpled and crying under that swing set for half an hour. No one came outside to check on me even though it was after dark. Finally, I got up and went to bed.

I peaked in Nani's room to tell her I fell down. "You fell down, Spit? That's nice," she said, then turned back to watching a Tigers game while sipping her way through a six-pack of *Bud*.

27June1973: Maris and I went to live with Joe and his fiancée, Jenny, tonight. He had come to fetch us for the weekend and saw that Maris had kicked the living shit out of me again. Joe went berserk, damn near killing Mary. He picked her up with one hand and threw her backwards against the screen door so hard that it fell apart - splitting at the lock and hinges. Mary rolled down the stairs and onto the walkway. She tried to crawl away and had made it to the lawn before Joe straddled her and gave her the kind of beating you only saw in movies.

It was terrible. Blood was everywhere. Maris stood at the door crying hysterically before finally running to hide in the coat closet with Jack. I stayed out on the porch in my pajamas, smelling of fresh cocoa butter. It took six neighbors to pull Joe off her. The veins in his neck swelled up like garden hoses. Mary's face looked like...she had just gotten the kind of beating that you only saw in movies.

I walked down the stairs, staring at Mary as she groaned with her blouse ripped open and her milk-stingy tits flopping everywhere. Joe hovered over her, swollen up like a white bull in a rodeo ring, so ready to buck it took six clowns to hold him back.

I was the first to notice the cops were coming. I ran to Joe's car and jumped in the passenger seat. "Come on, Dad!" I yelled, but those clowns were still holding him. The cops drove up onto the front lawn, maybe five cars in all. It looked like Christmas in June. They hopped out with guns drawn on everyone until they sorted it all out. In the end, Doctor Joseph Bosco, outstanding member of the community, was never even arrested. Back then, a man could beat his wife like it was his second job and the cops would blame *her* for stepping out of line.

04July1973: Today was Joe's thirtieth birthday. He went out to celebrate with his insane half brothers. Jenny stayed home to nurse me through the measles and she treated me like a king. Orange juice, tomato soup, *Petticoat Junction, Gilligan's Island...* the works!

But later on, after I had fallen asleep, Joe came home and tried to ass-rape me with an enema. I screamed for help, like a kid being ass-raped with an enema, but who can help you when your Dad is the one hurting you?

Jenny held my arms down on the couch while Joe shoved the frozen piece of chalk up my ass. But my sphincter rejected it, shooting it back out to bounce off the TV and land on the coffee table. Joe and Jenny died laughing and that's all that saved me. I cried for a while but I was okay. I kept my manhood.

24September1973: Today is Marisa's birthday so she gets to pick what we have for dinner. Burger King is beneath her royal highness; she wants Little Caesar's pizza with slimy-ass mushrooms. I wanted to try anchovies but Joe said they were really fish pussies. I did not believe him though. I believe nothing he says since what happened last month:

Since we moved in with him in June, Joe warned us to stay out of the backyard but he never said why. Maris and I finally went back there anyway and discovered there was a giant German shepherd living in the garage! At first, I understood why he said it; he was worried the dog would hurt us. Then I thought about how many years he had left me with Mary while she was kicking my ass just for looking like him and I came to believe he was only protecting the dog.

It was insane. First, who would want to hurt a dog? Second, Tiger (the dog) was three times my size. Plus, I liked Tiger – he was beautiful and soft. But Joe taking so long to mention him made me wonder what other secrets he was capable of. Was I really his "main man" like he said or was he secretly planning to ditch me somewhere again? How long had he been taking care of this mutt while I had to walk around smelling like fucking cocoa butter? After a few days, my *like* for Tiger changed to an intense and sincere *loathing*.

I became obsessed with Tiger or rather with the absence of him. He was like a tangled, knotted telephone cord that had to be straightened out. Joe told us to keep our hands out of the backyard fence and not to touch Tiger because he might bite us. He had also once told us that the berries growing along the fence were poisonous. That was three rules...three rules too many...so I combined them into one: "Feed Tiger poisoned berries through the fence with your hands."

I mixed rose petals, bread, peanut butter, and shrub berries together. Then I hand-fed the concoction to Tiger. He lapped it up like candy and the next day...he was just gone! I never asked and no one ever said anything to me about it. We all just went on like nothing happened. Living with lies is what it means to be a Bosco.

Chapter 3

My drive back from Metro Airport was a nightmare. Usually, I could make the trip back up I-275 in about twenty minutes but Michigan roads are notoriously icy in January. A truck had spun out entering I-275 and jack-knifed on the freeway's circular entrance ramp. Its cargo of toilet tissue bounced everywhere, creating a slalom course that caused a virtual standstill clear back to I-94. White snow fell like frosting, coating the brake lights on all the gridlocked cars.

Traffic is really the only problem with being a Global Media Field Representative; it really is a cake job. We install computerized meters on the television equipment of randomly selected homes and monitor how television is viewed. We drive an average of eight hundred miles per week and read at least fifty e-mails per day. There are no problems really, unless the homes unplug our stuff without telling us or small animals eat some of our wires. Yeah, it really is a cake job, but until my meeting in New York today, I had not considered how much my cake job was changing the world.

I came home to a dark apartment and an answering machine blinking a message from GM; my expense account increase had been confirmed. Green called my cell phone soon afterward to talk shop. "We're telling everyone you're on emergency family leave," he said. "We'll have Tom Kingsley run your area until you're back so don't worry about it; just keep the equipment in the car. Can you leave the car in the carport so Tom can get to it if he needs anything?"

"Sure, I can do that," I said.

"It should be all right there, right? Novi?"

"Sure, it'll be fine. I'll have maintenance keep an eye on it while I'm gone. And I'll give them your number in case of emergency."

"Can you leave the key under the passenger floor mat and make sure nothing's left out on the seat?"

"Sure, Mom."

"Hey, it's company equipment; you know how they get. I may have Tom come and keep the car at his place. I'll let you know."

"That's fine too."

"Okay. Well, you know you don't have to get shots or Malaria tabs; you're only going as far as Cape Town. What else…we're sending a limo to take you to the airport; don't forget to be there early. Did I tell you Joe missed his flight over there?"

"No, you're kidding."

"Yeah, something about his bike. He said he was taking his bike on the plane and the Northwest people hassled him. He was running late as usual anyway, so he missed his flight and had to spend half the day in the airport here and then half the night in Amsterdam."

"Why would he try and take his bike on the plane?"

"I don't know; Joe's nuts. He always does stuff like that and always at the last minute. Who knows why; ask him when you see him. Be sure and call me when you get settled into your room no matter what time it is. I think we're seven hours behind them now. What else…your passport will be stamped over there allowing you to visit for thirty days. But if you can't find him by Tuesday, I wouldn't worry about the thirty days."

"Is that like…a threat? I thought I was helping you guys out."

"Seriously, concentrate on finding Joe ASAP because…" Green seemed like he wanted to tell me something but he was hedging. Then one of his kids spilled something and he used that as an excuse to get off the phone.

"Okay," I said, "I'll talk to you soon. Sure there's nothing else, old mensh?"

"Mensh? What is that, Italian?"

"It's Yiddish for *Dave Green*."

"Yeah, right. No, there's nothing else. Just be careful over there."

"Okay. I will," I said before hanging up the phone. But I knew I would not be careful. I was not raised to be. Maybe that's why I love speeding down the freeway, racing my dates back to my apartment; rewarding them if they win and leaving them unsatisfied if they lose. Unfortunately for them I win most of the time, probably because I take risks most people are not willing to take.

I never had an interest in white-collar guys or even in White guys in general. The poor are always the ones with the passion, so for them I risked my family's wrath. Like when I was dating Kilo, my Jamaican boyfriend who played steel drums in a ska band. Kilo was also a wanna-be gun and drug dealer. Dad would have tossed us both into the Detroit River if he found out about us, so why did I do it?

Kilo used to ask me that all the time. He used to say I had jungle fever and that someday I would simply recover. Whenever he came home and could not find me, he would first check under the bed to see if my suitcase was gone. He wrote and recorded a song for me called "Suitcase Señorita" that actually made it onto the international dance charts. It must have been a case of life imitating art because soon afterward, both the suitcase and the señorita were gone.

I kept switching in and out of the past as I ran my bath water, trying to recall exactly when I became so competitive. My childhood was normal – whatever that means. We had a big yard and all the neighborhood children played there. I remember loving the game of dodge ball. I used to stand there, willingly absorbing the sting of the ball, just for the chance of catching it and exacting my revenge. After a while, none of the boys would throw the ball at me.

During grade school, I could whip most of the boys in my class, probably because I was tall for my age. The girls resented me for spending so much time with the boys but there was nothing they could beat me in either. They dissed me behind my back and excluded me from their cliques as my punishment for being better. I never understood that.

Middle school was even worse – a suburban wasteland where the inept faculty mistook my indifference for leadership, pairing me with the mentally and physically challenged. But I never tormented those kids or any of the others deemed "special" by the popular kids. I befriended them instead, sticking up for them when they were bullied. I always tried to understand what made them different, maybe because I was different too. Growing up a Rosatti would make anyone different.

My father always tried to make sure we ate as a family. He also insisted we watch TV together. I think he just wanted to add his own commentary or on occasion, his shoe. When I was eleven, we saw my father on the Channel 4 Evening News being released from booking along with some of his other "business associates". We were all treated differently after that, but we continued living in denial. We continued believing and insisting to others that Angelo Rosatti was merely a self-employed investor in capital ventures.

As teenagers, my brothers and I became heavily involved in after-school activities. Family dinners and TV time became more difficult to regulate. Eventually, family time dwindled down to just Sundays, followed soon by the divorce. Cause and effect.

I toweled-off after my bath, slipped into my U of M sweats and began the drudgery of packing. Mom called but I let it go to voicemail; I knew she would worm the news out of me and then I would never get to finish packing. My flight was tomorrow night so I would have most of the day to spend breaking it to them at their separate residences. I was thinking lunch with Dad and then dinner at Mom's.

I could feel my stomach gurgling at the thought of food and I realized I had not eaten anything today besides honey-roasted peanuts and a turkey sandwich. It was almost midnight and way too late to order pizza so I whipped up some spicy chicken wings, ranch dressing, celery stalks and a margarita. Sam Cooke was singing in the background about how change was going to come. I took it as a positive sign.

Afterwards, I nestled into bed to finish reading more of the blog. I felt like some kind of peeping Tom, gleaning pleasure from the private details of someone else's life. I was also curious as to what the blog's name meant. Was *Head167* a clue? A location? Green believes the blog is all true and something in me hopes it is as well. Its bluntness made it seem…pure…and immune to the falsities of reality.

Maybe that is why so many readers continued to find it appealing. Millions of people are sick of being lied to and having the truths they "can't handle" filtered out for them by the media. It was more than that for me though. To me, Joey was like one of those special kids from back in school and I had been appointed his protector. With a Rosatti as a friend, you had no enemies.

I felt cold, even tucked in my flannel sheets. Michigan in winter is no place for a single girl. It was that windy, drafty kind of cold – the kind that rattled against windows and seeped under doors. I got up, adjusted the heat to seventy-four, and jumped back into bed. I had been without a lover (real or electric) since I kicked Noel out last August. Noel...the bastard that gave me herpes. He probably never would have told me himself. Unfortunately, one of the tramps he was teaching salsa lessons to called our apartment one night looking for him.

"No, he's not here," I told her. "By the way, this is *my* phone, not his, and I don't want you calling on it. Did he give you this number?"

"Look, just tell Noel that he needs to get checked out," the tramp said. "Tell him my doctor said he needs for him to come in."

I confronted Noel in my own way, by packing all of his things in trash bags and setting them in the hall outside my apartment. Taped to one of the bags, I left a note telling him to leave the keys and which doctor to contact. The next morning, I found his keys at my doorsill and his bags gone. I never saw him again. He called once or twice to try and make peace but he never came back. He knew the only thing keeping him breathing was that I was too ashamed to tell my family.

In some way though, I felt I had brought the whole thing on myself. I knew he was no good when I hooked up with him. Maybe I wanted him because I thought I was no damn good myself. But I was never as fucked up as he was. What an asshole! In just two months of living together, he had given me a disease, wrecked my car, raised my insurance, run up my phone bill, lowered my credit score, fucked up my laptop, and cheated on me. I was stupid to get involved with him. None of my friends liked him – that should have been a big hint right there! Noel was a helpless, hopeless, selfish, one-night stand I was dumb enough to try and domesticate.

If I had already been ashamed to let people know I was dating Noel, I was definitely ashamed to tell people that the bastard had given me herpes. I never even told my parish priest. Because Royal Oak is so small, I kept running into people that would ask me about him or why we split up. I felt like the truth was bound to come out there, so last September, I paid off my lease in cash and bought a condo in Novi.

That was one of the lowest points of my life. Noel had caused me so much heartache and humiliation that I just could not cope. At one point, I was even suicidal. Thankfully, my doctor recommended a herpes self-help group that I have been meeting with once a month ever since.

At group, I learned that Noel was only a symptom of the problem, not the problem itself. The problem was my unsafe lifestyle. If I wanted to feel good about myself again, I had to admit that *I* was the root of my own problems. So I accepted that I was my own worst enemy but it took many long talks with my group mentor to find out why. I had been trying to prove myself; overcompensating to prove I was just as strong and as virile as either of my brothers because I was seeking my father's approval. After all that time, I still needed it. I needed his unconditional love.

Novi itself was also having a calming influence on me. It was no Royal Oak but it has its own small town charm. I am a lot calmer now; I have quit barhopping and drinking myself into numbness. Maybe that is another thing Joey and I have in common: maybe we both needed to run off by ourselves to find ourselves.

I became a new woman last September. I am now Mrs. Right but I only meet Mr. Wrong: the married GM co-op who hounds me to run off to Europe with him (he keeps unplugging our equipment so I can drive out and fix it), the ten pound Korean nail tech who fondles my hands, and finally U.N., the exotic dancer from Toledo.

I met U.N. at Lucia Bartolli's bachelorette party; it was held at a club in Toledo that her father owns. U.N. is the star of the all-male review. He is tall and muscular with long dreadlocks and a full beard, giving him the look of a mocha-drenched lion. His stage name is U.N., like the United Nations, because he has allegedly slept with a girl from every nation in the world. That was a big red flag for me, especially after Noel. So when he came over and asked me out, I had already decided not to honor his passport.

U.N. was just too…uncomplicated. I feel like I deserve something more now. I needed a healthy, stable relationship. I need Joey Bosco. I need his smell…his smile – everything! Joey had moved me so much with his words and with his passion that we were making love within three hours of meeting…and I was never that easy.

There was nothing *easy* about sex with Joey though; it was full throttle. He bit, licked, and sucked me like his life depended on it. We made love at least four times by the time the sun rose the next morning. I lay back on his chest as he held me in his arms, nuzzling my hair. Our mouths spoke of inconsequential things like mass transportation, the decline of the L.A. Lakers, and the negative effect of trees on lawns and pavement, but our spirits spoke of love. After we dressed, he walked me to his front door and disappeared from my life forever, leaving me only memories to combat the wolves and Noels of the world.

***

01October1973: Today we moved into a huge house on Asbury Park. The attic is filled with old secrets, like 73-rpm glass records and an old phonograph. We used the records like *Frisbees* until they shattered. I found two old books of nursery rhymes up there – *Mother Goose* with *Disney* characters and *The Brothers Grim Fairy Tales*. We have a big maple tree in the backyard and a garage. Dad says we're going to get a van and just travel across the country. He said we are getting a swimming pool too.

16May1974: School is a joke to me, like the Easter Bunny. Rabbits do not lay eggs; neither do they wear glasses *inside* their masks. I hate this school and their dumb songs: "...Purple mountains majesty above the fruited planes..." What the hell are they talking about? Were our founding fathers high?

18May1974: Today is Jenny's thirty-second birthday but I gave her nothing. She asked me why and I said, "Because you and Dad don't give me an allowance."

"Even if you didn't have money," she said, "you could have still made me a card or something." She missed my point about the allowance and I missed her point about the card.

Jenny and I have not been getting along for a while. She just lost her son to crib death. It was difficult for me to feel anything because I was hardly allowed to touch him. There was an ambulance at the house one night and Jenny was crying. Afterwards, Maris and I were sent to stay with Jenny's mother for a few days. When we came back home, my cat was gone!

His name was Kitty or used to be before Jenny gave him away to one of her sisters. She told me she gave Kitty away because I did not take care of him or clean up after him but that was bullshit! I heard her tell the lady across the street that she blamed her baby's death on cleaning Kitty's litter box. It was something she saw on *Phil Donahue* – fucking toxoplasmosis. I know why she did it and I empathize with her but Kitty was *my* cat. How could my parents punish me for crib death? Family...what a big lie. What a fucking mirage.

Chapter 4

I think we are flying over…Afghanistan? It seems strange to look down and see snow, ice, and sand together. I wondered if Al-Qa'ida could have an anti-aircraft missile aimed at my kosher meal. "Get the kosher," Dad told me. "It's just as inedible but they deliver it first; that way you don't have to wait around like all the schmucks."

I sat in my first-class KLM leather seat staring out of the window, thinking about the last chat with my doctor. He prescribed enough *Famvir* to last three months, which was good because I had the feeling this job would take longer than Green and Nelson thought. The doctor warned me of possible drug interactions and confirmed that I did not need malaria pills for Cape Town.

He also said to avoid taking any medication without calling him first, because it could throw off my immune system and cause me to have an outbreak. I never once had an outbreak. That somehow made it easier to forgive Noel, because I know it may not have been entirely his fault. Some people are asymptomatic but still contagious. Anyway, it already happened; all I can do now is deal with it.

There should be some kind of cure though. If doctors know that one in every five Americans has herpes, we should have a cure for it by now. We have pills to prevent and cure malaria, which you can die from, but for herpes – which is non-lethal – there is still no cure. It seems like that one would be easier to fix. Is it selfish not to want to spend the rest of my life paying for prescriptions of *Famvir?*

I needed something to clear my mind…I began reading passages aloud from a pandemic diseases brochure I picked up at the airport.

"Malaria: An infectious disease characterized by cycles of chills, fever, and sweating, caused by the parasitic infection of red blood cells by a protozoan of the genus Plasmodium, which is transmitted by the bite of an infected female anopheles mosquito. Also called paludism. Also called swamp fever…"

That was no help at all. I turned on the in-flight movie and ordered a double *Stoli* and orange juice. Soon I forgot all about diseases, kosher meals and terrorists...but I could not stop thinking about Joey. I opened his file again and gazed at his pictures.

Just then, a baby's bottle came rolling up the aisle from coach, startling me. "So sorry," the stewardess said. Apparently a baby was unsatisfied with his meal selection and wanted the whole world to know it. That seems like the kind of kid Joey was. No one can say because no one knows who wrote the blog or even if it is true. All I can go by is the Joey I know – the one who is cute, charming, and in control. People like us never lose control.

In high school I knew a lot that did, like this one kid named Ron Pollock. Ron was deemed a burnout but I befriended him anyway. We shared homeroom for three years. On graduation day, he wrote a note in my senior yearbook thanking me for talking to him for all those years, adding that I had probably saved his life. He told me his fantasy of shooting his bullies and then himself in his American History class. He said talking to me everyday in homeroom actually kept him from going through with it.

There were times when I thought of checking out too. Although I had many friends at school – mostly guys – I really didn't have anyone to talk to. They were always busy talking to me. Over time, I just...shut down. My problems stemmed from feeling virtually abandoned by my father at age thirteen. He took a good look at me, noticed I had tits, and then built a wall between us. I would have sold my soul to have been born a boy, to have been the one my father loved most instead of least.

I turned out okay though. I graduated with honors, men find me attractive, and I make a decent, legal living. In a perfect world though, I would have a career helping others. Maybe I would even adopt an orphan or two, since my doctor recommends I not have children of my own.

The most important thing to me now though is to feel a connection to my work – to my career. How could anyone feel a connection from collecting statistical data? I know why I took the job and after I find him, we should both move on; this is not the right career choice for Joey either. I see him as a schoolteacher and maybe even a loving parent.

I remember the night we met at Gracie's...Liz Tataglia, my best friend since third grade, called and asked me to meet her there. My brothers Jimmy and Johnny showed up, which delighted Liz. She always had a crush on Jimmy.

We all drank a lot that night, which is bad for me because doing so gives me jaundice outbreaks. My family doctor assures me it is congenital, caused by an excess of bilirubin. All I know is when I drink a lot, my eyes look like lemon wedges.

It was about ten-thirty and we were all drunk off our asses when you walked over. You asked if anyone was using the two empty chairs at our table. Jimmy said "Nah, go ahead." You thanked him, planted your *Corona* on our table, and went back to the bar to retrieve your friend.

You came back with a handsome Irishman whom you introduced to us as Frank but you kept calling Francis. Then you went off into your own private world, scribbling on a stack of cocktail napkins. Your ignoring us only intrigued me more but it seemed to piss everyone else off.

Liz and Frank got into a mortgage lending discussion that bored Johnny, who wandered off to talk with others. Jimmy stayed, noticeably upset that Liz had turned her attention elsewhere. This was funny to me because, normally, Jimmy never noticed Liz was alive. He used to call her J-Lo, right to her face, because of the size of her ass. Now she was suddenly his turf. Guys are a joke.

At some point, Liz asked Frank something about "Fair Market Value" and you let out this hollow, sinister laugh, causing all of us to stare at you. "That's Joey for you," Frank said, continuing to talk to Liz.

Impatient from being ignored, I went over to your side of the table to see what you were scribbling. I was expecting it to be the cure for cancer, since it was clearly more important to you than any of us were.

"Hi. I'm Lisa," I yelled above the crowd.

"Yeah, you said that earlier," was your smiling reply. Your voice was sharp, almost shrill. Eyes…dark and intense. You stared straight into me. Such an odd man…an odd combination, like honey drenched over the edge of a razor.

"Are we boring you?" I asked.

"No. But you're not as intriguing as that girl at the bar. She's definitely not from here; I think she's from Poland. Maybe Germany."

"How can you tell?" I asked.

"I don't know. Experience. The style and shade of her jeans…her teeth, her hairstyle…the scarf around her neck."

"What are you drinking, *Corona*? I'll bet you a drink," I said, and hardly had the words out before you walked over to the blonde by the bar. I saw you saying something, smiling, and then leading her back to our table. I read your napkin while you were gone:

Red raspberries swimming in a vodka mote,
Black paint backdrop kaleidoscope.
Blood-drinking girl from the city of Krakow,
She called it a Manhattan; it looked like a Cosmo.

Buzzing from girl on sofa: 'FMV?'
Francis answered the couch potato
Who rudely mixed business with fermented potatoes,
Decaying the ambiance with Fair Market Value and
Destroying the memory of our last martini.

"Now, tell Lisa where you're from," you sneered triumphantly, introducing us all to the au pair with the strange name. The girl, who seemed too young to even be in a bar, said she was from Poland. You even shared pleasantries with her suspicious boyfriend who had eventually followed her to our table. You toyed with both briefly, yawned, and then set them free.

I bought the next round of drinks – two *Belvedere* martinis. You offered to pay, saying you did not want to break my bank. I smiled and thought how refreshing it was to meet someone in Royal Oak that did not know I was a Rosatti.

Another two hours had passed before I knew it. Liz interrupted us, saying she was ready to go home and that I should not worry because Jimmy was driving her. Johnny, the youngest twin by about two minutes, was ready for bed also but refused to leave without me. I could tell that you wanted me to stay so I tried to include Johnny in our conversation. This did not go over too well with you. It ended up being Frank, Johnny, and me on one side of the table, versus you and your napkins on the other. Soon, Johnny was damn near pushing me out the door.

You smiled, leaned over the table, and whispered something in Johnny's ear. Then you whipped out one of your GM business cards from a silver case and gave it to him. For some reason, he still has that card. He never told me what you said to him but he turned to me and asked "Are you sure you're okay here?" I told him I was. He kissed me, glared at you and left.

Frank called it a night soon afterward and I felt bad when he mentioned that you should have a safe trip. I made the connection with what you wrote on the cocktail napkin and realized you guys were meeting for a goodbye drink. I apologized for interrupting your farewell martini but Frank was really cool about it. He said he knew you would be back soon.

"He'll be back when his bird gets bored. I know he seems strange but it's all an act to get laid," Frank said. "Chicks just fuck him and see how it goes in the morning." We both laughed at you, then Francis left.

You and I stayed until closing time, listening to Teddy Richards sing folksy renditions of the Stone Temple Pilots and eating the bleu cheese stuffed olives from our martinis. You staggered with me to the bathroom and when I came out, you were sitting in a chair across from it. I was never intoxicated to the point of making out in public but there was something arousing about the way you were sitting there in regal solitude. I looked to see if anyone was around before straddling you in the chair. We kissed passionately, my aggressiveness startling us both.

Still kissing, we stumbled like barflies out of Gracie's back door. We walked a little before catching sight of a recessed doorway below ground level, immediately to our left. You dragged me down into the shadows of the doorway, ripping down my panties with one hand, while still kissing me. You shoved your fingers into me forcefully, causing me to shudder.

"Shut up!" you growled, covering my mouth with one hand. Then you raised my legs off the ground, wrapped them around your waist, and impaled me. I grabbed the security gate behind me and held on tight; writhing uncontrollably while you took me, plunging deeper and deeper into me.

I held nothing back from you; I was all yours to do with as you willed. And you did as you willed, at times hurting my back with the force of your thrusts. The thought of us somehow being watched or filmed only excited me even more. I came so hard that I bit into your finger. The bite broke your skin, oozing the taste of salt and metal into my mouth and causing you to thrust even harder until you came. I could feel you swelling to explode and I begged you to cum inside of me. Instead you pulled yourself free at the last possible moment and came all over my skirt.

We tidied up quickly, calmly walking to our cars like we had just left the bar. I was still tingling, trying to figure out what had just happened. I kept trying to figure it during the drive to your place but gave up when we got there and the same thing happened again.

I never really slept that night because you had this talking alarm clock that called out the time every half-hour. If I began to doze off, a woman's voice would wake me up. Then I would realize that it was your clock and not some deranged girlfriend with keys to your condo. I just lay there, staring at you sleeping, and realizing something important was happening to me.

As I lay there, part of me wanted to get up and snoop around the place or at least the medicine cabinet. You could have been an axe murderer; I knew literally nothing about you. But I decided to just lie there, afraid to ruin my most perfect night out by snooping and finding out you wore dresses when no one was watching.

"Five-thirty a.m.," your clock said.

Usually, I would not have bothered sticking around. The Suitcase Señorita…I would have rushed home to shower and be in my own space by now. Instead I lay there, staring at you sleeping, listening to you breathing, and I pretended that – just this once – things would work out.

You must have sensed me watching because you opened your eyes, formed your luscious lips into a smile, and pulled me into your arms.

"Tell me something about yourself, Joe Bosco."

"I'm strange," you muttered.

"No, be serious."

"I have morning breath."

"So do I. Now, where is your family from? You don't sound

like you're from Detroit. What's your background? Like…your ethnicity?"

You were silent for a while. You looked into my eyes like you were watching an old movie. "I never met anyone past my paternal and maternal grandmothers. The grandfathers don't get talked about – ever – but over the years I heard my father's father is from Sardinia, Italy. My father's mother's mother is from Dahomey, Africa. She came to this country by force. She had no clothes, no money…all she had with her was a tree branch that she planned to grow so they called her 'Lonetree'. And that's all I know because my father never said more about them. It was a kind of unspoken rule; we just didn't talk about them."

We were silent. Your stare was blank for a while. Then you blinked and came back to me again. "Of course, I could have heard the old man wrong. Maybe he said my grandfather liked sardines…and my great-grandmother was homely."

I laughed, causing the bed to shake. "So what would you define yourself as on a GM questionnaire?" I asked.

"Not Interested."

I laughed more. "Can you be serious?"

"Why? Is race so important to you?"

"No. I just want to know more about you."

"Whatever you see when you look at me, that's what I am."

"Do you want to ask me anything?"

"No. Not really. About the past? Definitely not. So what am I? What do you see?"

"An African-American."

"Then that's what I am."

You went quiet again, your eyes having the empty look of someone watching television or dreaming with their eyes wide open. "I remember my father's mother…Maggie? Maggie Lonetree. I remember her sitting in a rocking chair, snapping string beans on her wooden-plank porch, and flinging them into a paper bag. I remember long black slugs somehow springing themselves onto the sides of the bag. I remember her killing a snake with some kind of…golf club-looking thing. I can see her making blackberry cobbler…or spanking me with a thick leather strap. In the backyard, there was this…huge spider, the size of a fucking eyeball! It lived in Granny's mulberry bush, in a web as thick as human hair."

You were captivating to listen to, like a star who had fallen off the movie screen and landed in my arms. We watched each other while you caressed my face with your hand.

"The past is the future is the past," you said. "Everything is everything."

"What kind of spider was it?"

You stopped smiling and swam back upstream into the past. "I called it the God's Eye Spider, because its web looked like that macramé design: the god's eye."

"You know how to knit?"

"I used to."

"What does your father do?"

Your jaws clenched tight.

"He burns," you said.

"What does that mean. He's a fireman?"

"Yeah," you answered smiling. "He's on-fire-man."

Then you laughed that hollow laugh that – still even today – cuts through to my soul. The sweet danger of it was like red licorice-arsenic, making everything else seem irrelevant.

Suddenly, *I* was the one on fire. My hungry hands slid up and down your muscled frame, clawing you, as you reached one arm behind yourself into the nightstand drawer, retrieving a condom. All I could think of was having your lips on me and your cock thrusting inside of me.

"Fuck me..." I moaned in pleasure, freeing my mouth from your kiss. I kissed your neck, your chest, your nipples, and had begun working my way further down when you pulled me up. You draped my arms around your neck and rolled the condom down your shaft. Then you lifted me on top of you and plunged me down on your cock, using my hard breasts like handles, pulling me down onto you repeatedly as I screamed out your name. I was all yours!

You pulled me closer, clutching my hair in a knot and biting my nipples as I rode you to your climax. Heightened by your orgasm, I raised myself up from your chest, arched my back, and came harder than I have ever cum in my life! I was crying, repeating your name, and trembling all over...I could not stop cumming.

I was barely conscious when you pulled me back down on your chest, placing my face next to yours. The stubble of your boyish face was like the whiskers on a cat. We lay there, two sweaty and spent love cats, having just mated for life. Our breaths were as one. I could no longer hear the clock. I could no longer hear anything but your heartbeat. Our heartbeat. Beyond exhausted, I finally fell asleep.

I woke up around noon to the smell of breakfast, wondering if there was anything you could not do. You made scrambled eggs, sausage, grilled cheddar on white bread, and tomato slices sprinkled with virgin olive oil. Then you hand-fed me, and I you. Where had you been all my life? I finally felt…loved.

I had no idea that when you walked me to your front door it would be the last time I ever saw you again. Otherwise, I would have left an earring behind as an excuse to come back. Everyone has always fallen for me so I naturally expected you to do the same. I gambled, lost, and stupidly went back to the dating game – even though my night with you had been the most amazing, most romantic encounter of my life.

***

20June1974: Today is my sixth birthday. Maris and I both got our first bikes without training wheels today. Joe sat me on the bike, held it steady, and told me to push the pedals forward. But he didn't tell me how to steer or press the brakes so I ran smack into a fucking tree a few feet from where I started. They all laughed at me. I cried.

I resented sharing this birthday with Maris. I never got presents on her birthday. In fact, I was beginning to resent Maris in general. She keeps speaking to her friends in pig Latin so I can't understand her and she whispers behind my back like I'm deaf.

Tye, our cousin, is babysitting us for the summer. Tye practices yoga and has the biggest tits I've ever seen. Sweet Lord, they are perfect! I recommended to Maris that she take up yoga but she failed to make the connection.

Tye lets us talk to her while she bathes and I pretend not

to notice her mulatto melons and cherry nipples floating above the water like surfacing submarines. Sometimes I kept a list of questions prepared for the times I knew she was taking a bath.

I drew a naked lady with the lower body of a cobra and a quiver full of poisoned arrows. Old Joe happened to see it and now keeps it with him in his briefcase. He says I could be a great artist someday. I wonder if he knows those are Tye's tits.

20June1975: Today is my seventh birthday. School is out for summer but I wish it were open so I could see all my friends. Eric Campbell, Lori May Brown, John-John, Ian, Jimmy, Cecilia, Warwicka...I have too many friends to count.

Eric and I both like Lori May. She is the only chick we have not pulled into the bushes yet. Actually, I just sit in the bushes and wait while Eric and Jimmy pull them in so I can interrogate them.

Lori is pretty, with soft skin the color of *Wonder Bread*. She is also very tough but cannot catch my dodge ball. I never met a girl who could catch my dodge ball.

Jenny always keeps my birthday card money for "back-to-school shopping". I never see a dime of it. She's such a tight-ass; she keeps the water temperature set at lukewarm and the heat at sixty-five, only turning it on in November. Does she even know it goes past sixty-five? We never need the freezer in my house; when we want ice, we just fill the ice trays with water and leave them on the fucking counter.

Joe got me a lefty baseball glove, a *Louisville Slugger* bat, and a baseball, which he tortured me with by throwing me fastballs until I cried.

Joe has been taking me to work with him at the hospital on weekends because "Jenny can't handle me." I get to play in the whirlpool spa there and the nurses all flirt with me. But Joe is still an asshole. Last week, I called Jenny pitiful during dinner. Joe picked me up and slapped me so hard I'm still seeing stars. This guy is completely off his fucking trolley. He came home late the other night and tore the rain gutter off the side of our next-door neighbor's house. He never apologized and Martin and Malcolm's parents never pressed the issue.

I discovered I could burn those huge mosquitoes right out of the air if I spray them with *Right Guard* then light the spray-stream. They burst into flames and fall like fireworks. The smell is awful. Sometimes I go down to the basement and torch the centipedes by the water meter. Their legs burn up so fast the fire is out before it hits their bodies. Afterwards, they lay there squirming. Writhing white worms. I imagined their little mouths screaming, then I finished the job. The smell was just plain awful.

27June1975: I made a clubhouse out of the garage and got everyone to join: Martin and Malcolm, Darryl and Duane from across the street; even Maris joined. I charged them fifty cents each per meeting and Maris convinced me to make her our treasurer. Surprisingly, she really came through for me. When I was grounded for shoving a banana up Mister Dixon's tailpipe, she kept the clubhouse going.

She even cleaned out the garage, including Joe's old *GM Javelin* that I kept my stray cats in. It was the closest we had been in years. Then she stuck the knife in my back; she hijacked my clubhouse while I watched helpless and grounded from my upstairs window.

She renamed my club from The Boys Club to The All Stars and spray-painted a big white star on the wall. Then she took my treasury money and threw a fucking PARTY! She spent everything on *Doritos* and *Faygo* pop, and the bitch knows I hate *Doritos*! All I could do was cry.

By the time I got sprung from house arrest, there *was* no fucking club. Maris had convinced my friends that the club was "dumb" and "immature." Everything I had planned for them...the spears we would make from broom sticks, the secret notes made from writing in lemon juice and holding a lighter under it, the sheep's brain Joe brought home that I was waiting to dissect with them, and the glow-in-the-dark skull model that we would build...all of that fun was now completely fucked up.

Mother Mary hated calling me *Spit*. She had her own nickname for me, "Head". She said it was because my head was so big that I almost didn't get born, and because I left stretch marks on her belly. But I like to think she called me that because I was so smart. Now I'm going to show some people how smart I am. Maris has to go.

03July1975: I've decided to postpone Maris' flight-of-stairs accident. Some of her girlfriends from school have come over for her slumber party, including that hot girl, Angie. Angie already has great tits and she's only nine. They all danced together in Maris' room while I took pictures (special pictures) with Maris' camera.

Yeah, Maris has a camera. She also has a tape recorder and a record player. Can you believe that shit? My parents won't even buy me a radio! I have one, but it's a *Six Million Dollar Man* AM-only radio and it has to be clipped to a fucking metal surface to work.

Sometimes I imagine Maris falling out of her upstairs window but not as much lately; Region Four Open School really helps keep me calm. It was in all the papers when it opened and had a mile-long waiting list for enrollment. All I do there all day is write, draw, read, and play. They try and get me to do math but they call it *Open* School; I am not yet open to math. Not unless the subject is flies or insects in general, then I love to subtract.

There has been a particularly bad spell of ants since spring so I organize ant raids. I take some of Joe's blood vials, fill them with rubbing alcohol, and add a dash of *Ajax*. I pass them out to my friends and we hunt around the yard for those huge black ants trying to find a way inside my house. We collect them and drop them in the vials where they change color from black to brown before they die. Some turn almost white.

This is fun but not as much fun as the slug hunts. We pull up rocks and logs in my backyard to find slugs – those super-sized snails without shells. Then we sprinkle the slimy bastards with table salt and watch them explode.

Everyone seems to like Bug Kung Fu best, where we capture spiders, wasps, hornets, and honeybees in jars and let them fight it out. If there is more than one honeybee, the bees mostly win. Except in the case of black hornets that are always the winners, no matter what else is in the jar.

The winner wins nothing because they all die in the end anyway. We drop in a smoke bomb and the jar turns milk-white. When the smoke clears, everything is dead.

13July1975: Joe got an old cast iron water heater. He cut it open and hinged it to make a barbecue grill. Every time he lights it, he yells, "Fire in the hole!" and jumps back five feet. He never painted it though; he left it sitting out in the rain to become another rusted piece of junk like the car in our garage. Joe never finishes anything. We never got our swimming pool and we never took a road trip in a van. He may have come back from Vietnam but as my dad, he was still MIA.

We had a new baby-sitter almost every week. The last ones were my cousins Tye, then Annette, and then Tye again. Annette falls asleep the minute Jenny leaves for work. Then I steal one of her cigarettes to smoke later with Malcolm. The skinny ones have the best flavor but they make us cough more and then we eat up all the cereal in the house. I always feel sleepy afterwards. No wonder she sleeps all day.

Annette was really nice though, unless you pushed her too far, and one day I did. I went through her purse and used up all her nail polishes repainting my *Matchbox* cars. She flipped out and quit the job on the spot, cursing and crying. I got a beating from Jenny for that but it was much better than getting one from Joe. She ties my hands in front of me with a sock to keep me from shielding my ass, while she forces me down on the bed and spanks me.

After Annette left, Tye came back but they had to double her pay. They thought she was the only one who could handle me. She ended up shaving her head bald and driving to California with some guy. They blame me for that too. How could I make someone become a Krishna when I have no idea what a Krishna is?

14July1975: This morning, after Joe and Jenny went to work and Maris went across the street, I put charcoal and newspaper in the water heater/grill and soaked it all with gasoline. I took one of my stray kittens from the *Javelin,* wrapped its mouth shut with electrical tape, set it inside the grill, and closed the lid.

There was a hole in the water heater for lighting the pilot light; I dropped a match in there. Immediately there was this big WHUMP! The concussion from the blast slapped me hard in the face, knocking me backwards and singing my hair. The tape must have melted off the kitten's muzzle because it screamed loud enough to wake the dead. It kept throwing itself against the heater's cast iron frame. My heart was racing. The kitten was making too much damn noise!

I went back into the garage and took out Joe's old coal shovel. He used it for shoveling snow; I used it to pry open the burning grill and break the kitten's back. The lid slammed shut again.

Smoke was everywhere. The smell was like broiled meat drippings and women's hot-combed hair.

There were voices behind me coming quickly up the driveway - Maris with Darryl's sister, Linda. Maris asked me what I was doing, obviously looking for something to tattle on.

"I'm cleaning out the grill for Dad," I said. "You gotta burn out the rust and old meat and stuff; otherwise, we'll all get sick."

She and Linda moved closer to the grill to investigate, waving smoke from their eyes and coughing. Maris reached out to open the grill but Joe never installed a handle and the lid was piping hot. She backed away, placing her hands on her hips in aggravation.

"Spit, what are you burning?" Maris asked. "We can smell it all the way across the street! Dad didn't say you could cook on here! I'm callin' Ma!"

"I think there must've been a rat's nest under it," I said. "That's why we've got to cover up that pilot light hole or clean out the grill sometimes. You can look inside if you want; I'm gonna wait."

I knew she would never try opening the grill now; she was terrified of rodents. She just shook her head, called me weird, and walked back down the driveway with Linda.

"Fire in the hole," I mumbled.

I liked watching Linda's ass. While Maris had literally no ass at all, Linda was endowed with certain curves that made her windowpane bell-bottom jeans seem more like circles than squares - inviting circles that held a hypnotic effect when viewed as she walked...her ass swinging side to side like a pendulum.

I waited at least twenty minutes before opening the grill, afraid of what I would find. I imagined the kitten jumping out on me as I held open the lid, pulling me forward into the flames. I deserved it; I botched the job terribly so the thing had suffered needlessly and I was almost caught.

I finally lifted the lid and examined the carnage. There was nothing left but a charred, curled ball. The eyes and most of the head were gone or just indistinguishable. The top of it looked like a melted carpet; the rest was black and cracked on the bottom. I looked down, feeling at first curiosity and then something else - something new. I prodded it with a meat cleaver before cutting it completely in half, right inside the grill. The inside was all dark meat, stuffed with something like...chicken gizzards.

I checked to make sure no one was watching before I picked up the top half of the carcass and hurried into my garage, locking the door from the inside. Next, I lifted it to my nose. My throat was dry; my heart was banging out of my chest and I became overwhelmed by an unyielding desire to taste it.

Chapter 5

We were coming down from the Netherlands and over Northern Africa. We still had a few hours left before touching down in Cape Town. I suddenly missed my family. Explaining to them my temporary assignment in South Africa was more difficult than I anticipated. I told Dad the news over lunch at D'Amatos to prevent him from creating a scene but when I showed up at Mom's for dinner, Dad was there waiting for me and staged a family intervention.

Dad had them all imagining Cape Town as a bigger version of Detroit but with even less cops. He really hit the roof; I was afraid he would have to be wheeled back into surgery for another bypass.

I had begun noticing similarities between Joey's father and mine – assuming Joey was the blog's author. Both fathers were headstrong, dominant, philandering men who readily excused what they did as long as they provided for their families. Both men were respected in their communities and were leaders among their circles. Both had an underlying current of…rage, but the similarities ended there. Joey's father was a doctor while my father just sent people to the doctor.

As Friday night's interrogation concluded, my family saw that I would not change my mind and they finally conceded. There was a group hug followed by a toast of anisette. I knew, no matter what, I could count on them. Coach Rosatti had raised us to be there for the team, no matter what the circumstances. "Family," he would say, "are the only people you can truly depend on."

On the subject of dependability, Dad did not trust Green and Nelson's description of my assignment.

"What did I teach you?" he asked. "If something seems too easy, it usually is."

"Dad, you don't know these guys; these are very powerful men."

"They're always powerful," he said, "until they're *not*."

Angelo Rosatti always had charisma. When I was growing up, the kids in our neighborhood loved Dad because he was pretty much a big kid too. If he was home and not stuffing his face, he was pulling some kind of ball out of the closet and dragging us kids onto the back lawn.

Big Ange, as Dad was affectionately known, was also an assistant baseball and football coach for the PAL teams my brothers played for. He could not be bothered with being made head coach because that would have meant responsibility. By just being an assistant coach, he could show up just for the games and prowl the sidelines, screaming at my brothers whenever he thought they "fucked up the play."

Dad could not make all their away games but he made most of their home games. During the drives back home to Washington Avenue, in Royal Oak, he never gave up an opportunity to critique his sons' performances; sometimes leaving them in tears. Looking at the strong men and better athletes they became, I cannot say that Dad did not influence them.

My dad worked many late nights. "*Mary-Jesus-and-Joseph*!" he would say to Mom, if she nagged him about being home at decent hours. Angelo would say he had to meet his investors and business partners whenever it was convenient for them. Sometimes Big Ange would stay out until morning, coming home reeking of a business partner's heavy perfume; my dutiful mom always had a hot meal waiting on the range for him.

Every summer, we went on family road trips. Sometimes Dad would let one of my brothers steer the wheel while they sat on his lap, but only if there was no traffic, and he was in a good mood, and the AC worked. If it was too hot or we were stuck in traffic, Big Ange became a big asshole. Once, he reached back and backhanded my brother Johnny, spraying his orange soda all over us kids in the back. To this day, Johnny refuses to drink orange soda.

Backhanding was a rarity though. For the most part, we were all well-behaved children; we knew what would happen if we got out of line. Our parents always took us out in public. We genuinely enjoyed being around each other and were always seen together. Dad did not wear his wealth but people seemed to know he was somebody. He knew a lot of entertainers and business people that always paid their respects if they passed through town, giving us kids the chance to meet them. It was good being his children, as long as we remembered we were just children.

***

20June1976: Today is my eighth birthday. At least a month has passed since I dissected anything. I put all of Joe's syringes back and tossed the scalpel down the sewer grate out front, after I damn near cut one of my fingertips off while trying to trim my nails.

I was too afraid to tell anyone, especially Maris. There is a long scar there now and I cannot feel as much in that fingertip as in the others. The good news is that there is no infection like last year when Malcolm cut my left hand with my own saw. What an asshole! I could neither write nor draw for weeks and wiping my ass was damn near impossible.

Speaking of assholes, Joe has cuts on his hand too. Actually, they are on the inside of his left wrist and they are old...years old. Days of Mother Mary old.

Jenny bought me the same cake as every other year: Sanders fucking *Colonial* with white cream frosting. She must really like that cake. She also kept the card money - as usual.

After all us kids ate cake and ice cream, we went outside to play hide-and-go-seek. I was barely off the front porch when a cicada mistook my green shirt for a tree and landed on my chest (a cicada is like a fly on steroids or a small humming bird). It stared up at me with huge, bug eyes and made this eerie, high-pitched whine while buzzing its wings on my shirt. I screamed bloody murder and pissed my pants while all my friends ran from me - even my own sister.

Finally, I tore off my shirt, tossed it to the ground, and ran like hell down the block. I hate bugs. I fucking HATE bugs! Ever since I was clamped into this world, it has been me against the bugs. If I die and there is still one bug left in this world, people will know I died too soon.

A couple of weeks ago, we got a new baby brother - a Gemini like me. His name is Edward but we already call him Teddy. He's tiny as hell, with Chinese eyes, and cries like a mule. He so freakin' small! Where does he get the lungpower to keep that racket up all night and day? Everyone has gotten into the habit of calling me downstairs to take his shitty diapers out to the trash. This kid is theirs; they should do it! I was never consulted in the decision to have him. If I were, I would have ordered something bigger. This kid is sickly and so fucking frail. I bet if I hugged him...I could accidentally crush him to death.

30June1976: Today...was one of the most painful days of my life! Dressed in toy shoulder pads and a helmet, armed with two bricks and all my spineless friends, I assaulted the wasp nest residing in the clothesline pole of my backyard. We all agreed to the war on bugs and we all said we would kill the wasps, but by the time the first brick left my hand, those motherfuckers had left me!

As a consequence, I was the only one that got stung. I took two in the chest and Jenny had to take care of me – again. Crazy Joe told her to lay me in their bed so she could keep an eye on me, and then put cigarette tobacco and water on my stings, which had swollen up like cow udders. There is a muscle at the end of a stinger that keeps pushing it in, deeper and deeper, until the muscle dies, until all the venom has been injected, then it just switches off...and this motherfucker prescribed *Kool Filter Kings*?

I cried so hard that I fell asleep. The only thing that woke me was the sound of my friends, playing together outside. When Joe came home, he set fire to the clothesline pole, smoking out all the wasps. Maybe he loves me after all...in some demented way. Or maybe he just thinks no one should be able to hurt me but him.

I had not considered fire as a viable method of extermination in this case, but Joe killed them all in one blow. Piss-poor planning had left me confined to bed, while my friends rode their bikes and played tag. Smoke and fire...I will experiment...learn how much/how little is needed. Bugs may have won today, but tomorrow they'll pay. And tomorrow, and tomorrow, and tomorrow.

04July1976: Dad stayed out late again. He called me to his room this morning and told me, "Go find something to feed the dog." I looked in the backyard and there was this big-ass St. Bernard tied to our maple tree. Joe said his name is Luther and that he won him playing cards. Great...more shit for me to clean up.

17July1976: Martin busted his head on his back porch. Their house has these green iron rails that they can flip under, by bending forward and passing themselves between the porch and the bottom rail. It was cool to watch, until Martin cracked his fucking head open. The scar looks horrible, like he was cursed by God.

23August1976: Luther is gone and I had nothing to do with it! Yesterday, we left him outside roped to the garage door while we went to a family reunion. There was a bad thunderstorm while we were gone and we came back to a broken rope and no dog.

Our sliding garage door was busted and hanging off its track. Worst of all, the Plexiglas screen over our front door had been completely shattered. Strands of Luther's jaw were hanging from jagged pieces of Plexiglas. Blood was all over the porch. Our front door was all scratched and dented to hell. Joe made me clean everything up and I cried. Fucking asshole.

Neighbors say Luther had been frightened by the thunderstorm and ran off into the darkness. Nobody here was looking for him; he has heartworms, a bad temper, and no legal tags. Luther was on his way out anyway; he was already banned from inside the house. These assholes were afraid he would eat the baby.

I wish I was the one banned from the house. I keep waiting for the hospital to call and say it was all a mistake – that I was actually some other family's kid. Loving things never really works out for me in this family. Whatever I love either beats me or leaves me.

25December1979: This morning, Dad surprised me with the best Christmas present I EVER got! A Daisy pump-action .22 caliber air rifle. He also got me a bow and arrow set but the arrowheads are not sharp enough to do any real damage. Jenny got me the usual clothes but I am still so very happy! I am the only fifth-grader I know who has his own gun!

26December1979: I began executing all of my old toys today. Martin and Malcolm helped. We started with the paper bull's-eyes that came with the gun and then moved on to soda cans. Later, in a stroke of genius, I put my *Spiderman* action figure in the maple tree and blew his fucking head off.

After that, we gunned down all of my toys: the *Micronauts,* the *GI Joe*, *Batman* and *Robin*...whatever I had. I was born for this! But I cannot trust Malcolm with the gun. It is only a matter of time before he shoots someone, and it just might be me.

27December1979: For Christmas, Maris got some pattern designs for dresses and some electronic stuff, including a new stereo. She got more records too. She always gets more crap than I do. Maybe they should just come out in the open, call her their favorite, and get it the fuck over with.

After dinner, I was talking in our driveway to the kid that lives on the other side of us. Malcolm was playing with my gun at his house, leaning out of his bedroom window and watching us in the driveway. The kid was talking to me about comic books when Malcolm took aim and shot the kid in the ass! Actually, the BB ricocheted off our driveway and hit the kid in his rear thigh.

What is his fucking problem? Four years ago, Malcolm damn near amputated my hand while horseplaying with my saw. I had stitches and everything, but the wound got infected, oozing yellow and green pus. Crazy Joe had to drain it and re-stitch it. I cried, but he told me to shut the hell up or he would smack the shit out of me. This was my father...my father the doctor.

I had an intense dream about Mother Mary last night. I dreamt she was dead and warning me to avoid water. It was like she was warning me to avoid drowning or choking. Great advice, Mom. A bit vague, though. Should I also avoid walking into traffic or setting myself on fire?

I am also worried about a dream I keep having of an old Black man who looks like Bojangles. He follows me home from the school bus stop but I have to pee so bad that I take no notice. As I come out of the bathroom, he chokes me to death with a long red Chicken George scarf.

04April1980: Last night, Joe made me shoot a rat outside in our trashcan. "Always confirm your kill," he said. He made me dig through the trash with the rifle barrel and find it. It was on the side of the can near the bottom. When the barrel touched it, it dived through the watermelon rinds, shitty diapers, and tampons. The can was shaking. I shot six more BBs into it and the shaking stopped. There were at least a thousand white maggots everywhere, crawling all over the can and the lid. The smell alone made me want to vomit, but the look of them gave me nightmares.

Joe made me clean out the can today. "Put a bag over the lid and just flip it over," he said. Before I did, I found a can of *Raid* and just sprayed and sprayed. The maggots melted in the noonday sun. I washed out the can when I was done.

I really like to hurt things. I guess I even *need* to hurt things, and I cannot...correct the problem by myself. At school, the staff raves about my writing and artwork. Are they blind? Do I need to stab some kid in the eye with a pencil before these dipshits connect the dots?

Yesterday, I was shooting some *Busch* beer cans with my air gun. I filled the cans with milk and used pellets instead of BBs so the cans would explode on impact. Soon, my backyard looked like I was the unholy lovechild of Andy Warhol and Tyree Guyton.

I never missed a shot, and all the anger had gone out of me. But as I turned to go inside, I heard this annoying chirping above me...from a robin on a wire behind our garage. It was laughing at me. Mocking me and telling me what a lousy shot I was.

The sun was behind it and it was some distance away, making for a more difficult shot. There was the popping of compressed air and then the robin began to rise. It fluttered about eight inches before dropping like dead weight behind the garage. I peeked around the corner and saw it lying on its back. Its legs were bent inward and its talons looked like they were clutching air. Its twitching wings were outstretched and jumbled and its eyes were closed.

I ran in fear, leaving it there in that death twitch. When I returned the next day, the robin was gone. I thought perhaps a stray cat had gotten to him but then I remembered...I had long ago rid the neighborhood of strays. "Always confirm your kill," Joe once told me. And from now on, I always will.

Chapter 6

This was the longest flight I had ever taken. There was a real-time map of the plane's progress on the back of the headrest in front of me; it looked like we had not moved in six hours. My legs were cramping up. No wonder people freak out on planes.

I am grateful to have this blog to read and I hope to God that it is fiction. Still, beyond the insanity, I find we have more and more in common with each word I read. We are not twins like Jimmy and Johnny but so…similar.

For example, there was a time when Dad and I could not get along. Unfortunately, that was most of my teenage years. I was growing up to be just as stubborn as Angelo. I really back-chatted him a lot but he never disciplined me like he did my brothers. He just seemed to give up on me around the point that I reached puberty – and that is when I acted up the most.

After the inevitable divorce, Dad broke down in tears and apologized to me for not being there when I needed him. That was the only time in thirty-four years I had ever seen Big Ange cry.

On the other hand, Mom always seemed to cry. Ironically, we all considered her to be our pillar of strength. She was more than just the soccer mom who ran us around because Dad was working; she saw to our needs and worked full-time too.

Mom did not take a job because she needed money or to get away from us; she just hated sitting around the house like other suburban housewives. She used to say, "If God wanted me to be housewife, I would've been born with my ass stapled to a sofa."

Although Dad taught us to be competitive, Mom was the one who taught us work ethic. While Dad taught us the importance of standing up for your friends, Mom taught us the importance of family. She made sure we knew that our father loved us, even if it was difficult for him to show. If we thought Dad was being too hard on us, Mom would tell us to forgive him and let go of the anger or give time a chance to turn our hate back into love.

Mom did not support my decision to go to South Africa but she did not try to prevent it. In reality, it was no longer their decision to make anyway. I think Mom finally understood that. I think they are all starting to realize that I am all grown up now – a thirty-four year-old woman with no husband and no children.

They should be proud of me; I am sticking by a friend. I am helping someone who – given the right circumstances – could become the newest member of our family. Joey and I only had that one night together but I am completely convinced that he is the one for me. Nothing has happened to him that we cannot fix together. GM has their plans for him…but I have mine.

I wonder why it is always the smart ones that go crazy. Ted Kaczynski (the Unibomber) graduated with honors from U of M, just like us. Kaczynski also had some kind of blog…a manifesto. He had it published in national newspapers as a condition for ending his mail-bombing campaign. He was pissed off with American industrialization so he began blowing up university professors in the name of Mother Nature.

Actually, Kaczynski's insistence on being published is how he was caught. His family recognized his manifesto and turned Fed on him. His own family did that. Fucking unbelievable. I guess a person's writing style and subject matter could be like a fingerprint – like how Green is so confident that Joey has been writing the blog. But there seems to be no motive for it. Had Joey just gone nuts like GM thought? Nelson and Green told me what he was doing but they stopped short of telling me why he was doing it.

I was considering Joey's motives when I became faintly aware of bells and the clicking of safety belts. I looked around. Although I could not make out the Captain's Dutch over the PA system, I saw everyone preparing to land. My heart began to race. All I could see was Joey's face!

Exiting the plane into the airport, I ran smack into a wall of humidity and the omnipresent scent of human body odor. These people smelled bad! A driver met me there, holding a sign that said only "LR", as was prearranged by GM. We got many long looks on the way to retrieve my bags. I checked my clothing self-consciously several times, eventually accepting that South Africans just love to stare.

Outside in the sun, the heat became unbearable. My driver hobbled along with a pronounced limp in his right leg as he toted my two large bags. He was tall, sweaty, and light-skinned, wearing a dirty white dress shirt under a black leather jacket. I offered to roll the bags for myself but he smiled and mumbled something unintelligible in Afrikaans through the space that used to be his front teeth.

I tried hinting to him to walk faster – anything to get out of the heat! I packed for warm weather and had worn a sundress but this place was beyond warm. It was the middle of winter in Michigan, but in Cape Town, it was the middle of hell. My hair hung from my neck like wet noodles.

The driver, whose name may or may not have been Martin (I gave up trying to understand how he pronounced it), finally pointed out his red Land Rover and threw my bags into his trunk like he was tossing out trash. "The boot," he called it. Then he raced us out of the parking lot like he had warrants on him. I was too tired and sticky to object, plus motion circulated air in that rolling oven.

All I wanted to do was get out of my bra; the underwire felt like it was surgically grafted to my skin. Out of boredom, I glanced over the front seat and noticed the dashboard included all the standard dials, including one with the color blue.

"Martin," I said coldly.

"Yes ma'am?"

"Does this car have AC?"

"Sorry Miss?"

"A – C…That thing right there; does it work?"

"Oh, the air conditioner? Yes it does. You want me to turn it on? No problem."

The air from the AC took ten minutes to make any noticeable difference; perhaps because Martin still had his window down while he talked me to death about the differences in our two countries. They did not call it AC here and they try not to use it because it is bad for the car, he said.

The jet lag from the twenty-two hour plane ride, coupled with this intensely humid weather, had left me nauseous. I was overwhelmed and tried to fake sleeping for the rest of the drive. We went over a big bump and I opened my eyes to see what it was. I thought it might have been Joey. I inherit my sense of humor from my father's side of the family, where joking about death is occupational therapy. When we were kids, Dad never took us to see *Disney* films, only murder films, like he was keeping up-to-date on new techniques. I used to pretend I was a spy with a license to kill. While the other girls were playing with *Barbie* dolls, I was scheming on ways to seduce and destroy my target. My code name was Luna.

We all have alter egos. Others might find them laughable but they carry us through the tough times. Sometimes they even have the strength to carry others. I always imagined Luna's tombstone would read: "She Mattered". There is really nothing else people want out of life except to matter to someone.

I was asleep when we finally arrived at the Metropole. This time, I had no qualms with allowing others to carry my bags. In the lobby, I dismissed Martin for the day and followed the porter to the antique elevator taking us to my second-floor suite.

Once there, I discovered the softest bed I had ever plopped into. There were no snakes or scorpions under the pillows, despite rumors spread by the head of the Rosatti family. Speaking of which, I thought I should call home to say everything was okay. According to the nightstand clock, it was 3:12 p.m. I knew it was Sunday, January 30th, and Michigan was seven hours behind us. So it was…8:12 a.m. there.

I decided I did not have the strength to talk to either Green or my family; I had not slept more than thirty minutes in the past twenty-four hours. I would let Sunday be my day of rest and get a fresh start tomorrow. I was already beginning to yawn uncontrollably. Goodnight Secret Agent Bosco; Agent Luna is self-destructing in ten seconds.

***

25December1980: Merry Christmas. I got nothing I wanted – again. Jenny's son got an *Apple* computer, Maris got a full tuition to *Barbizon Modeling School*, and I got clothes. Fucking corduroy pants.

Last night, we went to a party at Ken and Dottie's house (Joe's friends). They have a huge house somewhere in the woods of

Southfield where they host an annual Christmas party. Jenny and Joe probably only took us so we would not search for our presents. There were toads in those woods…toads that came right up to their patio door. I took some for pets.

Later, while Maris was in one of the bedrooms sleeping with Teddy, and I was watching *ON TV* (cable), Jenny yelled my father's name so loudly that it made the hairs on my arms stand straight. I ran to the living room and saw Jenny and Ken holding back Joe, who was towering over some guy he had just laid out flat on the carpet.

Jenny and Ken were begging Joe to go home while the guy was just lying there, staring up at him in terror. Joe was breathing hard and had turned beet red. "Come on, let's go," he said. And we left.

The ride home was tense. They argued about what the guy had said, which amounted to "You look sexy tonight." I became very upset at Joe. Not because he clobbered the guy but because I could not finish watching cable! They had twenty-four channels; can you believe that? And this asshole ruined it for me.

When we finally got home, upstairs I did run. The asshole followed me, calling me a "motherfuckin' slob" and a no-good son. As I was crying, shaking, and cowering on my bed, he punched a hole through the wall, right next to my head. He slammed my door behind him and stomped down the stairs. I wish I could sneak up behind him with a shovel and catch him unawares.

As I undressed, I realized I had crushed my toads to death by sitting on them while Joe cursed me. There was a wet spot with a little blood on my bed. I was so sad. I had planned to dissect them alive.

I wanted to run away last night but I had nowhere to go. If I say something at school, I'll end up in an orphanage or with some freaky family member. I remember back in the days…when Maris and I were passed around from relative to relative, like a joint at a Jimi Hendrix concert. Fuck that…anything was better than that. All my belongings in a ripped plastic bag, having to call everyone Auntie This or Uncle That…

I have not heard from Mother Mary in years. Her other son, Jack, has been sent to Don Bosco Hall boys' home, for forging checks while he was living with an uncle. I feel so alone. I am the loneliest kid on Earth. The only places I have to go are here and to sleep. Sometimes, they don't even let me sleep.

Teddy woke me this morning to show me his toys. I could never stay mad at someone that beautiful, but sometimes he could be really selfish. Did he not notice the lack of toys bearing my name? Jenny sent Maris upstairs to make me come and thank Old Joe for my gifts (sox and pants).

Downstairs, Jenny was repeat-playing "Silly Of Me" by Denise Williams. She always did that when she was pissed at Old Joe. But this time, through his hangover, he finally listened to the song's lyrics. He got up, stomped to the record player, and smashed Jenny's album to pieces. He marched back to bed while we helped Jenny clean up the carnage, but it was useless. Not even J. Edgar Hoover could find all those pieces.

It was silent after that. Jenny was too stunned to cry. She just kept making Christmas dinner...and burning it. I felt bad for her so I offered to do the household's laundry as her Christmas present. We still hated each other but I needed to wash my coat and sheets because of the toad guts. I kept their bodies in the attic until today, until I could take them outside and bury them.

The ground was cold today. Not a good day for burying smashed toads but I knew that our shovel could break through anything. Old Joe had brought it with him from Kentucky. A cast iron shovel, used for shoveling coal; I had broken through inch-thick ice with it. The earth was snow covered and flint-hard as I struck it repeatedly with the shovel. It felt like I was striking bone. Maybe skull bone.

CHAPTER 7

I PICKED up the *Cape Times* in front of my suite door on the way downstairs. Today is Wednesday, February 2nd; it says it will be another hot one. I got an earful last night from Green, who sounded like he was either going to be fired or contract-killed. I acknowledged missing the deadline, and reminded Green with what relative ease a person of color could lose himself in this country – a country eighty percent Black and whose infrastructure was only ten years old.

I spent Monday and Tuesday meeting with GM's list of South African Expansion contacts and got zilch. They had not met with, nor heard from Joey, since before December 2004. If the leads were any colder, I could have dropped them in my *Jack* and *Coke*.

I had Martin meet me at the Metropole to brainstorm. We had an early dinner of guinea fowl with a hybrid Merlot/Sauvignon, during which, Martin seemed nervous and out of place. This was understandable; he had no idea what I needed from him or why I was looking for Joey. He only knew GM had booked him a room at the Metropole to escort me and to be on call twenty-four hours a day.

In exchange, Martin would be paid well; enough to suffer through staying at a four star hotel, even if it meant not seeing his family for a few days. Martin said GM only gave him one clear instruction: he was not to let me travel alone under any circumstances.

I sat across from him as the waitron adjusted my chair then dashed off to fetch me a glass of water. "I'll be with you now," she said, and then disappeared for twenty minutes.

"So…why do they call it guinea fowl?" I asked Martin. "That's an insult to my people."

"Sorry ma'am?"

"Dinner. I asked why it's called guinea fowl."

"I don't really know, Miss. Maybe because it comes from Guinea, which is up north in West Africa," Martin answered seriously.

"I was only joking Martin. And you've been driving me around for four days now; you can cut the ma'am crap and just call me Lisa."

"Are you sure?"

"I insist."

"Okay. Lisa."

"Better. Um, I'm not really getting anywhere with my contact list. I think I'll just stay in for the day. There's a suitcase of Joey's – Joe Bosco's – that the hotel kept for GM. I'd like to go through it. Maybe our guys missed something.

"You might as well know, we really don't know how or when Joey disappeared. All we know is the date – December twenty-third of last year. He got a call in his room around seven-thirty that morning from a payphone on Long Street. The call lasted under a minute. His laptop was left in his room but erased, and he hadn't used his cell phone in over a month."

Martin rubbed his chin curiously, like he was trying to solve the riddle of the sphinx. "Do you mean December of two thousand four?"

"Yes. Why, do you know something about it?"

"I was just trying to remember if I saw anything in the papers or heard something…"

"You wouldn't have; a police report was never filed." I was noticeably irritable and chewing on what was left of my fingernails. I was in way over my head. Another day or so and I'd be drowning.

"Lisa, you seem upset. You've been working very hard this past week. Why don't you rest or let me take you to some nice clubs, neh? Are you married?"

"No. Maybe soon, though. Listen, just…hang out in the area and I'll call you if I need you."

"If you let me, I can take one of those photos and show it to some other drivers and see if they recognize him."

"That's a great idea! Just be kind of discreet. And keep your cell phone on, please."

"Yebo, my mobile is on."

"Thanks, Martin."

I took the stairs back to my hotel room, having not worked out since I left Michigan. I feel like I'm gaining a pound a day from cakes and alcohol, but it was better than having an anxiety attack. I ordered a *Belvedere* martini from room service, settled on *Absolut*, and sat down at the desk. I stared somberly at the large gray *Samsonite* suitcase that room service also brought up…the last remains of Joey in this world. A cursory search of the contents produced shirts, socks, *Jockey* briefs, *Rembrandt* toothpaste, and a small pyramid. As I picked up the plastic pyramid, it beeped and said, "three thirty p.m." It was Joey's talking clock! I thought again of our night together, sensing his presence so close to me.

I had picked up a crumpled napkin with the pyramid. I unraveled it and saw Joey's handwriting in quotes: "…The world forgetting, by the world forgot." More scribblings from a beautiful, fucked-up mind, I thought. Poetic insanity was part of Joey's charm. Shit! I hoped it wasn't a suicide note! I thought of Ron Pollock back in high school…and shuddered.

I must have been insane to think I could pull this off. I needed the family now. Dad wanted to send my brothers with me but I refused his offer; that was a mistake. Jimmy and Johnny were always effective at solving problems for me.

They basically ran our neighborhood, influenced by Dad, no doubt. As a result, the boys in our school region considered me untouchable all the way through high school. I would have crushes on boys but they would never even look me in the eye, let alone ask me out. For a while, I though it was because I was ugly. I was gangly and skinny back then, plus my nose had been broken once while riding my bike. I had no semblance of an ass until college, and I'll have to give birth to get out of a B cup.

"Five thirty p.m.," the clock squawked.

I realized it was two hours and three martinis later, and I still had no leads. I was smarter than this. I had always been smarter than this. I graduated with honors from U of M. I could have been or done anything I wanted to, but all I wanted to be was with you. So I was glad Johnny held onto that card you gave him. It was a red carpet rolled out for me, right through the hidden doors of Global Media. Now, almost a year to the date we met, I am being paid to find the only man I have ever loved. I came to find you, Joey. Please…help me find you.

***

20June1981: Today is my thirteenth birthday; I got the usual cards and cake. Whoop-Dee-Fucking-Doo! I beat up our paperboy with my *Louisville Slugger*. We had a disagreement regarding newspaper delivery etiquette. I have delivered *The Detroit News* since April, so I should know. The newspaper belongs in the customer's door, not on the lawn, and not in the driveway.

Old Joe should just cancel *The Free Press* since we get *The Detroit News* for free, but he prefers *The Free Press* funny papers. That's how they get you...with the funny papers.

But I'm the one who has to pick the paper up off the lawn or the driveway, because I get home before Joe and he expects his paper dry; so I beat the shit out of the paperboy because his dumb ass can't find the door unless it's collection day.

Sooner or later, everyone takes a beating at our house. The other day, Jenny woke up Joe by waving his hairbrush in his face to ask whose blonde hair was on it. He jumped out of bed, chased her to the dining room, and beat her with it.

24December1981: It's Christmas Eve, but since Maris and I hate each other, and Jenny does not speak to me directly, referring to me as "him upstairs", I guess I can sleep in late tomorrow.

Joe called and told me not to go to bed because he was coming to take me out with him! Maybe he knows about my experiments with lighter fluid and *Coke*! Or the lime *Jell-O* and antifreeze! The only way he could know...is if someone found my diary. Not possible; I keep it in the dishwasher that sits unused next to the bathroom. It's not even hooked up (he came home from playing cards one night last year, drunk and dragging a dishwasher). So what the hell does he want suddenly?

25December1981: I am barely able to write this; my arm is broken at the shoulder, or my shoulder is out of joint, or both. My eyes hurt in the light, and my brain is throbbing like it's twice the size of my skull. Last night, Old Joe said he was coming home to take me out with him after work, and he actually showed up! Something was obviously wrong.

We started out at The Blue Chip, where everyone treated him

like he was the Mayor. They let me sit at the bar, even though I am only twelve. We ate chicken wings and I got to drink *Jack Daniel's* and *Coke*. Women kept pinching my cheeks and telling me how much I looked like him.

Then we went to another bar, Ted's, where they treated him like he owned stock in the joint. No wonder I never got shit for Christmas. The kitchen doors swung open and a short, dark, damn-near bald woman came over to us. Maybe she knew Maris; she said she needed money for his daughter's gift so Joe gave her a wad of cash. The troll kissed him on his lips and vanished. This man needed to either put on his glasses, stop drinking, or stop telling people that we knew each other. I felt her nasty kiss on MY lips.

Old Joe and I shot the breeze for a while. We ate more chicken wings, while he drank *Jacks* and I drank gins with *Vernors*. I believe I was drunk. I am not sure because it was my first time, but I must have been. I kept thinking Old Joe was a great guy.

After a while, he began to get serious. "Son, tell me something. I'm not gonna get mad at you, I'm not gonna hit you, I just want you to tell me why you don't like my wife."

"I like her just fine," I said. "Who says I don't?" I was drunk, not crazy. You never knew what could set Joe off. I wore my brand new Adidas *Dragons* in the snow once to play street-football. He called me to the front door, picked me up, and bitch-slapped me in front of my friends. But the alcohol worked like truth serum. So with no regard for personal safety, I gave Old Joe what he wanted.

"Okay, it's not that I don't like her, it's just...she's not my mother, and she makes it clear to me that I'm not her son. Every time you go out, she says, 'Don't leave me here with your kids.' How do you think that makes me feel?"

"You know," Joe said with a steadily rising voice, "I married her to take care of you guys. So I could finish school and still work. She's given up a lot for you!"

"I know and I'm grateful. But her kid got an *Apple* computer for Christmas. What did I get? Pants and socks! And every time I wanna go somewhere, I can't because I have to clean up the house or babysit Teddy! She only calls home during the day to make sure he's okay. Nobody cares about me. I already know I'm the stepchild; you don't have to treat me like it!"

Old Joe stared at me in amazement. I had never spoken to him that way, not before nor since. But I was on a roll, and the gin continued to take its toll. "It's not that I don't like her...I HATE HER! She's not my mother! She's YOUR wife and I want nothing to do with her!"

Joe looked down at his drink, finished it, then picked me up and threw me across the bar. I landed half on a booth seat and half on the floor. It was like I was watching the *Six Million Dollar Man*...Joe walked over to me in slow-mo, grabbed my jacket and lifted me into the air. His right fist was raised. Lots of people mobbed him. There had to be a lot...otherwise, I'd be dead. I was saying something to him and then I passed out.

I woke up in the front seat of his *Cutlass Cierra*. After a while, I recognized the Southfield Freeway. The ride home was like a commercial for Mothers Against Drunk Driving. That we did not flip over was a miracle. I wanted to reach out, grab the wheel, and flip us myself, but I was still drunk and trying to block my face in case he felt like slapping it.

The car had not even stopped in the driveway before I fell out of it and ran into the house. Joe must have really been mad enough to kill me because he didn't follow me upstairs. I could hear him and Jenny arguing downstairs, then he went out again.

Hours later, Joe came back home and walked upstairs. He opened the door enough for the hall light to shine through on my face. I pretended to be sleeping, but I was awake and smelling the whiskey and the chicken wings. He closed the door quietly and left, but I could not sleep. I prayed that Santa would bring me a bigger gun, but this morning, all I got was shirts, slacks, and socks...and a hangover.

20June1982: Today is my fourteenth birthday. Jenny surprised me by getting me a Sanders caramel cake. Now I kind of miss the *Colonial*.

Joe's lost it. I'm trying to stay out of his sight. In April, he made me dig up the backyard – the ENTIRE fucking backyard – pull out the weeds, and till the soil. And he never even planted any goddamn grass seed! I was so pissed off that I took photos of him from our family albums, took them out back, and repeatedly shot them.

Joe is allergic to black widows. He was bitten in the hand once while repairing the rail that he ripped out of our porch in a drunken rage. His hand swelled up like a red balloon.

I'm leaning toward rat poison but I am not sure if it has a

pleasant taste, or how much it would take to kill a six-foot, two hundred thirty pound man. Too bad laxatives aren't fatal...been mixing them into Jenny's leftovers since June 1st. I know just how much to add now...all depending on how they treat me.

Sam, Martin and Malcolm's dog, bit me once while we were horseplaying on their front lawn. I got two puncture holes in my side, plus I had to get a tetanus shot. I forgave him...publicly.

I hand-feed Sam now and let him defend me from strangers, but his scent disgusts me, and I once found his fleas on my socks. I thought of taking him for a walk and tossing him over the Southfield Freeway's Fenkel overpass, but there would be way too many witnesses along the way. No, poison is best. It has to be poison.

After all, Sam could have gotten poisoned anywhere. It could have come from someone's backyard, or from roaming through trash. They leave him outside on Sundays because they go to church all day. Can you imagine being in church all day? All that praying? Maybe they should start praying for Sam.

Chapter 8

On Thursday, February 3rd, I was startled from my dream by a knock at the door. I lay there a while, trying to see if I had dreamt it. When I finally got up and went to the door, there was no one there.

I called for room service and had a quick breakfast of rocket salad, escarole and cherry tomatoes. Then I called for Martin to meet me in the lobby at 9:30 a.m. I grabbed my bags, checked my neck for the flash drive's lanyard, and then headed out the door. Just then, my room phone rang. I went back and answered it.

"Hello?"

"Hey, kid."

"Dad?"

"How's my girl?"

"I'm fine! I'm great! What's wrong? Is everything okay?"

"You tell me; we haven't heard from you in a year."

"Dad, it hasn't even been a week!" I said, smiling.

"Don't forget, they stoned an American girl over there so you be careful."

"How did you hear about that? That was years ago."

"You think I don't research things? I'm all over the place. I'm thinking of sending your brothers down there to get you back here."

"Dad! Will you let me handle this?"

"Alright, alright." There was silence next, with both of us trying to avoid the long brewing fight over my independence. "So, how's it going? You find this guy yet?"

"Not yet. But I got some new leads. Nothing much."

"Well, what kinda bait you usin'?"

"Bait?"

"Try spreadin' around a little American green; that always does the trick."

"Dad. In the first place, you're not allowed to pay for things with American money here. Second, I…it's just a bad idea."

"Didn't you say those bums gave you an expense account?"

"Yeah. For things work related."

"Well isn't finding this finuch work related?"

"Okay, I see your point. But he's not a *finuch*; he's not gay!"

"Oh? And how would you know?"

"We've…met before." Damn, how did he get that out of me?

"I'm listenin'," he said.

"Dad! I'm not accountable to you anymore…this is MY life." Again, silence.

"So what time is it there, kid?"

"It's…nine forty-five. Oh shoot! Dad, I'm late. I have to go."

"Okay. Uh, call if you need anything."

"I will, Dad. Thanks."

"And you should call your mother, she's worried sick about you."

"Tell her I'm fine, Dad. I'll call her soon. Maybe on Sunday, but I can't promise."

"Okay. Hey, kid?"

"Yes? I'm still here."

"Take care…take care of yourself."

"I love you too, Dad. Ciao."

I hung up the phone first because I knew Dad would not. He loves me. Always. Even when he doesn't quite know how. Down in the lobby, I apologized to Martin for being late as we headed out the hotel's main entrance.

"So where to today, Miss?" he asked.

"Okay, here's the plan. We need to go to an AMEX office, a printer's, a cell phone place, a-" I paused, leaving Martin holding the Land Rover's door open for me. I had just noticed something across the street. It must have always been there unnoticed: a CCTV camera jutting out from beneath the awning of an African food store. By its proximity to the Metropole, it would have been impossible for the camera to miss people coming and going via the hotel's entrance. And by people…I meant Joey.

"Is everything okay, Lisa?"

"Yeah…everything's great if that's a working camera over there. Do you think it belongs to the hotel or to the city?"

"It actually belongs to neither one; it belongs to the CCID security. All these cameras belong to the CCID."

"The what?"

"The City of Cape Town Improvement District. They control all the security in the central city. See those people over there? All those people in yellow bibs are security officers for the CCID."

"Is their office here in town?"

"Yes, it is. Yes, just down the street."

"Okay; we'll add them to the list as well."

A few hours later, I was sitting across the desk from Derek Bach, security czar for the CCID. Bach was a thin, efficient man of about forty-five; clean-shaven, with hazel-blue eyes that seemed bored beyond belief. He spent most of his time during my spiel monitoring his cell phone or glancing at his PA whose desk sat immediately past the glass door behind me.

Bach was a bottom line guy, unlike the convivial natives I had met here thus far. Life for him seemed more like a tedious formal gathering than a celebration. His listless eyes looked across at me like he was watching a late-night infomercial on the miracle cleaning powers of citrus. I could have stripped naked and beaten him with a rubber dildo and he would have sat there with that same jaded look on his face – that total, unblinking lack of interest.

I segued into Plan B, handing him one of the business cards I had printed earlier.

"Securities and Exchange Commission. Special Agent Lisa Rosatti," Bach read aloud, almost mockingly. "It's not that we don't want to help, it's just that you're asking for a tape from December of last year."

"Right, which was…not even two months ago."

"Yes, well, we don't keep these tapes for very long; we reuse them."

"How long before you reuse them?"

"Well, that depends on…the camera location, how many tapes are available, etcetera… Just think: there's a tape every eight hours per camera, which is three tapes per day. That's ninety tapes per month. So you see it wouldn't make good economic sense to save them. We just tape over them here; this isn't America."

"No need to be so glib, Mr. Bach. We tape over them back home too."

"Good, then you should understand. And please call me Derek."

"Okay. So what do you do in the case of a crime?"

"Well, in the case of a crime, we catalogue the tape and send it on to the SAPS – the South Africa Police Service."

"So if a crime happened on a certain date and street, that tape would still be available?"

"It's possible, but...not certain. We'd still have to locate the tape. And in your situation, the incident happened in December of last year. I don't want to make light of your investigation but we have serious crimes that go on here quite frequently. This is still the high season, which means we now have upwards of eight million tourists pouring into the city. As of now, we just don't have the resources here to help you with your problem. Try the SAPS," he said impatiently.

I studied Bach for a while, using everything I learned at GM, listening not only to what he said but how he said it. He was a businessman and businessmen always had a price. I began speaking calmly and pleasantly. Even flirtatiously.

"I don't want their help; I want yours. The SAPS are…saps! If they were any good, they'd be telling *me* what happened instead of me having to ask them. Those are *your* cameras. Off the record, if getting your people to look for a particular tape is a matter of manpower, then tell me where I can invest in your resources."

I removed a white envelope containing $1,000 in travelers cheques from my handbag and placed it on his desk. "You're the boss over many people, Derek; I'm sure you've leaned on a few of them to get things done. Well, my boss is leaning on me…hard, so I need your help," I said, demurely. GM's research showed that men cooperated more often if they were made to feel needed.

"We're under a lot of pressure to find this missing American," I continued. "We believe he's involved in an international stock swindle that may cost investors millions."

Bach's countenance began to soften as the growing wall of tension between us crumbled. His stiffness dissipated but his hands never left his lap. He looked at the envelope, then back at me, then past me toward his assistant who was busy fielding phone messages.

"What is this man's name again?"

"Bosco," I said. "Joseph Bosco. There's a thousand in signed travelers cheques there. That's almost seven thousand rand. You can get all the help you need to find that tape. Just make sure it's the right tape – the one for the camera across the street from the Metropole. The date was December twenty-ninth, about seven-thirty a.m. I could really use your help on this, Derek. My local cell number is on the back of my card. I'm staying at that same hotel. So if you get *any* information, please call me immediately…day or night."

"We'll see what we can do," he said, "in the spirit of cooperation. But this is South Africa, not Washington; we don't take bribes."

I reached across the table, covering the envelope gently with my hand. "It's not a bribe, Derek; it's just…to allow you to facilitate the necessary manpower."

"As I said, we'll see what can be done. If I get any information, I'll contact you."

I smiled alluringly as I exited, leaving the envelope on his desk. A man is a man, no matter how jaded. As sure as I could feel his eyes on my ass, I knew he would take the cash, and I knew I would get that phone call.

***

18August1982: Joe has become unglued. Last night, I awoke to guttural screaming. I ran downstairs…Joe was drunk and chasing Jenny around the dining room table with a fucking machete. He was wearing black shoe polish on his face and dressed in all black. He slashed the air so hard the machete sang.

Jenny was screaming for help. Maris and Teddy shielded her, begging Joe to stop. I stood in the kitchen watching, unable to move. After forever, Joe dropped the machete and they all had a group hug. What…the fuck?

After regaining my senses, I slipped back upstairs. I would have called the police but Jenny would never back me. Plus, he never actually hacked her so what could they do? No one can protect me. This is beyond critical now. One of us has to go.

01September1982: This ASSHOLE is making me dig up the entire fucking yard - again! I cried most of the day, between digging, swatting mosquitoes, and listening to WNIC. I counted the quarter hours by the number of times they played Joe Cocker's "Up Where We Belong".

Martin and Malcolm came over to sympathize (laugh at me) before they all left for Wednesday night service. The next thing I knew, Jenny was calling me in for dinner. Joe Cocker and I had been digging up the backyard for eight hours straight.

After dinner, I rolled some burnt spaghetti into balls. I went to the garage and smashed up *D-Con* cubes, placing the crumbs into each ball's center. Certain no one was watching, I jumped the fence separating our houses and called Sam to the farthest corner of their yard. I looked over my shoulders once more while petting him, and fed Sam his last meal.

Ten minutes later, Sam began eating grass and vomiting violently. I could see chips of *D-con* in it, so I hosed it all away. Sam flipped out, whimpering incessantly and scratching to get inside of his back door. I heard cars pull up in their driveway...in my mind. I thought of burying him in our backyard, but Joe might actually plant grass seed this time, and find him.

I couldn't wait much longer; the boys would be back soon. They'd kill me, then Joe will defibrillate me just to kill me again. This was different than when I told Malcolm peanut butter came from orange poppies and convinced him to eat one. Different than when he asked me to watch his hamsters while they went on Christmas vacation. I left them in my attic too long and they froze to death. I told him not to wake them because they were hibernating. It took him two days to realize they were all dead.

Sam's stomach swelled up like a black whale's and he was at death's door. He just lay on the back porch, scared shitless and looking confused. I had given him six cubes of *D-con*; Sam weighed about fifty pounds. Now he was just fifty pounds of dead weight.

02September1982: Early this morning, they took Sam to the vet but it was too late. The doctor needed tests to say what was poisoning him, but said he was going to die anyway. The boys' parents chose to have him euthanized (it was cheaper). So they had Sam put to sleep, incinerating his remains along with my sins.

Chapter 9

It was Friday morning, February 4th. I lay in bed, listening to a constant series of alarm beeps because I did not know how to turn off Joey's talking clock. I left the batteries in it to remind me of him, as if I needed to be reminded of the one man I could never forget.

The sun shone through the open curtains, fixing itself upon my hotel room door and turning it into an oblong projection screen. My mind replayed snippets of Joey laughing, Joey smiling, Joey sleeping…

He and I both took a while to decide what we wanted out of life. I was thirty-three when I graduated and joined GM; he was thirty-six when he moved to South Africa to run the AEP for them. Since then, they said he had become deeply deranged. He had gone over the edge of reason, and wasn't reaching back for a rope.

Someone was tapping at my door. I sat up in bed, thinking it was room service and hoping they would go away if I did not answer. My projection screen morphed back into a door and I noticed there was now an envelope under it. I ran to it excitedly, hoping it might somehow be from you, but it was only a note from Martin, who was already gone when I opened the door.

His note said he was going to meet a traffic officer named Woodward who had some vital information. Martin had been flashing your picture to other drivers, and word of mouth yielded a result. I thought of making him come back for me, but he might be able to make more headway without a nosey American.

Around 8 a.m., I ordered a breakfast of muslix, hot cross buns, and a Bloody Mary. After showering and dressing, I settled down to check my e-mail. Then my cell phone rang; it was Bach.

"Hi, Miss Rosatti?"

"Yes?"

"This is Derek Bach, CCID. Good morning to you."

"Good morning."

"I am calling to follow up with you about the security tape from our Long Street camera."

"Yes?"

"Apparently there was a stabbing at one of the office buildings on Long Street, on the date in question, and we forwarded all the tapes in that area to the SAPS. In cases such as this where charges are pending but have not been laid, due to not being able to locate the suspect, they hold onto the tapes until the suspect is apprehended."

"That's great news, Derek!"

"But sorting through the tapes and liaising with the SAPS is going to take more manpower than we have right now. If we had the funding, we could employ a casual worker or a police volunteer to get us that tape, I would say, over the next couple of weeks."

"Well…let's try this: I'll double what we talked about yesterday but I really need that tape in my hands by tomorrow. It's extremely urgent."

"Sorry, tomorrow is Saturday. Most people here don't work on Saturday."

"Then it should be easier to find the tape with less people in the way."

Bach sighed with masculine exasperation. "When are you coming through? Are you prepared to bring something by here today?"

"I can. Does that mean you can get someone on it today?"

"Yes, I'll get someone on it."

"Great. I'll see you in about half an hour; I'm just waiting for my driver."

"Then I'll see you now. Cheers."

I grabbed my handbag and went downstairs to the lobby. No sign of Martin. I left messages for him everywhere and then hailed a private taxi.

Once at Bach's office, I was assured that he had "good people working on it," so I handed over a few more travelers cheques and left. I decided to walk back to the Metropole, keeping an eye out for Martin's red Land Rover.

To keep his cell phone on and to not let me travel alone was all GM asked of him, and even that was asking too much. Martin had been gone for hours. Working with stupid people is always a drain to my patience, even back in my field area. Sometimes I want to tell them how stupid they are. Instead, I walk them through different scenarios, hoping to God one will stick, all to help them understand simple tasks.

It was just past one o'clock when I got back to the hotel. I tried contacting Green, but his cell phone went straight to voice mail, and his office phone was being checked for trouble. I sent him an e-mail letting him know I made a second payment to Bach. I also noted my disappointment in the driver they had gotten me.

I closed the drapes, collapsed across the bed, and tried to figure out my next move. The Long Street video would not be available until tomorrow at the earliest and my driver was MIA.

I thought about Joey…it was odd that no one in his family had tried to contact GM. It was either that nobody noticed he was missing or that nobody cared enough to find out why. Maybe that's what happens to a tree without roots; when it falls down in the forest, nobody hears it.

***

16May1983: Jenny turned thirty-two today. I put thirty-two candles on her Sanders cake, while Maris and Teddy went to get her from her bedroom. I lit the candles like I usually do; I like fire. But this time there was a big problem. Because those assholes took so long to get her, the candles arced into a big flame.

We frantically tried blowing out all the candles, before giving up in fear, and dumping the cake into the kitchen sink. It was fucked up; there was wax, silt, and icing all over the damn kitchen. Jenny ran crying back into her room, while Maris and Teddy stared at me like I just killed Santa Claus.

When Joe got home, I told him it was an accident. Actually, it was more like one of those story problems from math class: Jenny is thirty-two years old, the cake is twelve inches in diameter, there are ten candles per box, and there are four boxes. How many candles does it take to fuck up Jenny's birthday? Answer: thirty-two.

30June1983: Jenny has moved out. And left me here…with a psycho.

03July1983: I was washing dishes, and laughing with Maris about how different it was without Jenny, when Joe walked into the kitchen. He picked up a pot of spaghetti off the range, poured it onto my head, and banged the pot down with a strainer spoon. "Now that's funny," he said.

04July1983: Today is Joe's birthday; he's thirty-seven, I guess. I have not kept track of his age nor looked him in the face since the night he threw me across the bar room.

Tonight when I came home, Maris was sitting in the living room alone, in the dark. The demolished remains of our glass and mahogany coffee table were laid at her feet.

"What happened?" I asked.

"Dad did it," she said.

"What the fuck?"

"We were talking about something and he got mad. He just started yelling, then picked up the table and dropped it."

"Mad about what?"

"Jenny might be moving back...and I don't want her to."

"And you told him that? Be happy we didn't have spaghetti for dinner."

19August1983: Joe is in the hospital! Maris said some guys tried to rob him while he was leaving Ted's bar. They asked him for the time and as he answered, they pulled out knives and tried to rob him. When he resisted, they gut-stabbed him. Jenny has to move back in with us for sure now. Fucking amateurs. Always confirm your kill.

12November1983: Joe slammed Jenny into the hall closet door, shattering the full-length mirror. He was trying to get out of the house and Jenny body-blocked the front door.

"No!" Jenny said. "You're not leaving me here with your kids! You stay here and watch them; I'm going out!"

"Bitch, move before you get hurt!"

(Crash!)

Maris, Teddy, and I cleaned up the glass for Jenny, while she tended the scratches on her arms and face. She was numb at first but soon burst into tears. "All I did was tell him not to leave me here with his kids. Where was I wrong? I love you guys, but in all fairness, you're *his* kids! Why doesn't he ever stay home with you? You should ask your father that. Ask him why he spends all his time and money in the streets!"

16November1983: I won the Detroit Medical Society's Oratorical Award. They announced it today at an assembly. I would have skipped school if I had known they were going to make a big deal out of it. I got a plaque and a $500 savings bond that doesn't mature until fucking 1988. I could be dead by then.

31January1984: Martin left for the Navy today. Tonight is my first shift at Taco Bell.

15March1985: I won the Stratford Poetry Award. They gave me a certificate, a collection of William Shakespeare plays, a poster, and two passes to the Stratford Festival! This is some cool shit, but how the hell am I going to get to Stratford, Canada? I cracked my tooth in half once and Joe wouldn't drive me the two miles to the dentist.

They published my sixty-eight-word poem in both newspapers today, but I never told my family about it. They would just think it was about them. They think everything I write is about them.

"The Chronicles of Phil Nush"

"Who might you be?"
"Phil Nush" says he.
"Have you the time?"
Nush: "Quarter to three."
"Hands toward the sky,
You're going to die!"
"Bullshit," reply.
"Phil Nush am I!"…

…I barely go to school anymore. I'm crumbling apart on the inside, but on the outside, I look damn good. I have a moustache now, and muscles too…probably from repeatedly digging up the fucking backyard. I barely recognize myself anymore. Everyday, I grow to look more and more like…the type of guy who would throw his own kid across a bar room.

Slappings, beatings, and writing punishments are regular now.

Sometimes I have to write a thousand times, "I will not disrespect my mother and father." Where the fuck are my mother and father? And when are they coming to get me?

I had a plant…once. But after I covered my bedroom windows with newspaper and spray painted them black, the plant turned all anemic on me. I re-planted it out front but it was too late. Nothing thrives on this side of the fence. But on the other side…

When I hang out next door and go to church with them, or do family stuff, it feels…surreal. Like watching a black and white movie, or an episode of *Leave It To Beaver*. I hate myself. I hate this life.

10April1986: I finally cracked. I was listening to Prince's "Sometimes It Snows In April". I had it on repeat, plus it was a gloomy day. It was raining huge *Hefty* bags of dirty rain, like God was cleaning out Heaven and dumping the mop water down on us. I sat on the porch in the rain, crying. The next thing I knew, Joe and Jenny were driving me to Kingswood nut house in Ferndale.

People in white weighed me and made a big deal about it. Just under six feet tall, two months from my eighteenth birthday, and I only weighed 135 pounds. Joe took over the show with all his "I'm a doctor" crap. He diagnosed me as clinically depressed. No shit, Sherlock; any clue how I got that way?

I was happy to see them drive off. They looked so plastic, hugging and waving goodbye like they actually gave a fuck. Like we were the family next door.

11April1986: At the crack of dawn, a nurse came into my room and tried to take my blood. I freaked out and sent her away.

12April1986: This morning, the bitch tried to leach me again so I reported her to James, the HNIC.

"No, you don't have to give blood," he said, "but I do want to see you drop a turd today."

"What the hell, is there a camera in my bathroom?"

"If you want to get out of here, you have to eat."

I'm getting to know this longhaired kid named Karl. He's an extremely talented artist but they are keeping him on something called *Thorazine*, which hampers his ability to draw straight lines. He also slurs and is given to spontaneous drooling. Today he drew a portrait of me that came out looking like Satan.

"You will lead the Blacks in battle against the Whites," Karl said. "There will be a new world order. You will be its head."

"Have you ever killed anyone, Karl?"

"...But the days of man are numbered. After your reign, Satan will return."

"Ever been laid, Karl? Ever seen a really great pair of tits?"

"You wear the horn of Satan!"

"Tits, Karl. Best things life has to offer. And wipe your face... you're drooling on my portrait."

17April1986: I'm leaving here, today. I met the shrink and convinced him I'm okay. Who knows why I was crying anyway. He said it was mild depression, probably caused by my impending graduation. I wanted to tell him the truth about my situation, but that digression would have led to another session. Anyway, he let me go home. What's scary is there's no prescription necessary.

30May1986: Tonight was prom night but I didn't go. No dough for a tux, no cash for a limo. I spent the evening with Malcolm at the Norwest Theater, watching a double feature of *Cobra* and some even *worse* movie. Neither moved me.

11June1986: Today was my last day of high school, so it was goodbye for what Mr. Jenkins dubbed: "The Bosco-Bryce Comedy Hour." Charles Bryce is my friend and classmate. I was voted Class Comic, but that honor could have easily gone to him. I was also voted Class Luncher, whatever the hell that meant. I did not attend the assembly where the class honors were announced; neither did I attend the Class of '86 graduation.

Bryce has gotten me hooked on marijuana, which I am fairly certain promotes my seclusion. It also seems to improve my writing...while keeping me writing almost nothing at all. The best thing about grass is that it helps me gain weight. I feel like calling the staff at Kingswood and telling them to pass out dime bags.

21June1986: Yesterday was my eighteenth birthday, as if that still means anything. I have made arrangements to stay with Bryce because...this morning, my father threatened to shoot me:

Maris and Teddy were gone with her friends while I was upstairs disassembling an old television set. Joe and Jenny began to argue. He accused Jenny of cheating; this was followed by some banging and bumping. Jenny screamed for help. I ran downstairs to their room where she was naked and on her knees in front of Joe.

"Joe, please don't kill me!" she begged. "Please! There's no one else but you, Joe! I swear to God, Joe! Please!"

Joe stood over her like a naked white devil aiming a Winchester rifle straight down at her forehead.

"Dad, don't!" I screamed.

"You better get the hell outta here, boy!" Joe said. "You want some too? Get the hell outta here before I kill you!"

He aimed the shotgun at me and I knew he would pull the trigger as easily as he scratched his crotch. I was nothing to him; no more than a smoldering cartridge he would chuck out before reloading.

I grabbed what I could and left Jenny there...naked and on her knees. I should have called the police but I was too fucking scared. I should have killed Joe, like in my dreams, but dreaming a thing and doing it are completely different.

I walked about a mile across Greenfield to Bryce's house. A kid walking down the street, crying, with a big-ass suitcase...anyone who saw me could guess what happened, way before I got to Whitcomb Street and knocked on Bryce's door. His mother, a schoolteacher, said she was familiar with "domestic situations", so she let me stay there. I was familiar with domestic situations too. I knew they all had a beginning and they all had an ending.

28June1986: I called over to the house about five o'clock. Jenny answered; she sounded stiff and cold. She told me to come home because she had some bad news. When I got there, the driveway and street were filled with the cars of our relatives. Once inside, everyone hugged me and told me everything would be all right, but I still had not heard the news.

"What is it, Ma? What happened?"

"Spit, I'm sorry to have to tell you this but...your father...has been killed."

"Oh God, NO! How? When? It's not true!'"

"It's true, Spit. The police were here late last night. And I went down to the morgue this morning with your uncle...to identify the body. I'm sorry to have to tell you this. Your father is dead."

"What are you talking about? How?"

"He was shot after leaving Ted's bar last night. They think someone tried to rob him again but they can't be sure yet."

"Did anyone see anything? No one heard gunshots? Where the hell was the security?"

"Spit, they just don't know what happened. He was outside alone and it looks like he was on his way to his car. I tried beeping him up until twelve-thirty to see what time he was coming home but he never called back. We don't know yet how long he was there, or who with, or anything. The police are working on it right now, though. They'll find whoever did it."

"Oh, God! Oh JESUS!" I fell down to the floor, leaning on the piano bench while family members gathered around and hugged me. "We need to find out who did this! It's not over! This is NOT over!"

23September1986: Well...it's over. The high school grads of the Detroit Police Department labeled Joe's death an unsolved homicide. Cause of death: five slugs to the chest from a .38 revolver, shot from a distance of about five feet. Several vital organs were penetrated. He had no money on him and his Cazelle glasses were never found. Motive: robbery.

Phone and pager records showed that Jenny called Joe like she said, so she was cleared. She had no idea where he was. I could no longer collect social security because I was eighteen and not enrolled in college; plus I had no car, and Bryce stated I was sleeping in his room with him at the time of the murder, so I was cleared also. Teddy was only nine and Maris was a bigshot print model in New York, so they were both cleared as well. Hell, everyone was cleared. The cops did about two days legwork on the case and then went out for doughnuts. Never get murdered in Detroit. Not without a witness.

24September1986: Being with Bryce was great. He knew everyone worth knowing, and it was good for me to see the procession of whores passing through his red revolving front door. It encouraged me to be more assertive with girls. Before long, I was bringing home one of my own. A little Greek/Irish girl named Lisa. Or "that cock-eyed bitch", as Bryce is so fond of calling her.

One day, she came over wearing only one contact lens, causing her to squint in one eye. I explained why she was squinting to Bryce, who nevertheless went on to tell his mother, sister, and friends, about the cock-eyed bitch I fucked in his bed. "Ma, that bitch is so cock-eyed, when she smiles, a tear rolls out her ass-crack and into her back pocket!"

They all found that funny. I guess I...I didn't quite see the... humor in it. Actually, it's not even physically possible, and makes no sense. But his teasing annoyed me so much that I stopped dating the cock-eyed bitch.

My reasons for leaving Bryce's house can be summed up into one sentence. His mother saying "Joey, you got to *GO*." She didn't like that we fumigated the house on my second day of living there...but we swept up all the dead cockroaches, and she recovered.

Bryce's sister finding a syringe filled with a brown liquid in his desk didn't help either (she claimed she was looking for a pencil). When I got home, they staged an intervention. So I squirted them all with *Lagerfeld*...the contents of the syringe, which I had I siphoned from Joe's bottle of cologne, and they recovered.

But she was right; economically, it was time for me to leave. I had been there for three months, sucking up food and heat from this woman who was taking care of a house, two kids, and a car, all on a Detroit teacher's salary.

Plus, I was tired of jacking off whenever Bryce's sister took a shower. What was she, thirteen? I could only pass her so many towels or so many bars of soap, before she reached her hand past the partially opened door, and instead of *Dial,* got dick.

28September1986: I was over at the house to take some of Joe's things, his colognes and some clothes, when Jenny and I had our first heart-to-heart chat.

"Well Spit, what are you going to do now?"

"I don't know. But there's only one of me now, so don't call me Spit anymore. My name is Joey."

"Okay, Joey, whatever you want," she said, and hugged me. I told her I would not be moving back to the house. I was driving out to San Francisco with a girl from Grosse Pointe, that I met at J.J. Morgan's.

"How long have you known her?" she asked.

"A few weeks, maybe. Her name's Heidi. She's a police dispatcher."

"Oh. Are you gonna bring her by so I can meet her?"

"You told me no White girls allowed at the house."

"I never said that, Spit; I said no girls I don't know!"

"But you meant *White*. And my name's not Spit! Who wants to be called that? How would you like to be called Shit?"

Speechless, Jenny left me to pack and troubled me no more. When I was finished, she walked me to the door.

"Seriously, Joey, what are you going to do now?"

"I don't know. Anything I want, I guess. You?"

"Oh...pay off the house. Go back and finish up my degree...I haven't really decided yet. Maybe I'll do just like you; anything I want."

We hugged goodbye on the front porch, maybe for the last time. The sun was shining. Jenny was wearing *Opium* perfume. Her hair was in a bun with bangs at the front, and her eyes were a pretty shade of soft brown.

Chapter 10

On Saturday morning, February 5th, my ringing cell phone awakened me. I answered it groggily.

"Hello?"

"Hi, Miss Rosatti; this is Derek."

"Hi, good morning."

"Good morning to you. Did I wake you?"

"No. No, it's fine. What's going on?"

"We've got the tape."

"You did?"

"I'm having it brought to my office at noon; can I drop it off at your hotel room?"

"Yeah, that would be great. Why don't we…wait, I don't have a VCR here. Do you have one at your office?"

"Yes, I do. But honestly, I wasn't planning on staying in town so long; it's Saturday."

"You've been a great help, Derek, but they're really pushing me for results. Can you give me just a little time at your office with the tape?"

"Of course, Lisa."

"Great. Also...while I've got you on the phone, I've run into another problem. My driver has been missing since yesterday."

"So…you want another tape?"

"No, he was supposed to meet this traffic cop and then get back to me but he never came back. I don't think he's been back to his room and he doesn't answer his cell phone."

"What's the officer's name?"

"Woodward. He left me a note saying he was meeting an Officer Woodward."

"I'm afraid I don't know any officer in Cape Town by that name. Are you sure that's it?"

"Yes, I'm sure."

"I'll make some phone calls and see what I can sort out."

"Okay. Thanks, Derek."

"Cheers."

I met with Bach at his office around noon. He queued up his VCR and poured us some coffee.

"Lisa, in the interest of time, my people edited the tape down to between six-thirty and eight-thirty a.m. Is that okay?"

"That's fine. That's actually great." I put a blank AMEX envelope on Bach's desk. He picked up the envelope, hesitated, and handed it back to me.

"Thank you, but...it's no longer necessary. Just take your time and look at the tape. We've been through it all and nothing stood out but...if you find something, just wave. I'll be on the other side of that door, making calls."

Something was up. My nerves were tingling. "What's going on, Bach?"

He turned to answer me. "How do you mean?"

"You just seem...different somehow. What's changed?"

"Well, Lisa...I like you. But I called the Securities and Exchange Commission last night, and it turns out they've never heard of you. Did you know it's a serious crime in both our countries to impersonate a law enforcement official?"

I said nothing.

"I also contacted the Metropole; they told me your room was booked with a corporate account by Global Media. I contacted their corporate offices and my call was returned by a Mr. Kleinhurst."

Bach watched me for signs of a response but I gave none.

"Mr. Kleinhurst and I have come to an agreement which...doesn't include you."

Still I said nothing.

"So I'll help you this last time because I like you and because I already agreed to, but know that anything we find, I must report to Global Media."

I sat down in his chair and swiveled toward his fourth floor window. "Things seem to have worked out for you all the way around." I tried seeming like I was still in control but I had none; my own company was backdooring me. They told me I was the only one who could find Joey, now they were hijacking my investigation. And who the hell is Kleinhurst?

"Fine," I said. "I'm still grateful for your help and I think my company and I have compensated you well for it. GM wants this man found, so do I. We share the same goal. So I'll get started now and let you know what I turn up."

"Yes. Well…I'll be just out here."

"I'm still worried about my driver," I said, swiveling back toward Bach. I picked up my AMEX envelope and placed it in my handbag. "If you find him, I'll be back with this."

Bach closed the door behind him, caught off guard by my composure. I wondered if there was anyone in the world that couldn't be bought. Then I remembered; GM had offered Joey a million in cash to make things right. He turned it down flat.

I skipped ahead in the tape, concentrating on Joey, trying not to think how easily GM had turned on me. At 7:15 a.m., the tape showed a white utility van with a logo on its side parked in front of the Metropole. At 7:28, a man wearing a business suit exited the driver door and walked to the payphone on the corner. He made a call at 7:29, spoke for a minute, and hung up. Then he walked back to the van and hopped in it, looking brazenly in the direction of the security camera.

At 7:45, the passenger door opened but it was impossible to see if anyone was getting in or out. The camera angle only showed the driver's side, the top of the van, and the very top of the passenger door. At 7:46, the van drove off.

I fast-forwarded through the rest of the tape but there was nothing else significant on it – homeless people, hotel guests, and porters hailing taxis. So around the time Joey's hotel room got a phone call, the driver of that van was making a phone call. A few minutes later, the passenger door opened and closed, and the van took off. This could be why Joey was never seen exiting the hotel on the day he vanished; the van was purposely obstructing the view of the CCTV camera.

I could not get the payphone records without Bach or the SAPS. Ditto for the license plate on the van, but I could try and make out its logo. I replayed that section of the tape over and over, pausing at the side of the van. Bach's set-up was sophisticated, allowing me to zoom in on the grainy videotape. I could make out the writing on the van: C-A-P…"CAPE COMMUNITY NEWSPAPERS". I scribbled that down on one of my fake business cards and zoomed in on the number plate *CF 45881*.

Bach was preoccupied with a phone call at his PA's desk, but I could feel him occasionally monitoring me through the glass door of his office. I tried looking disappointed with my results, but this was the best lead I had so far. There was still one more thing I wanted to check…I zoomed in on the van's driver. He was Black or Coloured, wearing a blue suit with blue-tinted glasses. I didn't want to risk Bach's attention by printing it, so I tried very hard to memorize that face.

Afterwards, I forwarded the tape almost completely to the end, to a silver sedan that had pulled up to the front of the Metropole. Then called in Bach.

"I think this might be a lead," I said.

"The sedan? Why do you think so?" Bach asked unimpressed.

"The tinted windows, the way they're just parked there…it's just a gut feeling. Can you find out who it belongs to and why they're parked in front of the hotel so long without getting out?"

"As I said, I can check it out, but I must pass the information onto your superiors."

"I know. Just check it out; a man's life is at stake. Contact GM as soon as possible. And…thank you."

"Pleasure. I'll contact GM by tomorrow morning at the latest. I'll zoom in see if I can run the tag, then check with Billy, the manager of the Metropole. But you must let me handle this part okay? Don't speak to them or anyone else about it."

"I think you can trust me with keeping my own investigation a secret. The question is can I trust you?"

"Of course you can. And please let me know what else you turn up. I'm only trying to help. Oh, about the missing driver…no one seems to know anything. We checked with his wife at his home in Khayelitsha and got no information. It could be serious. I can assign someone from my staff to escort you full-time."

"No thanks. It's just…it looks bad to have so many people come up missing. This is two thousand five; people don't just vanish anymore, right?"

I walked out of the CCID office and hailed a taxi to the Cape Community Newspapers office, checking as best I could that I was not followed. The office was closed, as if there was no news on weekends, so I returned to my hotel and checked my e-mail. I got a letter from GM – an Area Supervisor named Walter Reiter. He said he would be taking over Green's responsibilities "in the interim" and that I should not worry because my field area numbers were at ninety-five percent. It figures; my area runs its best when I'm away from it.

Reiter also told me GM was handling the situation with my driver and that I was not to get further involved. GM would assign me another driver by tomorrow, Sunday, at the latest. He also reminded me I was not authorized to take public transportation under any circumstances, and that I should spend any down time searching for clues in the blog. But he failed to mention what happened to Green.

After lunch, I sat on my bed and read more of Joey's blog, but curiosity got the better of me and I phoned the front desk to see if Martin had returned. They told me a representative from GM had come in, collected Martin's things, and signed off on his bill. I ran downstairs and told them I needed to see the bill to make sure the person was duly authorized to sign for the company. It was true; someone had checked Martin out of his room at 12:11 p.m. – exactly while I was at Bach's office!

I flashed back to Bach's face, chatting away on his cell phone. He fucked me. He had set me up the whole time. He made sure I was there with him at a time when GM could be here, closing the books on Martin. Scrawled on the dotted line of the checkout bill was that name again: F. Kleinhurst.

***

01October1986: Heidi is sleeping next to me. We stopped in Yosemite National Park for the night. Getting a blowjob here was great; like sinning in the Garden of Eden.

The sky is so wide, you can tell it really is round. The stars are close, too. Bright and close. They could fall right out of the sky. Rain down on the car, setting us and the whole world ablaze.

We left Michigan almost three days ago. We loaded up Heidi's VW *Rabbit*, hitched it to a U-Haul trailer, and burned rubber down I-75. It's a humbling experience to pass through places with trees taller than most buildings. They say a grocery clerk can become a movie star in California, and a whore a politician. What can a neurotic writer be?

12October1986: Heidi and I have been in San Francisco for about two weeks. Every day is cold and rainy. We live at the Leland Hotel on Polk Street, in the Tenderloin District. Heidi got a job at *The San Francisco Examiner* as some sort of copy editor. But I read the other paper, *The Chronicle*. This old guy, Herb Caen, writes a column about the young San Francisco. About its history and its politics; all the causes and effects. He does it so well that I never have to leave the hotel to see the city. There's power in printed words.

Equally as powerful is the view from our windows. The garish colors of the Tenderloin go hand in glove with its idolization of youth, of James Dean and Marilyn Monroe, life-lovers who lived hard and died young. This city is a still a shock to my senses. The loud music, the even louder motorcycles, and things like what I see right now...a man walking by with his ass hanging out of black leather riding chaps. The Greek pizza joint two doors down is as far as I'll go. It's all I need.

There's a *Twilight Zone* marathon on TV through Halloween. Heidi wants us to go dancing but it's still too strange for me out there. Heidi twists up her face and frowns; I stay inside. It's a freak show out there, more terrifying than the *Twilight Zone*. Never seen anything like it. Nightmares of being absorbed up into it...finding out I was always one of them.

"Which philosophy are you following today, Joey? The one where you reject everything? Even love?"

"Love is the only thing I won't reject," I answer Heidi. "It's the only thing I still believe in. And only with you." We cuddle. Rod Serling's eerie voice echoes in the background. Heidi licks swirls on my nipples, undoes my pants...

"You're such a bad liar; you don't love me. You just love fucking me," she mumbles, mouth full of cock.

"What's the difference?" I sigh, running my fingers through her brown hair, clutching her skull. Pulling it down onto me. "There is no difference."

26November1986: Heidi eventually fucked a sense of security into me and I ventured past the Greek pizza place. I took a job on the Pier 39 wharf, taking pictures of tourists on their way to Alcatraz. I am slowly adjusting. I see some stars like Robin Williams and Thelma from *Good Times.*

I made a new friend today, which was good because I hate the people I work with. And the hotel workers never see me when they talk to me; they see freshly grilled bratwurst. The city salivates on me, subtly trying to digest me whole. Monika Perini was different, though, maybe because she was a tourist here too, just taking in the sights. We met on the Polk 19 bus, coming back from Fisherman's Wharf.

28December1986: Heidi moved out of our hotel room a week ago and hasn't contacted me; not even for Christmas. I have no idea where she went. The entire hotel staff is keeping mum; eager for the day I have to sell some ass to pay the rent.

"You wouldn't have to do anything," says Tony, the night desk clerk. "Guys will pay you just to have you sit on their faces. Just sit on their faces! That won't make you gay."

As money dwindled, I considered the offer. I could see the rentboys across the street from the hotel. Denim jackets with collars up and no shirts on; youthful faces with ancient eyes and mouths rimmed with canker sores...

29December1986: Heidi called late tonight, thank God; the rent was due earlier today (a hundred forty bucks for the week). I answered the phone half asleep.

"Heidi...where are you?"

"Why would you do that, Joey? Why, does she let you fuck her in the ass like you're always trying to do with me?"

"I swear: I have never cheated on you, Heidi."

"Liar! What about the pictures in your briefcase! Can't take me dancing, but you can take that whore to the Hard Rock Café? And take pictures kissing her?"

"You know better than that! In Europe, friends kiss as a greeting. We met while I was there filling out an application. I can't even remember her name; she was nothing to me."

"Nothing? You have twenty pictures with that slut! You have more pictures with her than you do with me! Am I that ugly?"

"Heidi, you are not ugly. But what you DID was ugly. Leaving me here stranded with the rent to pay every week. And you broke into my briefcase? I trusted you!"

"Have your whore pay your rent! You embarrassed me! Everyone has seen you with her! Even people I work with!"

"Those are haters, Heidi. All haters do is hate the fact that you're happy and they're not. Fuck them! So is that it? You hate me now?"

"You know I don't hate you."

"Then where are you?"

"It doesn't matter. I've already decided. I'm going to kill myself tonight. You'll find out where I am in the morning."

"I love you, Heidi. You know that! There's no one else for me but-"

"Where is this love, Joey? I never saw it! I waited on you, hand and foot, and you still slept with someone else! Is that what you call love?"

"Baby, I miss you. I miss you so damn much. Come back to me. Just tell me where you are and I'll come find you."

She cried some more while I begged. Finally she whispered sullenly, "I'm upstairs. Room three twenty-five."

I raced upstairs to her room. She opened the door slowly, enveloped in darkness. She was pale, with punching bag eyes and unkempt hair. She slinked back to her bed, crawling onto it, and sticking her ass high in the air like a motel vacancy sign. She stayed like that, sobbing loudly, her face buried in her pillow.

I crawled into bed behind her, lifted up her slip, and fucked her with a week's worth of ANGER and hostility. I yanked her hair back, thrusting into her deep and hard, clutching her throat like I wanted to kill the bitch myself. I meant to pull out and cum on her ass, but the warmth of her cunt bewitched me, and I came inside of her. It was the first time I had ever cum in a girl. As I did, Heidi cried relentlessly.

01January1987: I partied HARD on New Year's Eve in Haight-Ashbury, spending it mostly at the I-Beam with Monika. A West German au pair named Suzy sent her friend over to ask if I would dance with her. Suzy was the most beautiful girl I had ever seen: Long, blonde hair, thin and shapely...

Monika felt tired and took a taxi back to her hotel. She left me cab fare and said I should stay and have fun. Fun to me meant falling in love with Suzy, the best kisser in the history of civilization. We danced to David Bowie's "Let's Dance". When I looked down and noticed Suzy was wearing red shoes, I took this as a sign.

Suzy and I left the I-Beam together with the Sheriff – some guy we had known less than an hour. We ended up at his house, smoking opium through a long glass pipe shaped like a dragon. I woke up naked on the cold tile of his bathroom floor. Suzy was naked and passed out in the bathtub. I have no idea what happened between the hours of getting there and waking up.

23February1987: I had lunch with Heidi today. We ate at the Greek's, for old times sake. This time I paid. After that night she threatened suicide, I worried I had gotten her pregnant. Thank God she still looked good and slim. It had been two months since then...since I had helped her move out of our hotel and across the bridge to the Oakland Hills.

She rented a house off a hilly road; one so narrow a mirror was drilled into the hillside to warn of approaching traffic. Her house (more like a shack) was just across from that mirror, planted precariously on a steep hill with a beautiful view.

"Please stay with me, Joey," she had asked.

"And do what? How the hell would I get up and down from this mountain?"

"You said you wanted to write a screenplay. You could just stay up here and write. I'll take care of you."

I got it then: the isolation, the remote location – I would be completely dependent upon her. "And if you should be run off the road by a truck coming up this mountain, how would I survive then? Do I look like Grizzly Fucking Adams?"

"You don't look like a gigolo but that never stopped you from sticking your prick into every bitch-in-heat in the city. You ruined San Francisco for me!"

She began crying again, and I held her. "I'm sorry," she said, "I was wrong. You do look like a gigolo."

"That's not who I am. That's not what I'm about and you know it."

"Then who's that blonde everyone's been seeing you with?"

"Blonde? That's just Suzy, a friend of mine. An au pair I met."

"What happened to Monika? I thought that was 'true love'?"

"She's...around. Things are...okay."

Heidi sat up and sighed, flipping back her hair, and looking upon me with a contemptible kind of pity. "Don't you see the pattern, Joey? You only want women you can dominate. You want girls with green cards; foreigners who worship you and put up with your shit because they don't know any better. Because they don't speak English!"

"What? My girls speak English just fine!"

"Yeah, they can say 'I do' and 'visa'!"

...But that was two months ago. Now she was sitting across from me at the Greek's, glowing and sensuously sipping *Coke* through a straw. I wanted her.

"Want to go upstairs?" I asked.

"Let's talk first," she said, playfully.

"Why don't we talk...upstairs?"

Heidi smiled and slurped her straw, pleased that I still wanted her.

"How is work?" she asked.

"It's fine. I quit the wharf. I'm a tour guide at Alcatraz now."

"How did that happen?"

"I got tired of just taking pictures of people getting on those boats, so I finally got on one myself, just to see what all the fuss was about. After we landed, I took the tour and asked for a job. Did you know Al Capone was locked up there? And in the seventies, the Indians took it over by force. Some kind of protest uprising."

"You mean Native Americans?"

"Yeah, whatever."

"Good, so you're working full time now," she smiled, batting her eyelashes and flipping her long hair over her shoulders. "I have some car trouble, Joey. I need a new clutch and it's going to cost me about two thousand dollars. I thought you could help me out with maybe half, since I spent so much money on you. Like you said, we were partners."

"Oh. So Heidi Troutman from affluent Grosse Pointe needs money from my broke-ass."

"I know you, Joey; all the money you spend drinking and hanging out. Did you ever once try paying me back? And if I didn't bring it up now, would you have even considered it?"

"In a relationship, you shouldn't have to pay things back. That's socially frowned upon, and legally without merit in California."

"Be honest, Joey, do you really think you could have gotten

this far without me? I paid for the gas, the car, and the trailer that brought you out here. I bought your clothes, your food, and paid the rent. Doesn't that make you feel like, as a MAN, you owe me something?"

"When people are cohabitating in California, everything – even money – is community property. And on a more personal note, let's not forget: when you were about to kill yourself, I was the one who talked you out of it."

"That's true...but do you remember the reason I wanted to kill myself? It was YOU, Joey. You're the reason I wanted to kill myself!"

Heidi's smile had disappeared, along with my appetite – my appetite for everything. I tossed enough money on the table for a tip, got up and walked out of her life forever. She thought she had a beast in a gilded cage, but I'm not a beast. I'm a man.

17March1987: Monika has gone back to Zurich. She said she'd be back, but no one ever leaves and comes back unless it is someone you really do not want to, like the cops.

Golden Gate Park is over six miles long. Today, Suzy and I walked to the very end of it. We do everything together. We loved the Japanese tea garden, the cherry blossoms, and Strawberry Hill. We walked all the way to the Dutch Windmill (too many people around for a quick fuck).

I have begun working as an usher at that theater on Van Ness and Sutter called the Omniplex. It sounds like a science museum, but it's a cheesy movie theater for cheesy films like *Fatal Attraction*. For the past few weeks, I have also been a bar-back/bouncer at the I-Beam. Best job I ever had. Sometimes, bar patrons tip me in crystal-laden chronic.

20March1987: Tonight at the I-Beam, I met this hot piece of Italian ass, named Jana Rimini. She's actually from fucking Sardinia! What are the chances? She said she never met any Boscos there, though. She told me my name meant "wood", and I was damn close to showing her my wood, before Suzy showed up.

The two are completely opposite. Jana is pale, dresses in all black, and has dark, short hair. Suzy is all blonde curls, baby-blue eyes, tanned skin, and bright clothing. Suzy is an angel and I am damn lucky to have her, but something is drawing me to Jana... something familiar between us. Maybe the bits and pieces I know about my family origins are all bullshit, leaving the only attraction between us to be our insatiable need for casual sex.

The truth died with Joe, since he never introduced me to my grandfather. He never spoke once of him either. I never even saw a photograph. Neither have I met Mary's father. Speaking of Mary, I haven't received so much as a postcard from her since the seventies, since Elvis died on the toilet.

21April1987: At the I-Beam, Suzy introduced me to "a friend" of hers named U.N. - like the United Nations. He seemed odd, and also seemed to be constantly staring at me. Perhaps that had something to do with amount of coke I snorted tonight. Being paranoid doesn't mean people aren't really staring. Waiting to hurt me somehow. Waiting to make me one of them.

05May1987: I have moved in with U.N. He lives in a two-bedroom flat on Grove and Masonic. He's an extreme Leftist radical - the whole fucking fight-the-power, Black Panther, Fruit of Islam bullshit. Ironically, his preference is for white chicks. Katerina, his main girl, is from Sweden, and hot as hell.

Today, Suzy and I saw Lombard Street, the crookedest street in the world. She was taking the bus with me to my new job at the Alhambra; I quit the Omniplex. The Alhambra is the biggest single-screen movie theater in Northern California. I helped restore it (at non-union wages).

I have three jobs now: the I-Beam, Alcatraz, and the Alhambra. Proving to myself, the pimps at the Leland, and Heidi, that I could survive here without her. Getting a new job is like getting something for Christmas. Everyone is so nice to you at a new job, and I like being liked.

I met a redhead named Janine who was blocking the stairs to the backstage area at the I-Beam. She was talking with her friend and I told her they had to move because of the fire code. We began arguing and screaming at each other; then we started kissing. Later, we went back to my place, downed a bottle of brut champagne, and fucked.

I woke up early in something cold and wet, and found Janine had pissed my bed. She apologized and then gave me head. I bleach-scrubbed the mattress 'til all the germs were dead.

I have been spending a lot of time at Point Lobos beach and the Cliff House. And also at the Legion of Honor Museum, drawn to its memorial of Holocaust survivors. U.N. and I go there alone sometimes, just to talk. We get high and talk of Voltaire, Emerson, the Koran...about anything and everything. I understand what he is saying and he understands me. I keep waiting for him to tell me he is gay, and fuck it all up. Things are too good right now. Life is just too damn good.

17June1987: I got fired last night from the I-Beam for being under twenty-one. The owners said the heat came down from the Feds. It was my own damn fault; I put my real age on the fucking application. I must have been high at the time.

San Francisco was dulling my edge. All I do here is get high, get laid, and get new jobs. Everything is too fucking easy here. My hair was growing long and chick-like. Even I was becoming chick-like. Neutered. My anger suppressed. The call for revolution blocked from my wax-filled ears. I no longer dreamt of writing the perfect screenplay. The only thing I perfected was the junkie nod.

20June1987: Today is my nineteenth birthday. U.N. got me an eightball (which he smoked half of), Suzy let me ass-fuck her, and I quit two jobs as a gift to myself.

I hate working for people and their little rules like "Be on time". I feel no connection with my work or with my employers. The most satisfaction I got from any job was listening to the music at the I-Beam while I worked, tripping off LSD, and watching Suzy and U.N. dance.

I liked the boat rides to Alcatraz but I always felt isolated on those trips. The other tour guides sat in cliques. I am the anti-clique. I gave less than a damn for their child-like chats about dating and parents. The only thing I dug was the view on the boat rides, so I quit.

The Alhambra was a work of art, painstakingly refurbished. It was the big dog; it made the news. Working there meant I could see movies for free anywhere in the city and I always did - always with Suzy, U.N., and Katerina.

But the pay there was so low that I fell in with a gang of ushers and cashiers running a scam. We would re-sell tickets, re-use popcorn and drink containers, and split the profits equally. We called ourselves the Mickey Mouse Club. Everything was jake until I got a dose of conscience and ratted us all out.

What an asshole I turned out to be. Everyone got fired but me. Samir, Russell, the little Chinese girl...even the redhead girl missing her right index finger – I gave them all up. So I quit.

All my life, I wanted to be nothing like Joe, but all I am is Joe: selfish and insane. I need to leave town and start over; find some place with no rules. See, the problem is control. Every job I ever had came with its own system of control. I hate the inherent impotence of being a cog on the wheel of someone else's machine. This is MY life.

I should be the one making the movies instead of just selling tickets to them. I should be the club owner instead of the glorified bus boy.

I remember once, as a child, swinging up to the stars and being crushed for the effort. What crushes me now...is making no effort at all.

05July1987: Last night, I carved my name on Suzy's right ass-cheek with a steak knife. Just my initials, though; I'm no monster. She screamed and cried. I silenced her by pressing her face into my pillow. The lack of air took her to the brink of unconsciousness, and seemed to be a real turn-on for both of us.

After sobering up this morning, I realized I should have carved her initials. That way, if she ever got killed, it would have been easier to identify the body. I can never think clearly after smoking heroin.

30July1987: Suzy and I just had our biggest fight ever; she's getting to be a real nut-job. I think...we are nearing the end of our journey. She brought me hot food and bread, but no juice. How was I supposed to eat dry-ass chicken without juice? I told her several times before, "Meat...bread...juice." When I protested, she said, "Wait! Can't you see I'm doing your laundry?"

I took the food and dumped it into the folded clothes of her bureau. She stared at me, tears welling (I had warned her before about the staring). Then she scraped the food up, dropped it into my bag of clean laundry, and shook it vigorously.

I grabbed her by her throat and flung her backwards onto her bed, while she kicked and punched at me. The more she struggled, the tighter I clenched her neck. She was three shades of red, crying and gasping for air. Once again, I released her at the edge of consciousness. Her color slowly returned as she gasped and coughed.

She lay there trembling and crying for about half an hour, speaking German and calling for her mother. But somehow, I felt she was just as turned on as I was.

After a marathon sex session, Suzy rewashed my clothes and fed me. And this time, she remembered the juice.

17August1987: Suzy and U.N. staged an intervention, coercing me to accept a job with him at the GLU (Global Labor Union). Doing so had probably saved at least two lives.

Working here is beneficial to me financially and spiritually. I like having the opportunity to help others instead of just focusing on myself. I met Reverend Jesse Jackson in person, and he shook my hand (along with a hundred others). GLU will be campaigning for Jackson to help him win the Democratic Primary.

29August1987: Suzy flew back to West Germany today. Sadness and mourning beyond belief! She IS my soulmate. I should have married her, but I was afraid she only wanted a green card. Deep inside though, I was really afraid we would end up like my parents. Now look at me...I'm lost without her. There is no state of intoxication strong enough to ever forget her.

Ashu (my good friend and a devout lesbian) went out with me tonight to help me get over it. We tried to fuck anything with tits and lipstick. We met a butchy German girl who encouraged us to drink warm *Absolut* with her, straight from the bottle. It was effective.

We all ended up at Firehouse Seven where, at last call, Ashu and I competed for this hot chick named Raquel. Ashu won. I ended up spending the night with some fat broad who seduced me with her massive tits and magic mushrooms. I passed out during sex, awaking to dazzling, psychedelic explosions, and this pasty blob bouncing up and down on what was left of my dick. The Talking Heads' "Burning Down The House" blared in the background.

30August1987: I made plans to meet one of Monika's friends, Jackie Vogelbach, at the Hard Rock Café. Jackie is Swiss German, like Monika, except her father is Egyptian. She has a great rack, and looks like a goddess. But this is California...everyone looks like a goddess.

My relationship with U.N. is becoming strained. I feel like his little puppet. He is stronger than me mentally and – purposefully or not – is cloning me into himself. I catch myself using his sayings like, "Everything is everything," or "Dude," and I often see things solely from his point of view.

There is more to U.N. than all the drugs people lay at his feet like roses. More to him than the acid, the coke, or the excellent muscle-debilitating grass. But my problem with U.N. is U.N. himself. He makes me think of things I never considered before...politics, global economics...even national healthcare. We never learned those lessons from Joe. All he ever taught us was how to give and receive pain.

U.N. is bigger than life to me. I have placed him upon a pedestal and, in lieu of drugs, have laid all my trust at his feet. If he should fall...I'll be crushed.

Chapter 11

It was about 4 p.m. on Saturday, February 5th, as I waited anxiously in my hotel room for news of a new driver – a driver who would probably be taking me by force back to the airport. The vultures were circling. GM had been monitoring me all along, waiting for the right time to swoop down and take over my mission. I was being set up to trap Joey. Things would not end neatly. They would end badly, maybe even bloody.

I was searching through the blog for clues when my cell phone rang. The number came up private.

"Hello?"

"It's Owen Nelson. I assume our boy is still missing."

"Yes," I answered surprised.

"Well? What are we doin' about it?"

"Like I said in my e-mail to Dave, I've got some clues to locating Bosco but the loss of my driver was a major setback."

"Your driver? You're tellin' me a multi-billion dollar global conglomerate hangs in the hands of a missin' driver?"

"No, I'm not telling you that." I felt caught off guard and suddenly defensive.

"Lisa?"

"No, I'm not saying it's up to the driver; I'm saying it would be easier to check out leads if I *had* a driver. It's Saturday evening and whoever is taking over for Green said a driver would be here as soon as possible and not to-"

"To hell with Green! I shit-canned his ass three days ago! The increase in your AMEX limit was to handle things like this; why aren't you handlin' it?"

I hardly had time to process Green's firing, and by the way Nelson was grilling me, I felt sure I was next. "Mr. Nelson, I feel like I need to remind you that I haven't even been here a full week yet. I'm in a country where people think Saturdays are holidays, and-"

"I don't want excuses Lisa; I want some goddamn results! Do you realize what is happenin' over here? The wheels are in motion! I need that sonofabitch found!"

"And I'm doing the best I can! You…you can't put all this on my shoulders! The entire company had six months to find him; I haven't had six days!"

"And you damn sure won't get a seventh! But I'll have one million dollars wired to you if you can find him by midnight tonight."

Now I knew the deal was crooked; Nelson and GM were splashing money around like water. But could I trust them? No; too many secrets.

"Who is Kleinhurst?" I asked.

"I don't know anyone by that name. Is that someone Green mentioned? Again, he is no longer under my employ."

"Don't bullshit me, Nelson! You want results? Then give me some answers!"

"Kleinhurst is…missin'. He hasn't reported in for several hours. Frankly, I'm concerned that Joe had somethin' to do with it. There are things you don't know about Joe. You didn't need to know them at the time but maybe now you do."

"Go ahead."

"Joe's lost his ability to distinguish between fantasy and reality. He believes he's the victim of an international plot to assassinate him. He's on the defensive now, makin' him a serious threat to himself as well as those around him; those who are tryin' to help him. We're-"

"I asked you in New York if this assignment was dangerous and you told me 'no'! Now there are three people missing! I want off this job. Now! I quit!"

"You quit now…and the glass ceiling will drop on your ass like an Acme safe in a *Roadrunner* cartoon. You'll never pass a background check in this country again!"

"I'll be sure and tell my father you said that!" I threw the cell phone against the wall, breaking it. The crashing sound was the destruction of my career. I needed this to all be for a reason. I needed to find Joey and get some answers. Not for GM, but for myself.

My room phone rang next. I expected it to be Nelson.

"What!" I yelled.

"If you're looking for a lost hand bag, you must try the newspaper," a deep voice said in a thick Afrikaans accent.

"I think you have the wrong-"

"*The CapeTowner*. There's a reporter there. A Mr. Bush. He's good at finding things. Long lost things."

There was a click and then a dial tone. I hung up the phone and checked for my purse. It was on the dresser. I checked through it, making sure my passport and travel documents were still inside; they were. But if nothing of mine had been taken, then the call was either a trick or a clue.

The CapeTowner...it was their paper delivery van I saw on the security tape the morning Joey vanished! This was more than a coincidence.

I got change from the front desk and called the paper from the payphone outside, hoping the line wasn't being monitored. The receptionist put me through to Bush.

"Hi, Mr. Bush? I'm Lisa Rosatti. Someone-"

"I know who it is; it's an American tourist who's lost something of great personal value and needs help recovering it."

"That's right. And I heard you're the last Boy Scout."

"What's all that noise in the background; where are you?"

"That's traffic. I'm outside the Metropole Hotel."

"You used a payphone. Smart. Flag a taxi and come see me now. Leave everything but your passport and some cash. Come to the *Cape Times* building – the Newspaper House. Go around to the back and have security send you up. And stay off the phones. In fact, don't bring your mobile or any other electronic devices. Si?"

"Si, capisco. Va bene."

"Grazie. Ciao."

Bush hung up, leaving me wondering how he knew I spoke Italian. There was no way, unless he was in contact with Joey.

On the fourth floor of the Newspaper House, a receptionist pointed out where Bush sat. I saw him, immediately recognizing the blue glasses from the videotape. He wore the intense scowl of a serious writer and was furiously clacking away at his *Mac* when I approached him.

Bush sat at a large metal desk surrounded on all sides by other *Macs* and other reporters. While the other desks were filled with family photos, news clippings, and index cards, Bush's was surgically clean. On the wall beside him hung a calendar of Table Mountain and a postcard photo of a young Marlon Brando. Bush was handsome but also stiff and tense. He was the oldest young man I had ever seen.

He stopped typing and looked up at me, studying me from head to toe before speaking.

"He said they sent you to tempt him. An offer he…couldn't refuse."

"Are we talking about Joey?"

"Easy, the walls have ears. Hell, even the ears have ears." He swiveled around in his chair, signaling me. I noticed that almost everyone in the newsroom was either stealing glances at us or just outright staring.

"Lost your hand bag, huh?" Bush asked loudly. "Well, try this place. I got a call from them earlier saying they found a red bag with some U.S. documents inside."

Bush scribbled some words on a piece of paper, along with an impromptu map. "Meet me there," he mumbled quietly. "It's not far, just past Green Market. Meet me upstairs. Ask for Lucky."

"Lucky?"

"We have to leave separately, so go now. Try and make sure you're not being followed. If you didn't know, they've been tailing you since you got off the plane."

"Who's been following me?" I asked.

"Who hasn't?"

I snatched up Bush's note and walked away. I felt eyes all around me. I kept repeating my name to steady myself: "Secret Agent Luna."

***

17September1987: My popularity is at its pinnacle in poetry circles and cafes. I'm producing my best work to date, as a result of being exposed to…new stimuli. But the exposure to things once verboten has changed me irrevocably, and manifests itself in my writing:

"The Pink Curtain"

"…In a few weeks, she had grown to disgust him completely.
Her unshaven armpits, her savage behavior and forwardness, even her muscularity –
Her overdeveloped thighs could crack a man between them like the shell of a pistachio.
Soon, she was forever naked…
And he once found her sitting casually in the living room
Upon a wicker chair, painting her toenails black,
While her labia slipped between the sparse meshing of the wicker…"

29September1987: There is something really wrong with me. When I cum, it feels like molten lava erupting up from my balls. I also have really bad gut-cramps. Taking a piss feels like I'm slicing my dick open with a scalpel and I'm pissing every twenty minutes. Neither Epsom salts, antibiotic cream, nor locally applied cocaine, can numb the exquisite pain. Jesus Christ, forgive me. I think I have AIDS.

30September1987: U.N. wouldn't let me work today and insisted I see a doctor. I just picked one out of the phone book and was grateful that Jenny's insurance still carried me.

The doctor I picked, Dr. Applebaum, turned out to be a real asshole. Obviously, he thought I was gay, and could barely mask his sarcastic homophobia.

"I guess I'm just trying to figure this out," he said. "You have a green discharge in your underwear, it hurts to urinate, and you don't think you should have come in and gotten medical attention?"

The doc gave me a shot in the ass and some Tetracycline pills. He told me to avoid dairy products and to wash all my linen in hot water. He also said to drink plenty of water or cranberry juice. Cranberry juice...from now on, I'm sucking that stuff in like it was air.

14October1987: After my test results came back from the doc, confirming that I only had a urinary tract infection (thank you Jesus!), U.N. had me assigned to a campaign with him in San Diego. We're leaving today to organize over seven hundred hospital healthcare workers. He hinted that doing well there would mean a promotion for me. If so, I would become GLU's youngest Lead Organizer.

I've thrown myself into my work the past few weeks, protesting for gay-rights and against harsh immigration laws. GLU also came out in support of panhandlers when the S.F.P.D was secretly evicting them from Haight District parks.

Jackie is giving me hell over my decision to remain abstinent for a year. I am ashamed to tell her the whole thing is a kind of penance for almost catching AIDS. Our government is fucked up; they spend all that money on space shuttles but cringe at giving one dirty dime to help cure "the gay disease".

AIDS victims look fucked up when they die, like modern day lepers. I would rather be gut-shot five times than die of AIDS. My near brush with it caused me to revaluate my way of living. I realize if I refrain from getting drunk or using drugs, I am less likely to wake up in bed with a stranger who has my shredded condom hanging out of her ass.

15October1987: U.N. and I have finally arrived in San Diego and are staying at the Holiday Inn. It was fun to wake up and dive into an indoor pool. It's been maybe ten years since I swam at all.

We took a detour on the way to San Diego, because U.N. insisted we stop off at UC Berkley to see a Dr. Weisenthal - a professor he once studied under. She tested my IQ with three different types of tests, including the Wexler. After administering these quite boring tests, she registered my IQ at 167.

"I need you with me in the struggle," U.N. told me afterwards. "I need you out there with me, instigating positive social change. Otherwise, you're just another black hole in the fabric of society. A wasted breath."

U.N. was more inspiring and more family to me than anyone I had ever known - even more than Martin. But though I loved Martin without reservation, I could not truly love U.N. There was something transitory about him, something impermanent. And something hypocritical.

For starters, I still have no idea what his real fucking name is. He has about ten fake IDs stashed in ten different places. "It keeps me off The Man's radar," is all he says about it. This guy must have warrants up the ass. He may have even killed a man. Most likely someone White.

The basis of his hypocrisy revolves around his penchant for

White girls. How does someone who feels so wronged by Whites, and such contempt for them, continue to fuck their women? Someone would have to rationalize that behavior in their own mind, and rationalizations are nothing more than intellectual lies. So somewhere inside, I don't completely trust U.N. If he can rationalize that today, he can rationalize something even worse tomorrow.

25December1987: Katerina left for Sweden last month, so U.N. and I planned to have last night's Christmas Eve dinner alone. Along with Christmas, we were celebrating U.N.'s having me promoted to Lead Organizer, effective January 2nd, and I was celebrating being sober and abstinent for just under three months (December 30th). Then...Jana Rimini called.

Jana is the Italian girl I met at the I-Beam, the one who comes from my grandfather's hometown. Her boyfriend was still on active duty in the Navy so she asked to come and celebrate Christmas Eve with us (I was probably her tenth call).

She was wearing that new Christian Dior perfume, *Poison,* apropos of her character. The mood changed the minute she walked in our front door. She was taller and shapelier than I remembered. She had lost weight, restyled her hair, and was wearing a red shirt with concentric white lines extending outward from its buttons. They were like arrows saying, "open me." Like lines of coke saying, "snort here." I tried desperately not to listen.

After a three-course meal including turkey and apple pie a la mode, U.N. stacked the dishes in the kitchen for the dish fairy to magically wash while I, the dish fairy, gathered his clothes and paraphernalia off the living room furniture so we could be seated.

I sat alone in the sofa chair, leaving the couch for them, but Jana chose to sit almost on top of me in the chair. We listened to Art of Noise, the only CD I owned. Jana served us some cannolis she brought with her, but they were too sweet for me, so I went to the backdoor and spat mine out, under the pretense of checking the lock.

When I came back, Jana was sitting next to U.N. on the couch, all her attention focused on the quarter ounce of hydro he had produced in my absence. I collapsed back into the sofa chair while he finished rolling a fatty.

"I got the best shit in 'Frisco," he said, obviously flirting with Jana. They smoked their humongous joint, laughing at me and my sobriety. Soon I was buzzed from the contact and laughing right along with them.

A while later as "Moments In Love" played, I grabbed the roach, smoking it all to the beat of the music. I sat down on the coffee table and exhaled the last puff into Jana's face.

"Do you like me, Jana?" I asked, tenderly.

"Yes," she said, becoming serious.

I put my arms around her, caressing her back with my hungry hands, breathing hotly on her throat and ear, chilling her. U.N. looked away, preoccupying himself with rolling another joint. I grabbed Jana by her hair and led her down the dark hall to my bedroom. She whimpered like I was hurting her, exciting me even more. We kissed passionately as I fumbled in vain for my keys, which had fallen out into the sofa chair. It was too late to stop and get them; I had not been this high or this hard in months.

I untied the drawstring of Jana's white denim pants, watching her sensuously peel her way out of them. She wore a red thong that was already sopping wet. Within seconds, we were fucking furiously against the wall. She gestured a couple of times toward my door but I kept her pinned there, like a butterfly. Much too soon, I pulled out, blasting three months of petrified cum all over the wall and bedroom door.

I heard the front door slam, signaling that U.N. had gone out. I retrieved my keys from the chair and unlocked my room door. We kissed and clawed our way to my waterbed, leaving a trail of clothes, as Jana whispered the most vilely erotic things in my ear ever heard in the history of mankind.

I ripped open her shirt and she moaned, exposing perfectly round bra-less breasts. I sucked and pinched them while Jana whispered, in broken English, all the sick things she wanted to do with me. I was well hard, and ready to fuck her again but she stopped me, laying me on my back and deep-throating me... sucking my dick like she had gone to hooker school and learned it.

"You like this dick, bitch?"

"Mmm!" she moaned, sucking harder and faster. I was about to nut when she got on top of me, sitting on my face. Her pussy was right there, thrust into my reluctant mouth, and before I knew it, I was eating it! I was mostly gnawing on it and sucking the lips because it was my first time, but the tramp had the nerve to cum anyway. It was slimy, funky, and disgusting. I vowed never to eat pussy again.

We fucked a few more times, ending the session as I called her a disgusting pig slut and came in her ass. I took a ho-wash (washed my dick off in the sink) and gargled several times with *Listerine,* staring at my father in the mirror and wondering what the hell had just happened. I lifted the toilet seat as the whore knocked on the door and slowly entered.

"Don't pee yet," she said. She pulled back the shower curtain and lay down in the bathtub, smiling enticingly and crooking her index finger at me. "Pee here," she said.

I'd like to say I did not do it, or that I was ashamed to do it, but what the hell...it turned me on. I called her everything but a child of God, as I pissed on her face and tits, and she writhed in pleasure. Finally, I went back to my bed and passed out while Jana showered.

I had never had sex so...kinky. It was so vulgar, so thoroughly raunchy, that I hoped it was all a dream. I even hoped she was just a dream. But when I woke later to the sound of her sucking me off again, I knew both were all too real.

She got on top of me and guided my cock into her while I gripped the soft cheeks of her ass. She pulled my duvet over us, buried her face in the crook of my neck, and rode me like Sea Biscuit.

"You filthy cum-slut!" I yelled, as she pinned my arms down.

"Yes!" she sighed proudly, riding me harder.

Before I knew it, I had cum inside a girl I met at a bar, and had known for a total time of less than four hours. What a fucking idiot.

She fell over to the side of me still shivering. I lay there, staring at the ceiling and picturing Dr. Applebaum.

"That was great," I said. "You liked that, didn't you?"

"Si," she said, putting my arm around her head and leaning into my armpit.

"Well, it's been like...three months for me."

"Yes, you said that. Are you sorry that you didn't wait longer?"

"No," I said, but I lied. I could feel the microbes crawling all over me, entering me through my pisser. "But this *is* San Francisco; have you been tested lately?"

"No, I don't have to. My boyfriend gets tested all the time."

"The one in the Navy?"

"Of course; how many do you think I have?"

"Two, now. I have to see you again."

...But that was last night. This morning, the whore woke me with a kiss. I slept so deeply, I had forgotten she was there.

"Merry Christmas Joey," she said.

"Yeah...Merry Christmas to you...Jana." (That was her name, right?)

I grabbed a *Hershey's Kiss* from the nightstand and gave it to her, taking one for myself.

"Oh, is this my present?" she asked.

"Yeah, I guess."

"Then I have to give you something as well." And she was off to the races again. Her head was back under my duvet, going up and down on me like an elevator. With each of her swallows, I resigned myself to the fact that I was going to hell, and nothing could be done to prevent it. She looked up at me, grinning; her black eyes gleaming like a demon's. I almost think I heard her laughing.

27December1987: Jana is STILL here and shows no signs of leaving. She keeps wearing my clothes or no clothes at all. U.N. seems not to mind; she even has the bastard vacuuming.

Her influence on me is growing exponentially. She stays home all day, cooking, cleaning, and fucking me. She's my sex-slave. My bitch. I can call her bitch freely because she prefers it. I have never once called her Jana in bed.

She's so perverted...never seen anything like it. The more I degrade her, the more it turns her on. Beside U.N.'s bedroom, there is no place in the entire flat we haven't fucked on or in. Last night, she had me lean over her face while she tea-bagged my balls. I came so hard I bit a chunk out of my tongue.

29December1987: Jana has FINALLY gone back to her hotel. She is having lunch with her girlfriends to exchange presents with them. Plus her fiancé is flying in from San Diego to spend

New Year's Day with her. Now that she is finally gone...I miss her. I have way too much free time without her and everything smells like her.

30December1987: Jana called me in a panic! Her fiancé found bite marks on her ass-cheeks and accused of her of cheating. It had gotten really ugly between them; her hotel finally convinced him to leave by threatening to call the police. I talked it over with U.N. and explained that she would be staying with us for a week or so, until her fiancé left town.

I have an assignment up in Eureka that begins January 2nd. About five hundred in-home healthcare workers are being fucked out of their benefits. The healthcare provider contracts out to temp agencies, who then employ workers just under full-time. That way, the healthcare provider receives maximum compensation from the state, the temp agencies get their fees, but the workers have no full-time benefits. They don't even get paid time off for giving birth. It is a scheme that is spreading, and GLU wants to nip it in the bud before it catches on throughout California, and the rest of the nation.

U.N. recommended Eureka as my first Lead Organizer campaign. Doing well would mean a lot to me personally, as well as to the workers being exploited. It disgusts me to think of children without health insurance suffering needlessly, because their single parent has no benefits package and can't afford independent healthcare.

On the downside, going there will mean being away from Jana. I want to take her with me but I know I won't get a damn thing done with her there. Jana is in almost every waking thought I have. I stare at her pictures constantly. I miss her accent...and the sound of her saying my name.

Still, this may be my last chance to even *try* and redeem myself, to make up for all my sins and debauchery. This is my time to give back to the world, to achieve my potential, though it already may be too late. When I killed one man, I killed two.

01January1988: Last night ROCKED! Happy freakin' New Year! Cheap Trick was playing at the Hard Rock Café, so U.N., Jana, and I went there to see them. Everyone there knew U.N. so he was quite occupied, allowing me to spend time alone with Jana. Usually, we looked like a threesome of swingers.

At the stroke of midnight, Jana and I kissed, and I told her that I loved her. It just came out. I think I really do love her, but she gave no reply.

By and by, I did spy, out the corner of my eye, U.N. kissing some fucking guy! I am refusing to acknowledge the subject, allowing for excessive drugs and drinking on all sides. It sure makes me feel better about leaving Jana living with him, though. Damn it! He's seen me naked!

Around two in the morning, U.N. summoned us to the bar for a private toast. Jana was already too drunk to stand without me. Three empty brandy snifters were already on the bar and Little Mikey, the bartender, was bringing two large bottles of something.

"We've had it pal," I said. "This dame can barely stand." Jana was falling asleep on my shoulder.

"Then you'll ruin my surprise," he said. He poured from the bottle into two of the snifters. "It'll be just us two, then. It's more fitting that way."

"What are we toasting?"

"The end of the world."

"And to the beginning of a new one? Cheers." I drank deeply. It was ale. Damn fine ale. "This is good," I said. "What are we drinking?" U.N. handed me one of the bottles. "*La Fin Du Monde,*" I read aloud. "Oh...the end of the world!"

Suddenly, Jana revived and snatched U.N.'s snifter. "I don't drink strange drinks from familiar men...but I'll drink a familiar drink from a strange man."

U.N. poured another glass and handed it to me, taking mine as his own.

"To the end of my world," I said. We toasted each other and drained our glasses.

"Those are on the house," said Little Mikey. "And your friends left these for you." He placed onto the bar a large butterfly made of hematite and other stones, a marble dragon's egg, and matching yin and yang candlestick holders.

We drained the bottles and both helped Jana out the front door. In his free hand, U.N. carried the blessings the New Year had given him. It was a magical night, stroked by a starry paintbrush. A bubble machine operated on the stairs, spinning up dreams. Each one popped was another year gone by.

The world had always been mine because I had reached out

and grabbed what I wanted, but when I woke the next morning, the world felt repossessed. And even though Jana slept next to me, I felt alone.

03February1988: Jana has been staying at the flat with U.N. while I've been working miracles in Eureka. We may actually have enough support here to force a vote on unionization. I feel pressured though, like I'm in the wrong occupation. Writing should be my only obligation, composing lyric about Jana, the love of my life, the cause of my frustration.

I expect to be finished here soon and again able to breathe her air. Until then, I compose sonnets ode to her eyes, her teeth, her smile, her hair, her body...her angel's feet. If I could just be left alone to write, what miracles of verse I would create. I'll sleep now, dreaming she loves only me, forever me.

10February1988: Well. I fucked up. I had gone six weeks without sex, so it was bound to happen. But this is bad...I slept with another man's wife. I fucked Mrs. Finley so hard that she bled. Her husband never liked sex, she said. Not even a blowjob would get him off. "He just goes in the bathroom and jacks off."

Just to make certain she would vote pro-union, I took her into her bathroom for round two. I leaned her over the sink and rammed my golden arrow into her quiver.

"Slower this time, okay?" she said. "Not like in there."

I didn't really stick it to her like I wanted to; she was old enough to be my mother. But in my mind, I was really fucking Jana, hard, like she liked it.

"And take your finger out of there, sweetie," she said. "That's not meant for that."

So we did it slow and I tried to stay hard, tried not to look in the bathroom mirror, and tried to remember this worker's name. Then I came.

On the way home, I could still smell her ass on my finger, even though I had twice washed my hands. I felt sorry for her husband. Finley was such a boring fuck; I'd probably end up just jacking off myself.

I also felt guilty too, like I had cheated on Jana. We need those extra votes though. Jobs are at stake.

13February1988: I was so successful at getting Eureka's campaign off the ground that they sent me to cover U.N.'s campaign in San Diego (he crashed his scooter and has his leg in a cast).

San Diego is a huge campaign and needs a good Lead Organizer, because they are voting on the union in less than two weeks. It was cool of U.N. to recommend me; it means lots of extra money - especially if we win. But I've been in San Diego for ten days without any comprehensive strategy. I cannot concentrate. I've lost all sense of coordination.

I delegated all the facilities and workers to the organizers. U.N. himself had trained them so they should be up for it. I, however, am not, because everyone and everything reminds me of Jana. It seems like a year since I last saw her. I asked her to come the other day, but she said U.N. needs her to help with shopping, cooking, and cleaning. What the fuck? Is he a paraplegic? I need her too.

I call home all the time. Sometimes we just hold onto the phone without speaking. Other times, just hearing her voice makes me cum. If I do well here, I plan to get us a place of our own. I'll even buy her a ring.

The vote here is on February 23rd and I have no idea how it will go. I know about El Cajon because I've been there myself. And they are for us at La Mesa. But the rest could go either way.

I feel like I should go out and survey everyone my fucking self. My workers are shiftless and untrustworthy. After our meetings, I'm certain Comrade Lamont parks somewhere and sleeps the rest of the day. There are workers at his facility who have never seen him. Comrade Ava keeps trying to get time off, bitching over kidney stones, and Comrade Miguel is only concerned with lunch.

This is the biggest chance of my life! San Diego's healthcare system is twice as large as Eureka's, but all I want to do is go back home...and fall asleep inside of Jana. I write poems about her, and scribble sketches of her. Everything around me sounds, smells, and tastes like her. And I miss her cooking. Dónde está mi leche con sweet potato pie?

Chapter 12

I arrived at The Purple Turtle sooner than I expected. Upstairs, there was no need to look for Lucky because Bush was already there. I walked over to his backroom table. Bush was sitting with a handsome brown-skinned man with long gray hair tied in a ponytail. The lone gold hoop in his ear gave him the look of an islander or a latter-day pirate.

Bush introduced us: "Lisa, this is Lucky. Lucky, Lisa."

"How do you do," said the husky voiced pirate.

"Why do they call you that?" I asked.

"Most people say I'm good luck to have around." I immediately recognized his voice as the one on my hotel room phone, the one suggesting that I call Bush for a lost handbag.

"Sit," Lucky insisted. He extended his hand to me and stood halfway up until I accepted. Bush could take some lessons.

There were about eight bottles of cold *Castle Lager* on the purple park bench they called a table. Lucky encouraged me to drink and soon left us to change the music. The blog's description of Lucky was so accurate, it gave it even more credibility.

Bush was craning his head past me toward the pool table. An attractive light-skinned woman was bending over it, angling up her shot. "Clearly, all men are dogs," I said.

"Do you see that girl over there playing pool?" He asked. "The one in the black and white striped shirt?

"No. I just see what you see – her ass."

Bush laughed.

"Is that supposed to make me jealous?" I asked. "She must be Pink, right?"

"Pink? Ah…you really have read the blog. Impressive. No, that's Cindy. Pink was beautiful but she never had an ass like that."

"What do you mean by had?"

"Unfortunately…the SAPS recently found her – what's left of her – on a litter-strewn beach in Guguletu. The only items of clothing left on her were the stockings used to bind her hands and gag her mouth. It was…obscene; too messy to tell Joey. He'd lose it and want revenge. And that would be bad for all of us.

"Rumor has it there's a contract on him here with the Russian Mafia; he's to be shot on site. In the past few weeks, several Coloured men have already found their way into the shallow graves of landfills and rubbish bins, probably just for looking like him."

"Is Coloured like…what is that here?"

"Black is dark, like the Xhosa or other Bantu tribes. Light brown, yellow, or any shade mixed with White, is called Coloured. It takes a bit of getting used to. How this country sidestepped a civil war is beyond me. If I were Mandela, after twenty-seven years of isolation on Robin Island, I would have had the streets flowing with blood. White blood."

"Aren't reporters supposed to be objective?"

"Aren't governments supposed to be humane? There isn't a Black in the entire country that owns a diamond or gold mine, let alone a jewelry store. After the fall of Apartheid, the ANC let the Whites walk away with everything but the desert land and the dilapidated infrastructure.

"This nation has been repeatedly raped for hundreds of years. They took the diamonds, the gold, and the ivory. Once, they even took the people. Look around you at the result. Most say it was much worse before, and that Blacks should be grateful. Why should they be grateful, when twenty-five percent of their population is infected with a death sentence?"

"Bush, the reality is that those things happened a long time ago."

"Bullshit! Watch CNN. Instead of sending monetary aid, American scientists say endangered African wildlife would have a better chance of surviving if they are preserved on the plains of the Midwestern United States! That's like us thinking the pennies we're sending third world children for rice money is being mismanaged, so we want the children raised in an American orphanage. Where do we get the balls? First we come here and take the elephant's tusks, now we want to come back and take the whole fucking elephant!"

"You keep saying 'we'; you still consider yourself to be an American?"

"Baby, I'll *always* be an American. So I feel…responsible when we raise hell all over the world while shit is falling apart back home. It's kind of like the Roman Empire; kicking ass everywhere else while rotting from the inside.

"And we're not done yet…we're taking something else from this land with its every breath. The pharmaceutical conglomerates, the militaries, and the statisticians, are all waiting to see how much of sub-Saharan Africa will be consumed by AIDS. Some respected scientists believe evolution will produce a natural cure for AIDS, when enough people actually die from it. The shanty towns of South Africa are the Western world's petri dish."

In between staring at Cindy, Bush checked his watch and the exits a few times.

"Are we waiting for someone?" I asked.

"I'm doing like I was told; waiting 'til dusk. I hope you did as I asked and didn't bring any metal. It may result in a strip-search once we get there."

"Get where?"

Bush stared at me intently. "What's that around your neck?"

I touched my neck, having gotten so used to GM's lanyard, that I forgot it was there. "It's my flash drive."

"What do you need a flash drive for?"

"The company gave it to me. They said someone would contact me when I needed it."

"Pass it here," Bush said suspiciously.

I pulled the cord over my neck and passed it across the table. Bush disassembled it.

"That's odd," he said. "A battery. I never saw a flash drive with its own little battery. And where's the hard drive? The memory?" He looked at me like I was the dumbest blonde in the world, and I was starting to feel like maybe I had been.

"I'm guessing this is some sort of short range homing device," he said, "which probably means you're being followed, if not listened to, even as we speak."

Bush broke the flash drive parts down as much as possible, then dropped them into an unfinished bottle of lager. "They're going to shoot him in the back of the head if they find him. You know what that looks like, don't you. Is that what you want for him?"

"No! I quit this job two hours ago! How am I helping them? I don't know what's going on! I don't even know if YOU'RE telling the truth! You may have just trashed my storage drive! I may need that to-"

"To what? What the hell are you going to do with a flash drive in the desert? Find Bosco? I'm taking you to Bosco! Open your eyes; try to make sense of the truth. You've been used and you're being used. GM's been pimping you since you stepped off the fuckin' airplane."

I calmed down enough to consider that…I had led a GM hit squad right to Joey. If Bush was right, I may just as well have pulled the trigger myself. "How many of them do you think there are?" I asked.

"GM agents? Shit, I don't know. It's about three a.m. in the States. By the time the sun comes up over there, they may be sending a small army. They'll have to; GM only has about twenty-four hours to hand over the cash. There's not much left of the blog to post. The December twenty-third entry will destroy GM with every e-mail and news report mentioning it."

"I work with these people; you think they're just going to fork over a hundred million?"

"Yeah, they'll pay. For what Joe knows, that's a bargain price."

We drank more lager as Bush waited for the sun to go down. "You know," said Bush, "he would have seen all this coming just a few months ago. He was brilliant when we met! He still is, but since he's been sick, he's become more erratic. Like a scary kind of genius, you know? So just watch what you say around him. I've seen things."

"If he's crazy, why do you continue helping him?"

"First, I never said he was crazy, I said he was sick…and scary. But he's still doing more for mankind in his sickness, than I've ever done for it in my health. And secondly, he's paying me a shitload of money, with exclusive rights to reporting his story."

"That all sounds familiar…like something I read in the blog."

"Maybe it is."

"So quit quoting the blog and start telling me what *you* think."

"Quit quoting the blog? I wrote the damn blog."

"That's bull! You don't know me; you couldn't have written those things about me! And you just met Joey; how could you know so much about his past?"

"Don't you think he'd be dead or captured by now if he had been the one posting the blog? He knew that from the beginning. He orates, I transcribe. He never wrote anything, which allows him to legally deny everything. This also keeps him out of town, which means out of harm's way."

"What does it matter what happened to him when he was three, or four, or twenty? What is the point to any of the blog?"

"There's a method to its madness. Its chief function is to entertain; this draws in readers. Its second function is to inform; this grabs the attention of the media. But the primary function of the blog is to remind GM that Joe can publish their dirty secrets at anytime, from anywhere, and that his following is wide enough for his claims to be taken seriously.

"Joe wants GM's hundred million to fund a radical genetic research program that may lead to the extinction of AIDS. The blog is like a time bomb counting down to the years Joe worked for GM. Every post to the blog brings us closer to his last day there, and closer to exposing their covert activities. Making public the illegal and unethical duties Joe carried out at their behest would cause their stock to plummet and dismantle their entire organization. Billions of dollars are on the line, and in some cases, entire governments.

"Right now, the blog is getting over a million hits per day and clogging up the entire server; we've had to pay extra *and* in advance just to keep the blog online. Even online news services are picking up the scent now, bringing Global Media, that erstwhile esoteric info-empire into the limelight.

"Of course, if they pay him, the blog would be shut down within hours. And the world will go on as it does, without ever really knowing who or what controls it."

"Bush, is it true though, the things in the blog? I need to know."

"I personally don't think anyone could make that kind of shit up; it's too horrible. His life, the things that happened to him, the things he did…if those things are true, perhaps he should be punished for them. Maybe he knows that. And maybe all this…this madness…is his way of atoning for that evil. Maybe a worm has gnawed through generations of his family for some sin long forgotten, and he is destined to be the spell-breaker, the unspotted lamb. The seventh son born of the seventh son."

"Can you give me a real-world answer, something that would

make sense to adults? Something that sounds like it came from an accredited reporter?"

"Adults. I didn't know him as a kid, and haven't known him very long as an adult, so I suppose the things in the blog could never have happened. But let's test it: the blog says he worked for Global Media and that he fucked you outside some bar. So: did he work for GM? And: did he fuck you?"

I glared at Bush, unwilling to answer either question.

"Then it must be true. Can you speak Afrikaans or Xhosa? Have you ever even been to Africa? Exactly what qualified you for this assignment? Perhaps fucking him was your only qualification."

"Okay, I get it!"

"They knew if they had sent anyone but you, we wouldn't even be talking. They're master manipulators! They manipulate world events all the time, baby. You think they can't manipulate you?

"GM has less than a full day to either pay him or kill him, because THEY know the blog is true.

"I think it's true too" Bush continued, "and I can damn sure swear to the parts about South Africa. I was here that day, outside on the balcony with Lucky and his crew; the day Joe Bosco walked up to us like we were old friends and smoked dagga with us.

"He had just come to town with all these bright ideas for a better South Africa. He was amazing to listen to, especially *after* he got high. The whole time though, he was preoccupied with the table behind us, with this homeless man scribbling ink onto *Popsicle* sticks. Bush dubbed him the Rune Man."

"I remember reading that in the blog, but what was he writing?"

"He was transcribing the human genome; the entire haploid set, and those associated with triggering the transformation of infected T-cells into AIDS."

"Was it real!" I demanded.

"It still is," Bush said.

"Oh, come on! You expect anyone to believe that a…bum in a bar wrote the cure for AIDS, on *Popsicle* sticks?"

"People are born neither homeless nor alcoholic; society makes them that way. In another life, the Rune Man was a microbiology student named Bevan Paulse. He was well respected in the Eastern

Cape, and on track to become the first Black microbiologist produced by this country.

"His only mistake was hooking up with the equally brilliant Dr. Bronwyn Kelswitch. It cost him his family, his career, and his mind. Shortly after her public humiliation and death, Paulse suffered a nervous breakdown. He abandoned all desire to live, and dissolved into the underbelly of Port Elizabeth."

"So how did he get here, to Cape Town?"

"Destiny drove him, compelling him to follow the train tracks for weeks…all the way down to Cape Town. He thought to live out the remainder of his tortured life here, but a new life was just beginning."

"And Joey is connected to this...how?"

"Western science got it wrong; the cure for AIDS won't come from evolution, but from destiny. GM's AEP project and the death of Kelswitch were destined to happen so that Joe Bosco and the Rune Man could meet over there – on the balcony of this very bar. This led to corporate blackmail, blackmail funding the genetic vaccinations against the most destructive plague in the history of mankind."

Bush seemed manic and more than a bit scary himself. I couldn't trust him. What if he had befriended Joey and then had him killed in order to blackmail GM himself? "I don't believe it…I can't believe anything you're saying. I need to hear it from Joey."

"At least you're honest," he said smiling. "I'll give you an 'A' for honesty."

He looked at his watch again. "It's dusk now. This is our best chance to slip out of the city unnoticed. They must know you're here so we can't leave together. There are cameras and tapes everywhere, but you already know that."

As we stood up, Bush leaned closer, whispering in my ear.

"Take a *public* taxi – not a *private* one – to Goodwood. It's a suburb just down the road. The ride will be dirty, dangerous, and overcrowded, but it'll be harder for GM to find the driver or where you got out. Get off at the corner of Voortrekker and Vanguard/N-2. Can you remember that?"

"Yes."

"You'll be right outside the Libertas building. I'll see you there, right on the corner. Hurry up; public transportation shuts down at eight o'clock."

I left before Bush, constantly looking over my shoulders as I walked to the taxi rank above Kaapstad station. The sky was threatening rain now. "I can handle anything," I kept telling myself. But each time, it sounded more and more like a question.

***

23February1988: We won! Preliminary results show that the workers have voted at least 90% in favor of the union, with a total worker/voter turnout of 75%. This is going to make me look damn good.

I didn't do this for myself or for the money. It was for the minority workers, and in particular, for that Somalian woman who was told by her asshole boss that she couldn't miss more than two days work after delivering her baby by C-section, or she would be fired. True story.

I did it for all the women who are too fat, too old, or too ugly to fuck raises and benefits out of their bosses. Those things should be guaranteed, not at the discretion of favoritism and management.

I feel great! I felt even better when Jana and U.N. called me to congratulate me. Jana promised to think about staying in America. I think she knows I plan to ask her to marry me. I can't let another Suzy slip by. For once, what I love will not leave me.

I have to spend another week or so here to finalize everything and help the workers to elect delegates. This is probably for the best because I have some sort of flu. It's the people here...I never saw so many nasty bastards! One out of every four people pick their noses right in front of me. I'm scared to look out my window at a stoplight. Some cab driver is always digging for gold, spreading diseases that have caused me to cough up a lung - red blood, yellow and green phlegm: a kaleidoscope of venality and pestilence.

I can catch it but not spread it because these fuckers have grown immune to it. Meanwhile, I can't even eat a value meal bacon cheeseburger without pissing through my ass for half an hour. These people must be part cockroach. Fucking indestructible.

05March1988: These are not tears on this paper; it's...eye-sweat. I have allergies. Anyway, I'm sleeping on Jackie Vogelbach's couch tonight because....because it's la fin du monde. The end of the world.

I landed at SFO at 9:45. I wanted to surprise Jana by popping the question to her with a $750 engagement ring I bought in San Diego, but I was the one that got surprised.

I opened the door to our flat and couldn't believe what I saw. I thought the joint had been tossed by cops. Clothes and dishes were everywhere and the volume was all the way up on the TV. I crunched over unknown things on the way to my bedroom, in the intermittent light of the living room television.

The door to my bedroom was wide open. I heard snoring. My heart fluttered and I became aroused. I had been almost faithful to Jana since I left town after New Year's Day. The things she had done to me were well worth waiting for. I flicked on my light switch and there was U.N., sprawled out on my motherfucking bed!

I dropped my bags loudly, startling him awake.

"What the fuck are you doing in my bed?"

"Hmm?"

"Where is Jana?"

"Hey bro', I got some bad news..."

"Some bad news?" I was blanking out. I felt sick but high at the same time. All I could do was to repeat what he said. "Bad news?"

"Hey, don't blame me. She just...up and left. Flew back to Italy last night. She left you a note. It's...around here. Somewhere."

U.N., obviously under the influence of something, swiveled his broken leg off the other side of the bed facing away from me. His long dreads hung in disarray along his naked back. He was wearing purple Speedos with a hard-on and nothing else, and I'll have to live with that imagery for the rest of my life. In the space where he had lain, there was ripped-open envelope and a crumpled letter.

Stumbling over his wooden crutch, I walked over to my bed, which smelled of him. I suddenly hated U.N. I thought about killing him.

I picked up the letter and sat on my nightstand. Before I uncrumpled the letter, which smelled of *Poison* and was undoubtedly from Jana, I already knew what it would say.

"Leave me alone, please," I told U.N.

He struggled to stand up, using the walls to support himself. I tossed him his crutch and watched him clumsily negotiate a path out of my room.

"Hey," I said as he reached the door, "did you fuck her?"

He said nothing, continuing to walk out the door.

I grabbed him by his locks and yanked him backwards onto the carpet. I picked up his crutch and began beating him mercilessly. He groaned and lunged at me desperately, clutching my pants, but couldn't get up having just one leg to bend.

I was having an out of body experience. I beat him like I was playing a video game and got points for maximum damage. When an unblocked swing cracked him in the head, the crutch splintered, and I came back to reality. U.N. was out cold now. I envied him.

Trembling, I dropped the broken crutch and sat facing him on my bed. I smoothed out the poisoned letter and began to read.

"Dear Joey:

"I have been seriously looking at our relationship and understanding what I need and desire from it. I think we are too different in our personality to be able to live together with joy and good communication and interactions. This is not about wrong or right or about some other person. It is about two lives that do not fulfill each other.

"I have asked you to visit me in Sardinia but please do not. I am very clear that we are not good together right now. I need someone who treasures me and also controls me. I am staying here alone for three months cleaning your house and waiting. I am not a person who likes to stay inside the house alone. You should offer me to come with you but I know you are working very hard. Keep doing what is important for you. We are no good for each other now.

"Please forgive yourself and forgive me. This is how we grow. I like you fine Joey. You are very nice and a nice looking man but I need to move on with my life and you coming to me to visit would not be for a positive purpose. Please accept this and know that God will find the right person for you. Be happy for what we had. Learn and move on from our experiences.

Bona fortuna,

Jana."

...And the bitch left no forwarding address.

I packed the few belongings I still wanted and called a cab. When it got there, I doused U.N. five times with a two-liter bottle of *Pepsi*. He regained consciousness, coughing and shit. I left him there, struggling to sit up on my bedroom floor. I took a mental picture of him, thinking that would be the last time I ever saw him. He reminded me of Old Joe, semi-conscious and struggling to get up, barely comprehending that he had been doused five times.

The cab sped toward Jackie's flat. I knew she would take me in, no problem. I knew it as much as I knew that U.N. had actually done me a favor; a whore can never be a housewife. Old Joe had tried the same thing with Mother Mary and learned the hard way. Some history didn't need repeating.

10March1988: I was so depressed today. It was overcast and Jackie had to work...so I went down to Haight Street and ran into Janine, the redhead. We had peppermint tea in the Chattanooga Café and talked about old times. She had a boyfriend that was different than me, and I had a fuck-partner that was different than her.

I missed the smell of her milky-white skin and henna-red hair. I missed the cleft in her chin and her sexy ignorance. There was no pretense with Janine. No wining and dining, no bullshit conversation about humanity; she was a sure thing – uncomplicated and completely honest.

"Hey," I said, "I'm going downtown to see *The Last Temptation Of Christ*. It'll be the last film I see here; wanna come?"

"I do but I can't," she said. "I'm meeting my boyfriend at New York Pizza soon. What time does it start?"

"Five fifteen."

"Where at?"

"The Cineplex Odeon. We can just take Market Street all the way until-"

"I really can't, Joey. I'm with somebody now. I really wish I could though."

"No problem. Shit happens."

I stroked the white kitten sitting on the table next us, paid the bill, hugged and kissed Ashu (my favorite cashier) goodbye, and walked Janine out the door. Outside, we hugged goodbye and both thought of kissing, but New York Pizza was right across the street, and there was no reason to mess up her life just because mine was fucked beyond repair.

I went to the film by myself. I still had juice around town so the movie house let me in free, but the film was so depressing, I felt like they should have been paying me to watch it. It still gave me a lot to think about, though.

It was pouring rain when the film ended, and as I opened the door to the street, I saw her. She was there, waiting outside the door for me, standing in the pouring rain. Janine: my last temptation.

My pal Ron used to work the dayshift desk at the Leland Hotel, but he was so good that the owner put him in charge of the Palo Alto. So that's where we went. I gave Ron $20 and he gave me a room for a couple of hours. This time, Janine didn't piss the bed...but she still gave great head.

16March1988: I'm leaving for Michigan tomorrow. Jackie woke me up, crying over it. She is really a great girl, but way-y-y to emotional for me. I've only been staying with her for a week. I just don't believe in our relationship like she does. To me, we are ships that passed during one beautiful night. To her, we are ships that collided, joined as one crew, and sank the other ship.

I told her I have things inside of me I need to fix, which is true. But the biggest reason for me not staying with her is to guarantee she doesn't end up like Heidi. Heidi went into seclusion after our break-up and moved into a shack in the Oakland Hills. I talked her out of killing herself but she may as well have. She's a fucking zombie now. She only comes down for food and work. Can loving me do that? Am I such a toxic person?

U.N. has been leaving me messages all over town. Some say he wants to tell me how sorry he is; others say he wants to kill me. Since I was leaving town tomorrow, I decided to meet with him. What we had, and the things we did together, far overshadowed his infidelity and my reaction to it.

We agreed to meet around noon at Coit Tower. I gave Sharky, the bouncer at DV-8, half an ounce of Humboldt to back me up (no one could refuse Humboldt County grass). I had scored some while working for GLU in Eureka, smuggling it through the airport by placing in it a baggie filled with coffee grounds and taping it to my nutsack.

Sharky was the last guy in San Francisco anyone would wanna fuck with. His neck was thick as a fire hydrant, and all his front teeth were filed into sharp points. He had always thought well of me (thank God) and that had always been a good thing.

U.N. was standing at the top of Coit over by the security rail, looking out toward the Embarcadero. I had Sharky hang back by the door while I approached U.N.

"I've resigned from the union," he said without turning, still looking at the horizon. He looked haggard and unkempt.

"That seems like a dumb-ass idea, but whatever."

"I'm moving back to Toledo if you want to know or ever need to reach me."

"You can live or die...I don't care either way." Sharky cracked his neck, flexing his muscles in the background, sensing my increased tension.

"Look dude, seriously, I've more than made up for what I've done. You realize if I was sober, I could have easily killed you for the beating you gave me? Even with *two* broken legs?"

"What beating? Those were love taps. You shoulda met my dad."

"Why did you leave me with her, for weeks? I mean...what did you expect?"

"Brotherhood? Trust?"

"Joey, again...I'm sorry. But why did you set me up so high? That's your main problem, dude; you idolize people. I'm only a man. I'm not your father figure, 'bro. I've got feet of clay."

"So did my father. Only, your feet weren't the fucking problem. It was your dick inside my girl."

"Are you gonna hold that over me forever? Didn't I take an ass-kicking for that? I damn near needed stitches!"

"What do you have to say to me so I can get the fuck out of here? Just get on with your life and I'll get on with mine."

"I wanted you to know that...the world needs you, man. The union needs you, the struggle needs you, and you need yourself. Don't reject the message because the messenger sinned, or because I didn't live up to your standards."

"At least I have some standards. Do you?"

"Yeah, man. I do."

"And did you live up to them?"

We turned away from each other and back to the San Francisco skyline. It was dusk; the pyramid building downtown shone like gold. Sea birds swooped and screamed above us, darting at all things shiny, and lighting down to swoop up the crumbs of tourists long gone.

"If you had to do everything all over again," I asked, "would you still have done it?"

"Hell no! Look what it cost us both. But why did you leave her there with me all those weeks? It was almost like you wanted us to fuck."

"Why did you keep having me sent to different campaigns?"

"Why didn't you bring her with you? Didn't you think she would get lonely? No offense, but you just met the girl. And what about me, did you think I was gay or something?"

"I wouldn't say absolutely, but I thought it was more than likely."

"Well...fooled ya."

I took one last look at the hobbled, matted figure facing the ocean. Watching the sun go down on him was like watching the end of an era. I began to walk away.

"Yeah," I said, "you sure fooled me." I turned and went back inside the tower with Sharky.

17March1988: Taking off from SFO, I was still thinking of some way I could win Jana back. I could fly to Sardinia and start asking around for her. How dangerous could that be?

To hell with women. La fin du monde. No sun, no truth, no time, no dreams...nothing but a persistent chill and disarray. I find it difficult to write when things are in disarray. My eyes are blurring and burning. My heart is vacant.

17March1988 (continued): I am stuck on the plane at the Detroit Metropolitan Airport. There was something on the runway...we ran over something, just when I need to take a crap. I refuse to sit on an airplane toilet, so I'm writing to distract myself.

The pilot began backing up the plane. "Do they have rear view mirrors on here?" I asked aloud. "Semaphores," said the guy next to me. "They got semaphores."

Ah, my city by the bay; from your heart I shall never stray. I thought about my last meal in paradise. It was a huge burrito from a joint on the corner of Masonic and Hayes. It was so big that I shared it with panhandlers in Hayes Park. Everyday of life there was like paradise...until one tramp fucked it all up. All women are whores. Something should be done about it.

19March1988: I have been back in the Motor City for a day and a half. Everything I used to know here has been altered in some way by crack cocaine. The way people live, the way things look, the bars on the doors, the number of people walking around the streets at all hours of the night...it seems like everyone is either selling it, smoking it, dying over it, or doing time because of it.

I'm staying with Jenny at the family house on Asbury Park. Our street is the neutral zone between the devastation of Ferguson and Murray Hill. Every home in those streets could have raised a black flag for a loss they had suffered.

Fat Charlie is in prison for drugs. Marcus Cloud, prison: murder and drugs. Kenneth Sarge, prison: murder and drugs. Marcus Tower, prison: murder and drugs. Big Daniel (basketball scholarship), prison: drugs. Little John, prison: armed robbery and drugs (robbed his own brother at gunpoint).

The only one that gave anything back to the community they sucked the life out of was Marcus Tower. He renovated an entire neighborhood park by himself. Maybe if the park had been there when he was a kid, he would have been playing with baseballs instead of eight balls.

Most of them will be incarcerated for life, but any life is better than no life at all. 'Magic' Juan, face blown off: drugs. Henry, tied up in his own basement and shot in the head: drugs. Bill (Jenny's brother-in-law), stabbed in a drug house: drugs. Bear, shotgunned getting into his car: drugs. Eric Jackson, stabbed to death running a drug house for Linda's brother: robbery/drugs.

It was madness! But the most fucked up thing, the most abhorrent thing, is what happened to Aaron Ishmael. He was a low-level dealer; strictly weed during high school. Ishmael was a handsome, friendly kid who wore patent leather Adidas with a different color silk shirt for every day of the week. He could have been anything he wanted to. Everyone loved this beautiful, articulate kid while I was here, but while I was gone people had found reasons to murder him. They not only shot him multiple times, but also shot up his funeral, turning the corner of Puritan and Schaefer into one big cemetery. Crack had changed everything. Cars, music, clothing...everything. Even pussy was cheaper.

But time stood still on Asbury Park, and it was nothing short of a miracle. Maybe it was because of how much the neighborhood respected Mary and me. Teddy had also grown up into a huge (and hugely popular) kid.

On my first night back, some dealer was shot on Murray Hill. He jumped Hank's fence and limped onto Asbury Park for help. "I'm shot! I'm shot!" he kept screaming. I told Hank's wife to call 9-1-1, while I applied my belt as a makeshift tourniquet to his thigh. I would have used his belt but kids these days don't wear them.

Asbury Park was immune to crack addiction, but not its collateral damage. The other streets treated Asbury Park like it was Chase Manhattan. It was nothing to have one's house broken into three or four times. Most times, crackheads had the decency to do it while people were at work.

After crackheads invented the bump-and-run, car alarms became ineffective. A bump-and-run is where a crackhead bumps someone's car late at night to see if it has an alarm, and if it does, will the car owner come out or just let the alarm reset. They attack in the wee hours of the morning, when most people are too sleepy to come out and just reset the damn alarm from the bedroom window. The next day some lady running late for work runs out to her car and ends up having to catch the bus.

Sometimes the crackheads have the nerve to leave shit behind they don't want and can't sell, like Top 40 music, text books, or baby shoes hanging from the rearview mirror. I heard that sometimes they even leave car alarms.

But all that shit stopped the day someone invented *The Club*. Putting one on the steering wheel ensured that no one could steer the car. Of course, thieves could always tow it away with a flatbed truck, but not many crackheads had access to tow trucks.

So they went back to simple break-ins – icing your car window with a screwdriver and rifling through your shit as you and your pit bull slept. Most people think it's better to wake up to broken glass and cigarette burns on upholstery than waking up to no car at all.

Asbury Park may have been a haven, but it was far from heaven. More people died there of natural causes than on either of its neighboring streets. Linda's brother: leukemia. Linda's father: heart disease. Linda: brain aneurysm. Mr. White ("Stay off my grass!"): lung cancer. Mr. Bush (math teacher): brain cancer. Martin and Malcolm's father: cancer. Martin and Malcolm's mother:

septicemia caused by intestinal surgery. Jenny's first baby: crib death. Joe Bosco Senior: instant karma.

Gino was the exception to the crack rules. Before I moved to California, Gino and I had smoked crack once or twice. It was still new then, and never affected me, other than the fleeting feeling of invincibility. But different people have different tolerances for drugs...

When I left town, Gino had been the sole beneficiary of both parents' life insurance policies. Since I came back, Gino doesn't even own his house anymore. No one has seen him for months, and some people here are REALLY looking for him, suspecting him of several daytime break-ins. It was strange; Gino never left his front porch, but never seemed to notice anyone getting robbed. I guess one side effect of crack is blindness.

It's all the same, you know. Crack and death are one in the same, and it doesn't care how you die, as long as you die. Overdose or old age, in the streets or in a cage, in the end, none of us will get out alive. Sometimes death dresses in drag, all seductive and allurin', leading drunken men to ruin.

Back in the day, my neighbor Maurice and his brothers helped me set the timing chain on my first car. Today, his brothers are both doing time for hacking up strippers and leaving their heads in local parks. Sometimes death could be two dudes dressed like Prince.

Life is like a Miles Davis album...forever changing in intensity and tempo. Today, I'm okay about Jana and Mary. Other times, I wondered why Mary bothered having me, or if that cunt Jana had given me AIDS.

It could be worse. Martin and Malcolm's parents, AND their aunt, all died from some form of cancer. The rest of the family is thinking of moving them to New York or back to Jamaica. Strange thing is...I never saw anyone eat healthier than them. All they ate was plantain, curry, and herb tea. It makes me want to go out and eat a whole chocolate cake, followed by a bacon cheeseburger and pack of *Newports*. When it's your time to go, it's your time.

23March1988: My half-brother, Jack, was doing well with crack. He had brought the game to a new level. He took me shopping with him today at Fairlane. He didn't buy anything; it was more like he was casing the joint. But he did hip me to the game.

"Crack is crack," he told me, "as long as you don't step on it too hard; you need that repeat bid'ness. And weed is always weed, no matter what you call it. The experience a nigga *has* wit' your shit, and the price of your product, are what makes the difference. Treat them crackheads fair, let them pay you wit' jewelry or quarters from the payphones - sometimes, not all the time - weight it up fair, keep your houses runnin' twenty-four-seven, and they'll always be back. Know why?"

"Because...they're addicts?"

"Shit! A nigga can get crack anywhere! You can get crack easier than cold medicine and it costs about the same. A nigga comes back because he found value in the experience and the price. Feel me? *Value* equals product and experience, divided by price."

"What's the price?"

"I put the crack out there for ten dollars a rock, Monday through Saturday. I let it go for eight on Sundays - that's my slow day. Crumbs always go for five. Eighths, eight balls, go on a nigga-to-nigga basis. Never sell that much to a nigga you don't know. If he willin' to pay crazy prices for it, you know that nigga Po-Po! And that's some Federal shit now.

"They givin' niggas life sentences for damn near anything more than personal use. But if I kept that shit in powder form, like the Whites, I could sell that shit all day long! I could get locked up for it in June and be home in time for the Super Bowl. Ain't that some racist shit?

"Weed is easy: twenty-eight grams or an ounce for a hundred. Seven grams or a quarter ounce for twenty-five, and one gram is a dime bag. Why? You thinkin' about 'rollin' wit' me?"

"Nah. Long on dreams, short on green."

"Well, if you wanna put in some work, I'm always lookin' out for industrial niggas who can count."

"That's *industrious*."

"Nigga, as long as I'm drivin' and you ridin', it's whatever the fuck I want it to be! Don't let that older brother shit go to ya head. My family is my fish and my *AK*. But still...I don't wanna leave your ass hangin' like Ma did."

"Have you seen her?"

"Hell no. I'm takin' you downtown tomorrow to get a chauffeur's license."

"Chauffer for who?"

"I'm not askin' you to be a chauffer, nigga; you just need it before you can get your cab license."

"You want me to be a fucking taxi driver?"

"Why not? You got the brains for it. And the balls. And you're fuckin' industrial! Most importantly though, you got a clean record. Don't worry about it. The tests are easy as fuck and you ain't gotta drop (no drug test). I'll pay all the fees, and when you're good to go, I'll make sure you get some runs. You can pick up and drop off packages for me every once in a while. I'll tear you off better than the meter. Maybe I'll use your license sometimes; drive for you."

I could finally see how we were related; he saw all the angles and played them well. In his own way, Jack - or Slim, as he preferred being called - was a genius. If I had stayed there after I graduated, by now we'd have an empire. But at what cost to ourselves and the city? How many cars, whores, guns, and fish would make me whole? Jack had sold his soul for two *Cadillacs*, two strippers, two *AKs*, and a six-foot aquarium. But my soul is priceless. It's all I have. My name, my face, and my mind, I share with a dead man.

17May1988: I've been back in Detroit for about two months working as a taxi driver. Jack, whose crazy idea this was, got locked up in Indiana for armed robbery of a jewelry store in South Bend. I guess he figured his soul was worth more too.

He's been gone about a month. His bail is ridiculous. One of his strippers was supposed to take everything and liquidate it but she said his rented house was broken into. She said they took everything; the cars...even the fish. At least that's what he told me when he called collect to ask me for help with his bail, but I'm still short on green and long on dreams. I put a hundred in his commissary account, though. I didn't want to leave him hanging like his Ma did.

I decided to keep driving a cab while I sort out what I'm going to do. I had given two years of my life to communal, *Animal Farm*, free love, hippie bullshit, and it was all a lie. So what am I going to do now?

Being here is no better. Crack had cheapened life in Detroit to about ten dollars per person. All the awards and shit I won, all the union votes, all the things I saw...only to come back here and have my life devalued to a piece of hardened coke.

I drive cab number 490. It's said to be one of the most stressful and dangerous jobs in the world. I think it's *the* most dangerous job because we're not legally armed, and we're driving crackheads all over East Hell in yellow ATM machines in the murder capital of America. Maybe I'm just looking for death because I heard he was looking for me. I don't want to wait on him. He could take seven to ten years.

Detroit is the place to find death; no place better. There's a city limits sign on Woodward south of Eight Mile, bearing a greeting which reads "Welcome to Detroit". Scribbled below it in red spray paint reads the dubious continuation "Sorry We Missed You".

CHAPTER 13

THE RIDE to Goodwood was more like a drag race, and the people in the taxi smelled awful! The stop light-running driver didn't speak to anyone the whole way and his toothless attendant never gave me my change. An older woman sat on my lap while the man next to me kept trying to nuzzle my hair.

All this only made me miss Martin more. I was ecstatic when we reached the Libertas Building and I saw his familiar red Land Rover waiting for me on the side of the building. I pried myself from the taxi, happy to step into the rain, like it could somehow wash the filth and stench of the city off of me. He didn't roll down his tinted windows, but blinked his headlights for me, and I headed for his bakkie.

I opened the passenger door, startled to find that Bush was driving. And he was alone.

"Where's Martin?"

"Hop in," said Bush, "I'm taking you to him."

"I thought you said you were taking me to Joey?"

"They're all together! Can you get in and close the door? We need to avoid being followed!"

Bush rambled on as we rocketed off but I wasn't listening. I was busy watching him undo his tie and wrap it around his wrist. He pulled off to the left of the N-2 highway and I reached for the door handle, wondering how Secret Agent Luna would get herself out of this.

"Hey, chill. What do I have to gain by hurting you?" he asked. "I'm famous here. You're just passing through; a tourist with a laptop. I HAVE to blindfold you. It's Joey's orders. No outsiders can ever know the way there. It's for your own safety."

So I began my journey into the desert blindfolded. In the darkness, and monotony of the drive, I fantasized of being face to face with Joey, but I suppressed my emotions. After a while, I began to feel disoriented and carsick. The night air seemed even hotter than the day's.

"Bush…for the love of God…turn on the air conditioner." After he did so, we drove on for miles without speaking.

"There are some things you should know before we get there," Bush said finally.

"For starters, Joe can barely stand on his own. He's subject to dizzy spells and has lost a considerable amount of weight. I wouldn't be surprised if we get there only to find he's been carried off by a strong wind."

"What's wrong with him?" I asked anxiously.

"I don't know; he won't see a doctor. He HATES doctors. Father issues, I think. He could have malaria or dysentery…even rabies. A kid actually died of that in one of the townships last December. Can you believe that? Fucking rabies?"

"Why don't you just make him get some help? You're his friend, right?"

"Because Joey Bosco only listens to Joey Bosco. You don't know how things are out there. You can't *make* Joey do anything; Joey makes *you*.

"How can I explain to you? You don't know who or what he is now. Of course it doesn't make sense to you."

"Try."

"I'll tell you a story: I was working on my first screenplay, in a café back in the States. It was one of those bookstore cafés – Borders, I think. It was noisy as hell. Kids running amuck, machines steaming milk, and behind the counter, a cheap radio actually played the theme song from *Flashdance*. I couldn't concentrate for shit; it was pure chaos.

"Suddenly, this skinny redhead walks in, sets up shop in the middle of the floor, and starts playing the hell out of his violin. No one made a sound. Even the few people annoyed by the guy sat up and listened to him playing. It was beautiful! And…for that brief period of time, there was suddenly this…great sense of clarity and order!

"At the end, everyone applauded him, and right in the midst of the applause, he packed up his case and walked out the café. I never saw him again, but I'll never forget him. I'll never forget that…for that brief moment he was there, there was order, and everything made sense.

"That's what Joey is to me: a person who can cut through the disorder of life, the red tape; a person who can walk right into the very heart of chaos and create order."

"Do you think…is it possible that he has AIDS?" I asked.

"Damn it Jim, I'm a writer not a doctor!"

"What?"

"You never heard that? From *Star Trek*?"

"No."

"Damn it Jim…!"

"Can you take this seriously?"

"Well, seriously, I'm a writer not a doctor. I have no way of telling what's wrong with him."

"You've seen AIDS symptoms before, haven't you?"

"All kinds."

"So you should have an opinion on if he has it or not; don't play stupid!"

"Don't ever again make the mistake of calling me stupid. He said I had to bring you; he didn't say I had to bring you alive!"

We didn't talk for a while.

"The hero doesn't always ride off into the sunset with the girl," Bush said. "Sometimes there's a kind of karmic reckoning. Did you read the entire blog?"

"Every word."

"There's a school of thought that says our genes are what's really running things inside of us. Selfish genes that only do what's in the best interest of our genetic code's survival. Even when we do altruistic things, underneath it all, it's still probably just for our own sake.

"In other words, I think Joey's done some really bad shit, so he's trying to make up for it by doing something equally good; you know, balance the scales. Whether he knows it or not, he's bartering his way into heaven."

"What has he done that's so bad? There are promiscuous priests, and certainly presidents. And what are soldiers but state sanctioned murderers? All have sinned…he knows that. He was raised in the Church; he knows there's nothing he could do so base or vile that would place him beyond the reach of God's forgiveness. All he has to do is confess his sins and ask to be forgiven."

"Let's assume he did all those things in the blog – and *that* was some crazy shit – but what if he's done even worse things too? Things so bad he couldn't even tell *me* about them? If he has a conscience at all, that must be a backbreaking weight upon his soul. Maybe even enough to break a true believer. Break his will to live."

"What kind of things?"

"I don't know, GM type things. You know more about what they're up to around the world than I do. If their hands were even remotely clean, the blog wouldn't be such an effective blackmailing tool. To me, it's more than just about blackmail though. It's Joey's final confession, and the extortion is an act of atonement. If God is good, then the person whose act of contrition facilitates the cure for the worst plague in the history of mankind should be a shoo-in for the pearly gates."

"Tell me about this cure again. I don't get why we have this cure but no one in the civilized world is using it."

"We don't have a cure yet, we have a theory; hence, the need for money. Doctor Bronwyn Kelswitch was a geneticist from Gauteng. In nineteen ninety-six, she went public with a theory that became a lightning rod for praise, criticism, and unparalleled scrutiny. Kelswitch theorized that you could live your whole life with HIV in a dormant status – three out of every ten infectees worldwide are believed to be doing so now.

"In all infectees, HIV inserts its own genetic material into the body's defensive T-cells and then replicates itself. The virus then waits years for some chemical change that triggers its virulency. Kelswitch hypothesized that locating and altering the gene responsible for the chemical changes in the body – the ones that trigger the conversion of HIV to AIDS – would neutralize the virus, like stopping the timer on a time bomb. Ultimately, hundreds of millions would be saved, especially in sub-Saharan Africa."

"AIDS is not just in Africa, you know."

"It *would* be if the rest of the world had its way. Come on, Black countries have always been the petri dish of Western civilization. The medicine they dump here is mostly adulterated and ineffective; a tax write-off that's immediately diverted to the black market.

"But you're right; AIDS no longer solely exists in Africa. Advances in travel and global trade have aided the spread of diseases. Eight years ago, corporations with common sense understood this and gave Kelswitch grants up the wazoo. In June of ninety-seven, she began conducting primate trials in the Eastern Cape, with money, praise, and the best of intentions. But those are the things that pave the road to hell."

"Keep going."

"In ninety-eight, some scandalous information came to light. Kelswitch – a white doctor from a wealthy family – was having an affair with a Coloured lab assistant, a man named Bevan Paulse. It was further suggested that Paulse was the father of Kelswitch's only child, Liesel, born in nineteen eighty-one, and being raised by relatives in Amsterdam.

"Kelswitch came under intense public scrutiny and character defamation. Not only were her grants and funding rescinded, but her entire family was systematically cut off from social circles and positions of favor. The media made out like she had shagged Paulse on the lab table and contaminated the test results.

"Next, it surfaced that the purpose of her original research was a genetic cure for obesity. Kelswitch had been looking for the genetic trigger causing some people to stockpile fat while others frequently burn it, when she made the scientific breakthrough concerning HIV. Since she herself was genetically predisposed to obesity, her humane and altruistic work was now seen as vain and self-serving. It was even suggested that Kelswitch fabricated results in order to receive funding.

"Soon afterwards, a personal letter she had written to a colleague while still in medical school was discovered. In it, she ranked the Avian Flu as a greater communicable threat than AIDS. This made her even more the object of ridicule and scorn by the media and her colleagues. They declared her promiscuous, fraudulent, and ignorant to the fact that the Avian Flu hadn't killed more than a handful of people in over eighty years. No one seemed to care that, in nineteen eighteen, it did kill…fifty million people almost overnight. Guess who dredged up all that scandalous and obscure information?"

I didn't answer. I didn't have to.

"GM doesn't collect enemies," I said, "they collect information. Who were they collecting it for? Who was paying them?"

"Informants told me that in early ninety-eight, six months after Kelswitch began her primate trials, representatives from a pharmaceutical consortium visited her private compound. They came bearings gifts, money, and fame. All they wanted her to do was publicly acknowledge a link between her genetic theory and continued pharmaceutical therapy; to say that drug treatment would be necessary to ensure the effectiveness of any genetic cure."

"Because...there's no real money in the cure," I mumbled in horrific disgust, "it's in the medicine."

"Exactly! Profit margin is all that matters! The good people at Murk and Smyth-Klein would rather keep you sick and treatable for years, than cure you outright in a day.

"Kelswitch refused the men and had them escorted off her grounds. Within hours, a media shit storm began. She rode it out for the rest of that year, using her family's name and wealth until there was nothing left, until everything was mortgaged to the hilt. She believed in the project that much.

"But on the morning of January second, nineteen ninety-nine, her test monkeys were found dead in their cages. Mysteriously, the media printed the incident in the morning editions; hours before anyone at her compound even knew the monkeys were dead. Gene A-5, the gene in question, became instantly known as the Killswitch gene. The media always maintains a sick sense of humor, but with her, they smelled blood.

"Headlines like 'Kelswitch Flips Killswitch' ran for weeks. Even the South African government got involved, denying Kelswitch the authority to continue genetic testing on plants, let alone primates.

"After a lengthy inquest, the government ruled the monkeys had been intentionally poisoned, and that the cause of death had nothing whatsoever to do with genetic manipulation. But even this worked against Kelswitch, because the cause of death was ricin, a rare toxic biochemical reagent that was intentionally administered. Her compound was quarantined indefinitely, and since the primates were under her supervision, Kelswitch was held legally responsible and stripped of her medical credentials.

"Soon, creditors foreclosed on the entirety of her family's South African estate. This forced Kelswitch and her elderly parents to relocate with relatives in Amsterdam, reuniting her with her daughter, Liesel.

"Even there, the media hounded Kelswitch if she so much as left the house for a walk; so she became a recluse, gaining over two hundred pounds in less than a year. She died on September fourteenth, nineteen ninety-nine. The cause of death was listed as heart failure resulting from morbid obesity. How's that for irony? A woman goes into medicine to help fat people and stumbles on the cure for AIDS, but before she can prove it, dies of obesity."

"Yeah, that's really too bad."

"Too clinical is what it is. Hollywood would say she died of a broken heart, a broken spirit. And so would I."

"So…everyone just stopped testing? Just like that? I mean, no one has tried to verify the cure in all this time?"

"Nope. After the quarantine was lifted, creditors sold her compound to a steer farmer. It became an abattoir."

"A what?"

"A slaughterhouse."

"That's fucking disgusting! These people are so messed up!"

"Because it was considered the intellectual property of the government, Kelswitch wasn't allowed to leave the country with any of her work. All the research materials found at the compound, and at her estate, were confiscated by government officials, who then allegedly sold them to pharmaceutical companies…multiple times over.

"Four of her five assistants became independently wealthy from selling their versions of events to tabloids, making television appearances, and publishing smut books about working with her. But her original lab notes, the Rosetta stone to her theoretical AIDS cure, were said by everyone to be kept in an expensive leather-bound notebook, which was never recovered.

"The fifth assistant, Paulse, long since lost in the underbelly of Port Elizabeth, was rumored to be the sole possessor of that notebook, and therefore, the sole possessor of the key to Kelswitch's genetic research. He instantly became the subject of a nationwide manhunt. His credit was destroyed and his family dispersed."

"The Rune Man, you mean?"

"Who else?"

"So…what do you think drove him crazy? *Is* he crazy?"

"No, just traumatized. My guess is Paulse fled Gauteng for his very life, long before Kelswitch left the country and before anyone noticed he was gone. In the period directly following the fall of Apartheid, a Black man interracially involved – especially with someone of substance – would have found himself fed to lions or dangling from the end of a very short rope, courtesy of the Boeremag, a group of White Supremacists who still vow to take back South Africa and drive all Blacks into the sea.

"From a distance, Paulse had to watch the public shaming and death of his lover – the mother of his child. It could have been enough to push him over the edge…probably suffered a nervous breakdown… maybe even a schizophrenic split. Soon, he just wandered from town to town, getting high and-"

"Writing on *Popsicle* sticks. I get it now."

"Meanwhile, Liesel Kelswitch, now a twenty-four year-old microbiologist, has just returned to South Africa, after spending most of her life in Holland and the USA. She set up shop at a clinic in Lesotho, determined to find that cure for AIDS and restore her family's honor. All she needs now are her mother's original notes, and a shitload of cash."

"And that's where Joey comes in."

"He said you were smart…*and* sexy. I guess I'll forgive you for the whole flash drive incident."

"But how did Joey get involved with these people?"

"I was getting to that. This past September fourteenth, the fifth anniversary of Dr. Kelswitch's death, I eulogized her in my op/ed column. I blamed her death on a smear campaign spun by corporate greed. My co-workers took me to task for it, saying things like 'You don't know all the facts, man! You don't know the history of our country! You're not from here, you're an American; stick to what you know!'

"Then I got a phone call from someone who had actually taken the time to read the damn column. He was passionate and compelling, and reminded me we had met before through Lucky, the deejay at The Purple Turtle."

"Joey."

"He complimented my work, calling the truth of it vital to the future of this country. Honestly, it was a shot in the arm to hear that. I was just about to blow town…move to France, maybe. Writing here was becoming nothing more than beer money…a means to eat and see shit for free.

"He told me the article was an important start, but I was still tilting at windmills. 'I know all the players,' he said, 'and have proof of the blood on their hands. How would you like that story?' he asked me.

"So we met again at The Purple Turtle. Joey promised me exclusive interviews with Kelswitch, Paulse, and himself, along with communications incriminating GM and certain pharmaceutical corporations. But he would only make those things available at the completion of his 'project'. Then he offered me fifty thousand dollars cash if I would act on his behalf in certain matters regarding that project. I didn't agree to help because of the money, but it sure as hell didn't hurt."

"So he needed you to post the blog while he disappeared underground?"

"Right, I meet with him once a week to type out blog entries on a manual typewriter – he doesn't trust laptops. But there's more to it. Joey gave me power of attorney to negotiate all his financial and legal concerns. There was the setting up of Swiss numbered accounts, the contractual procurement of building materials and petrol, communications with GM, Dr. Kelswitch, and others…hell, he even had me buy a used helicopter. Who's going to fly it?

"I'm ashamed to say I accepted the money at all though, the cause being so worthy. But like I said…it can't hurt. Maybe I'll use it to publish my books. Who the hell am I kidding…I'll end up spending it all on whores and tequila. I should have done it for free. He did."

"What do you mean?"

"When GM pays – and they WILL pay – Joey won't see a dime of that money. It's all set up to go to Kelswitch for her research, to Voox for care of the seventeen hundred followers, to me for services rendered…and to you."

"Me? For what?"

"He'll tell you that when we get there. All I can say is…you have a part to play in this too."

***

04November1988: Just received the absolute worst news of my life: Martin, my next-door neighbor, my true brother, and my best friend, died last night in a car accident in Italy. He was driving his Peugeot on the wrong side of the road when he was crushed to death by an oncoming US military truck. K.I.A. by friendly truck.

I got the news thirdhand form Malcolm. Martin was stationed in Sardinia and was driving to buy kerosene to heat his girlfriend's flat. It was early in the morning when it happened. The Peugeot was crushed so badly that the engine was literally in his lap. He died of a massive coronary. What am I going to do now? What can I write? I don't understand it or who's to blame.

04December1988: Today is Martin's birthday. I celebrated it by sitting on our back porch and shooting things out of our maple tree with my Daisy .22 caliber. I hid her in the house rafters before moving to San Francisco. I thought I had quit her for good, but there we were together again, blowing things away like old times. Got a few birds today. Maimed a squirrel. I think the birds were finches.

The whole time I was back there, I kept trying to get God to notice me, maybe kill me right on the spot. What kind of...what kind of God would bless Cain and kill Abel? Is he blind? Can't he see me sinning every night? Taking blowjobs, weed, and crack for cabfare?

I'm always being shot at and set up for robbery. Robbers bump my cab like it's an accident, so I can pull over and exchange my insurance information for their hot lead. They're dumber than me though. At least God has the decency to not let me get killed by someone stupid. But I long to die.

Maybe there is no God. Or maybe he really is dead, like the philosopher said who went nuts over a horse. I thought God had plans for me, other than shooting birds from a tree. What is it God? What is it you want from me?

20June1995: Today is my birthday. I'm twenty-seven years old and a completely plastic motherfucker. There is nothing I want that I don't already have. And there is no woman I can't have that I want. What's left? What should I think of when I blow out the candles? Who are all these plastic, bleached-teeth people around me? And really, what's the fucking point of anything? I blow out the candles...and wish for a mother.

I earned my BA in Marketing from the University of Michigan; a Suma Cum Laude graduate with a 3.6 GPA, and a member of Phi Beta Kappa. I'm an account executive with a major ad agency. On the side, I do local theatre. I've been in three sold out stage productions (garnering favorable reviews for myself) and I'm frequently interviewed for local media. At the Actor's Workshop, I just completed a live reading on the genital mutilation of women in sub-Saharan countries. *The Metro Times* also serialized one of my short stories:

"The Secret Of The God's Eye Spider"

"...This was during the time in American history when many young men such as my father were compelled to answer the call of war. It was therefore out of necessity (being abandoned by my mother soon after childbirth) that I was made to live with my Nana in her one storied, simple, wooden house whose curtained kitchen door opened up to God's own backyard.

I remember there were bobcats that lived in the trees out back, enchanted, as I was, by the scent of the fruit cobblers my Nana seemed to always have cooling at the opened kitchen window. I remember throwing rocks and sticks at them to coax them from the trees..."

I like writing, but my life is no longer worth writing about. I feel like I've been living the same day, over and over, for the past two years: meetings, restaurants, bars, and broads. I'm sick of looking at computers all day. Who has time to sit in front of one at night to detail the minutia of their existence? And if I did, who the hell would listen?

I don't know myself anymore. I knew me when I rented a Checker cab, earning my way through college as a pretext for it. I miss the danger and excitement of it. I miss that beautiful broad who walked out of her Palmer Park home one night, demanding to sit in the front of my cab. She called me cute as she poured herself and her glitter-red dress into my front seat. Then she reached over to grab my crotch with her MAN HANDS...

I miss the guys who paid me extra to smoke crack and fuck whores in the backseat of my hack, while I cruised down Fenkel and the side streets of Old Redford. I miss the blowjobs from girls I picked up leaving their boyfriends' houses at two in the morning, still horny. Or the ones on their way *to* their boyfriends' homes who just didn't have enough on them to pay their cabfare. I always required payment upfront. Some kind of way, you had to pay the piper.

I miss the free food from my regular fares, fast food restaurant closers. I even dated a regular from Burger King, but it ended up costing me too much time and too much money. I was there to make bread, not break bread.

There was always sex around. It seemed to follow the cab, like kids chasing an ice cream truck. It was more complicated trying to find the cheapest gas than trying to get some ass.

Keeping business first was hard, as hard as doing homework on the side while waiting for fares. In the day I went to school but I drove all night. And that could get stressful, right? So sex was always a necessary and welcome distraction, always best while the meter was running. Like the time I picked up the girl from Mount Sinai Hospital; the girl with tits so big, one was the size of my entire chest – and I'm a 40 regular. I kept the meter running while I tittie-fucked her in the principal's parking space at Cooley High School. It was free for her; the hospital gave her a pre-paid voucher.

But all that was before I graduated and became Mister Respectable. Now I just sit in meetings and listen to clients bitch about the importance of their product message, or the incorrect shade of blue used in our representation of their logo. I brought some Italian broad up to my office one night and fucked her on my desk, thinking the memory...the scent of her...might spice the joint up for me, but it didn't work. I'm still BORED BEYOND BELIEF. My departure from the agency is imminent.

I'm thinking of leaving Michigan altogether. I can't have a conversation of any depth with anyone! The only subjects my guy-friends know are pussy and sports. I ask them about books and they think I'm trying to place a bet. And the broads...the only books they read are the magazines at the beauty shops.

I've been living in Royal Oak for a few years now, and though it's safer and friendlier than Detroit, it's just as dull. People here suffer from the same fears: of thinking, of dissenting, of giving a damn. The Midwest is the kiss of death to anyone with a mind.

01September1995: Francis, my new best friend and personal Zagat guide to Metro Detroit, turned me on to this underground club called The Shvitz. It's a gentleman's club, which means they behave like animals. A female companion and $40 were required just to get in.

I decided to go there last night but none of my usual skanks were available. I ended up taking Beth, this shaineh maidel I met at a pro-Israeli rally. Thank God it was Thursday and not the weekend or she wouldn't have been able to go either.

Beth is very charming and has this whole innocence thing working for her, making her doubly attractive. She invited me to synagogue with her a few times and I actually accepted. Heads turned, but I'll try almost anything once. I had to wear the little cap in the presence of God. It all felt authentic, except for me, Plastic Man.

Sure, I go to church and all. I splash water on my forehead and kneel for communion, unless it's a Black church, then I kneel at a Baptist altar. In either case, it's only so people can see the names on the bottoms of my shoes. I damn sure don't go for the communion. Churches have really gotten cheap on me. Back in the seventies, it was all *Mogen David* and unleavened bread. These days, I'm lucky to get grape juice and crackers. In another few years, it'll be *Kool Aid* and *Wonder Bread*. Yeah, the Church has gone plastic too.

When they look at me, people see this person...this clean-cut, youthful-looking, handsome person. But inside I'm rotten to the core, with every conscious thought dedicated to some kind of sin. The real me can see out, but no one sees in.

I'm like Martin's dead tooth – the one that turned all gray when the root died. It was one of his incisors so it was damn noticeable, but only if you looked at it just right, and only in the proper light. Martin had a beautiful, disarming smile, but if you looked closely, you saw something un-beautiful and alarming. You saw something quite dead. That's me. I'm Martin's dead tooth. But I digress...

Beth seemed relaxed on the way there, and looked stunning in her chiffon shoulder-strap dress and string of pearls. Beth was a real sweet chick, with huge, intense black eyes and hints of gray in her hair. We'd gone out a few times, to proper dining establishments, and for pastries at Astoria Bakery, so she trusted me. I told her we were going to a private dining club, only I didn't tell her she was the dinner. She was as a lamb led to the slaughter.

"We are not of the night, Joey. Nor of the darkness," she told me on the way downtown.

"So let us not sleep as others do," I said. "Let us be alert and sober."

It's good to know some of the scriptures...the spirit gum holding onto my mask of humanity.

Once inside The Shvitz, those upstanding gentlemen – husbands and fathers all – swarmed Beth like red meat dangled for a wolf pack. I didn't see her again for the rest of the night.

The things I saw there were...bizarre. I felt like I was living in a Bosch painting, full of contorted fucking positions never seen before. This joint made the Kama Sutra look like *Sesame Street*. I saw many a yoni entered with a lingam or even two lingams at the same time. Can you really fuck someone while she's upside down on her head and shoulders? This was the kind of fucking that would make even Jana blush. The best thing about it was I didn't have to participate. I just watched everyone fuck for a while and then I jacked off. I paid. I saw. I came.

But I got bored after a while, started dozing off, and realized it was time to go. I couldn't call Beth yet because my phone and clothes were in a locker. I was only wearing a cum-stained towel. I headed to the locker room to get dressed and call Beth, when I passed this Japanese girl with a ghetto-ass, eye-fucking me as I walked by. I had no choice but to jiggle and smack her ass while she rode some guy she'd probably just met. I smacked her ass while she gyrated up and down until she came. I never even asked her name. But by the time I was done, her ass looked like hamburger.

I never found Beth. I described her to one of the doormen and left him ten dollars to give a note to her but she never called. I don't even know how she got home. I left her several unreturned messages. Fuck her! No, I feel some responsibility for her. No, not really, she's an adult! Plus, she never fucked me, even though I am circumcised. And we dated for almost four weeks! That was a record. Newsflash: Beth, I'm of the night.

01January1996: I spent last night alone. I would have been alone with everyone else anyway. This way, I just saved a few bucks. I had a lot on my mind. Something is missing from my life...something I NEED. Milton said, "When Alexander saw the breadth of his domain, he wept for there were no more worlds to conquer." Goals are the key. Where the fuck are my goals?

14January1996: The year is beginning well. I got a callback from an anonymous company that posted an ad in *The Free Press*. I'm scheduled to interview with a senior Field Representative named David Green. They asked that I not discuss the interview with anyone, and I agreed, but I had to consult my main man Francis.

"It'll be the best thing that's ever happened to you," he said. "I'm telling you man, that ad job is weighing you down. And if your bird don't fly, you're Earth-bound, baby."

A funny thing happened today: I'm seeing this tall blonde with carnation pink nipples named Sherry. I went to her house for her kid's birthday and guess what she got him? A Lhasa Apso named Gizmo! It's the same color and temperament as Osh Kosh, Teddy's old dog from when we were growing up. I got all freaked-out about it. I hugged the dog, then broke down crying. I may have to see a shrink behind this. All the things I killed, all the people that died around me, and the only deaths that bothered me were Martin's and that dog's.

Osh Kosh was long since dead. She died blind and tumor-riddled, back in 1992. She had eaten her puppies – the ones that were born black and stillborn – and spent the remaining weeks of her life in the dankness of the basement, huddled under an old stove.

Thinking about her just made me spontaneously cry. Sherry put her kid to bed and we had angry sex. After a while, I fucked away all memory of the dog.

17January1996: Today was a most excellent day. I was running late for my meeting with Green at the Mc Donald's in Ferndale. I had to get my *Xanax* prescription filled and it took longer than I thought. I took the pill, and by the time I met Green at Nine Mile and Woodward, it was already a most excellent day.

Earlier today, I had my first shrink visit. If I had known there were pills that could yank me from depression this fast, I would've taken them a long time ago. Think of all the pain and suffering I could have spared the world, and the things living in it. But I digress...

Inside McDonald's, I saw who I assumed was Green, wearing a laminated company ID badge, and eating a burger and fries. He was a prematurely gray, middle-aged man, having the look of someone perpetually tired. He looked like a warning sign for me *not* to take the job, but it was too late.

Green rose, extending his hand when I approached him. "Hi, Joe Bosco?"

"Yeah, how are ya?"

"Dave Green. Good to finally meet you."

"Thanks; same." I took off my coat and sat down.

"Got a cigarette?" Green asked in a kind of desperation.

"I thought company employees aren't allowed to smoke."

"Are you a man or a mouse?" Green asked, smiling.

I passed him a *Marlboro Light* from my silver-plated cigarette case. "I read the package GM sent me," I said. "It was kind of vague. No explanations for things, like what's the point of their non-smoking policy?"

"Statistics show that smokers take more risks, that smoking leads to harder drugs, and that smokers use up more health benefits," answered Green. "Pretty soon, all companies will deny heath benefits to smokers. GM's just ahead of the game."

"Are you management?"

"No," he laughed. "If I was, I wouldn't have to give up smoking. I can still be tempted though." Green slid the cigarette under his nose, savoring it like it was a Cohiba Esplendido. He reluctantly passed it back to me.

"Keep it," I said. "Use it to tempt yourself later."

Green stuffed the cigarette into his pocket as I smiled approvingly. It was all office talk from there on, but I could tell it was the beginning of a beautiful friendship.

15March2003: I've lived in Nyack, New York for the past two years, collecting data from cooperative homes in the five boroughs. We estimate that each home has more televisions than the actual number of residents living there, and each resident watches an average of eight hours of television per day.

If the household makes over 50k per year combined, they drink table wine for dinner and have at least one pet. If they make between 30k and 40k, they drink only bottled water, and if they make less than 20k, they have several pets, several unuseable cars in the yard, several unused television sets, and several children. They drink soda pop frequently, and only drink water out of the tap. I have no idea why such information could be of use to anyone.

03May2003: I've been back from New York for about two months, and already I want to leave again. I realize now that most of Michigan is flat, vacant, and cold. It's a black, salty asphalt plain, populated with women as fat as cows. I don't know whether to milk these broads or fuck 'em, so most times I end up doing both. I have to, there's nothing else here; and even *Xanax* can't take the place of pussy.

I hung out at Tremors in Livonia tonight. The club is aptly named, seeing how the dance floor shakes when those cows step onto it. Francis teases me about the joint but where else is there to go? He always takes me to places where the broads are like ninety years old. Between old and fat, I'll take fat.

It's kind of a sick thrill to see which ones can actually lie down on the bench seat of my *Cadillac*. They never want to just suck. The fatter they are, the more they want to fuck. It feels like I'm fucking a waterbed, or a *Hefty* bag filled with *Jell-O*.

All I can have now is ANGRY sex. Otherwise, I can't have sex at all. I have to concentrate on things that piss me off, like Mother Mary and Jana. I'm not saying I want to have sex with them, I'm saying I have to be angry, and they still make me very angry. Just thinking of them is giving me a boner right now.

I'm bored tipping these cows while their kids watch TV or pretend to be sleeping on the other side of a slightly closed door. Michigan is such a bore. A dairy land. And suddenly, I'm lactose intolerant.

15June2003: I don't know what city I'm in...Fort Lee? How long have I been here? I'm sick today. Every time I work in another state or interact with large groups of people, I become ill. The cycle invariably begins the same: scratchy throat, constant pissing, and then a headache. Eight to twelve hours later comes runny-nose, sinus-draining, raw throat and sneezing. About ten days later, it ends with loss of voice, headache, yellow phlegm and even more pissing.

It's probably from working too hard. I have over thirty-four thousand dollars saved in salary and bonuses, my retirement benefits have vested, and I can leave at any time. But leave to where? For what?

There's something wrong with me inside. I feel empty. Something is missing from my life. I tried Church, but at every church I go to I end up fucking one of the PKs (Pastor's Kids), or some soon-to-be fallen angel from the choir. I went back to Mass for a while, but I felt like I was just paying lip service. Reciting lines. Plus there aren't a lot of single women at Catholic churches; choirs there are mostly boys.

Francis is a non-practicing Catholic but can't seem to feel my pain. My attempts to engage him in conversations of any moral or spiritual depth always end the same. "Keep things light and easy," he says. He's the type of guy you wouldn't know had cancer until he fell over dead.

When I think of all the broads Frank and I have shtupped together, all the vodka we've consumed, all the steaks we've devoured, the primo dope we've inhaled, the crack vials, the opium paste, the smiley-face pills, the blue pills, the red-and-yellow pills...I know I should be just as satisfied as he is. And all that film and music! All that wonderful music! I should be content...but I'm not.

I feel like I should be doing more, and no woman has tits big enough to hide me from that persistent thought. I feel...lacking, like God emptied a jar down on me from heaven, and emptied out everything but contentment. Why can't I ever be content? Why can't I just once be satisfied?

17June2003: Green has been promoted to Field Supervisor and is now technically my boss. I don't really have a boss though, since none of them can do what I do, and they all look the other way when I do it. I can pick the top ten shows of the season before the pilots have aired. Sweeps month in November is when I really make my bread and butter. It's so fucking easy to me. How did I fuck around and get this job?

20June2003: Today is my birthday; I'm thirty-five. It's another boring day here in Michigan. I've been back from Manhattan for two days. I spent most of today seducing Amy, this art student from Western Michigan University. I met her on Yahoo and we hooked up at the mall after she convinced her friends to drive her down here. I tried to avoid being seen on mall security cameras with them, just in case things went wrong later.

"I thought you were driving up here alone," I said.

"See? You don't listen. I told you my car got impounded."

"Impounded? For what?"

"I came down here to visit some of my peeps that live on State

Fair, and Po-Po started trippin', sayin' I was there to buy drugs. Plus my license was suspended, so they just impounded my shit."

"Sorry. That's fucked up."

"It's no biggie. I'm getting it out as soon as my parents give me the money. The good thing about it is having my car cleaned out for free."

"You mean...they stripped it looking for dope."

"Joey, I'm a glass half-full kind of girl. You think you can you roll with that?"

"Rolling is fine. It's what I do best."

I convinced Amy to come back to my Royal Oak condo, or maybe she just let me think I did. We talked on my couch for a few minutes and then hit the sack. I was doggy-styling her when she yanked her hair out of my hand and turned over on her side.

"Joey, stop it," she whispered.

"Why? What's wrong?"

"You're having angry sex."

"Angry...sex?"

"You're too angry. It hurts. It doesn't feel good."

"I'm not angry, I'm just...fucking."

"I don't want to be fucked; I want you to know I'm here."

"Okay. I'll be gentle."

I would've said anything to finish my nut. I was so close...and this silly bitch made me start over again. Now I REALLY was angry. And though I smiled lovingly as I doggy-styled her...ever so gently...I knew it was the last time I would ever see this freckle-faced twat again. And I thought about Jana as I came. Angrily.

04July2003: What does it mean to want a young piece of Japanese cunt so bad that you'd pull the tampon out her snatch yourself, before fucking her into semi-consciousness? What kind of depraved man would do that?

I slid out of Michiko and sat on the edge of her king-sized bed, smelling of young college girl, and trying to make out shapes in the dark. Closet...bedpost...candle jar...pants...bedroom door.

I stumbled to her bathroom to ho-wash, tripping over something twice, before blinding myself with the efficient cheapness of her apartment lighting. As my eyes adjusted, I made out my father's face in the bathroom mirror.

18July2003: No real reason to be in our field office on a Friday. I should have been on a Metro Park beach. I just wanted to snoop around; rumor had it that GM was going to promote me. A GM rumor has the same validity as a real world fact.

Lisa, the icy uber-bitch of an office administrator, barely glanced at me as I walked in the office. She was on the phone as usual, drawling out her ironically sexy phone voice. People would sue for false advertising if they could see the wig-wearing, bag lady they were actually jacking off to.

Orlando Ray, the GM Local Market Field Supervisor, peeped out of his office to see who came in. He'd grown a beard since the last time I saw him. It made him look manlier but probably wouldn't do much to dispel the rumors; as I said, a GM rumor holds the same validity as real world fact.

Ray's sexuality was pretty well confirmed for me when I happened by after hours and caught him scarfing down thin crust pizza, while singing along to "Seasons Of Love" from the musical *Rent*. He's stayed out of my way ever since. Information is power.

21July2003: I've been promoted to Senior Field Representative, effective immediately. It's a paper title, though. A reason to justify the ridiculous raise they're giving me because rumor has it I'm jumping ship. They're wrong though; I'm jumping an entire fucking ocean. GM markets are opening up overseas and I want in. Maybe Amsterdam.

"Good luck," Green told me over a few *Captain Morgan* and *Cokes*. "I wish you all the luck you have coming to you."

"You know there's no luck," I said. "And no coincidences."

Green thought I was leaving GM too, but I assured him I knew such a move would be ill-advised. The secrets I knew…they'd be enough to make front-page news for a whole year, if a publication ever had the balls to print them. So leaving at my level would probably be just as rumor has it: hazardous to my good credit as well as my health.

Anyway, I had spent the last seven years learning all their bullshit little rules - a system of control just like all rules - and I learned to bend them to my advantage. So why should I leave? Better just work for GM someplace else - someplace new and different.

I've been avoiding Francis, lately. I'd like to think I'm offended by his preoccupation with teen girls but that's not the case. I'm avoiding Francis because...he's not really a person. My shrink doesn't believe he's real. Is he real? Or just the line I've yet to cross between possible redemption and complete, irrevocable damnation?

25July2003: Was today my birthday? I'm up to 4 milligrams of *Xanax* per day now.

29July2003: I told my shrink about the possibility of a new assignment in South Africa. He said something about people taking their problems with them wherever they go. He's wrong though; my problems are all in the past. I haven't killed anything in so long, it doesn't even seem like it was me that was doing it.

Four milligrams seems to be the best dosage for me but it makes me sleepy as hell. Two days ago, I fell asleep driving and rear-ended a sardine can full of Mexicans. Fucked my new Acura up! Fucking Mexicans...slammed their breaks on a yellow light! Then they swarmed out of the car like roaches, holding their backs and necks in pain, while trying to keep me from fleeing the scene. How could I? My fucking car looked like an accordion!

The cops gave me a *Breathalyzer* test and everything. They're going to let me off with equipment failure. The Mexicans could still do a mini-tort, if they even know what the hell one is, but they don't deserve to. Fucking Mexicans! Who comes to a full stop on a yellow light? I'm lucky I wasn't killed! I can still taste airbag dust. I was tempted to take down their names and ruin their credit, but they're Mexicans. How could their credit be any worse?

11October2003: I really must go to Cape Town, that's the place for me. Sure of it. I don't know why though; I've never been there and I don't speak their language. It could end up being another place I just don't fit in. I've never fit in anywhere, except San Francisco. But I can't go back there yet. I'm not at that point in my therapy.

"How do you think people imagined you seven years ago?" Dr. Irfan asked me.

"Imagined?"

"What do you think people thought of you when they met you?"

"Before GM? Before I started therapy?"

"Right, think back to that time. How do you think others saw you?"

"I'm not really sure...a cute guy who didn't know what he wanted?"

"Can you see what you wanted now?"

"No. It doesn't matter what I wanted before. It's about...what I want now, which is South Africa. Neither does it matter who people saw or who people see. It only matters who I see."

"And who do you see?"

"Myself. Yeah, I see myself. Stop with the trick questions! My IQ is one sixty-seven, you know. It's been tested."

"You keep saying that. Is that important to you? Is it part of who you see yourself as now?"

"I don't know."

"Joey, you have to be honest with yourself or I can't help you. Tell me who you see in the mirror."

"I see...a little pill-popping sex-aholic, in a matching suit and tie, bored with what he does because it has nothing to do with his IQ, and NO connection to him! He's just a clerk...a collector of household data. No wonder my soul left me. I don't want to be me either."

"You have made some positive changes in your life since beginning therapy, right?"

"Yeah, maybe. But maybe not enough. You have no idea the things I've done. And if I tell you, I'll always have to wonder if you can keep your mouth shut. The only secrets are the ones you never tell *anyone*. There's a price you pay for that too, though. Secrets...they rot you from the inside out.

"Sometimes I see people on TV like TD Jakes, warning people about hell. For me, *life* is hell. If I could stay here and make it heaven, I would. I think about becoming a priest. I got the Sacred Heart Seminary on speed dial. See? 313-883-8500. But I never seem to make the call. It's...not my bag. I need to have SEX and plenty of it. Got a pill for that?

"Look, the whole continent of Africa is so messed up, there must be a million different ways I can help over there. Maybe I can even do enough to balance the things out I did over here."

"So...we are back to the bargaining again? You told me your religion only requires you to make an open confession to God and accept him as your personal savior. There are no deeds you can perform to deserve redemption. You cannot bargain your way into heaven."

"I'm not trying to bargain my way into heaven; I'm trying to trade my way out of hell. These pills...they just numb me to the fact that I'm in hell. Hell is real, you know. I've been in it since the day I was born."

"What do I always say? Medication by itself won't help you, Joey. Therapy is the most vital component of mental healthcare."

"Thanks; it's nice to know they have healthcare in hell."

"If you're in hell now, where will you go when you die?"

"What the fuck? You're my shrink, and even *you* think I'm going to hell?"

"I'm just providing you with an apagogical argument: you can't be both in hell *and* going to hell."

"Even hell has its own hell, Doc. Don't you know that? What are you, Hindu? From India, right?"

"I'm from Pakistan. A Muslim, as I have told you before."

"Right. Whatever, you know what I mean right? Don't Muslims have a hell?"

"Yes, we also believe in hell."

"Everybody believes in hell. That's funny. Everybody believes in hell, but nobody listens to God."

28October2003: I'm in Lexington. I just ate some kind of hotel food. It was a crapshoot, but it was too late to go to the supermarket. I have an install in the morning and a C-2 fault in the afternoon. Afterwards, I'll fly to Pittsburgh for a meeting where they'll try talking me out of wanting the South Africa Expansion Project. The mainframe is already online over there; the whole operation should be up and running by November. For their sake, I'd better be over there up and running with it.

01December2003: I'm being promoted to Field Supervisor, effective January 2nd, per a congratulatory e-mail from Owen Nelson himself. And the greedy bastard misspelled *congratulations.* I'm going to be put in charge of the SAEP – the South African Expansion Project. I'll be trained for it over the next three months and then fly over there.

African pussy. I wonder what that's going to be like. I wonder if it has, like...little teeth.

Chapter 14

We drove along without talking for perhaps an hour. I wondered what time it was. I felt no more than two or three hours had passed so it was still probably Saturday, February 5th, around ten or eleven at night. I slapped my thigh, upset at how easy it would have been to bring some malaria pills with me from Michigan. Maybe that was all Joey needed.

"What's wrong?" Bush asked.

"Just thinking…how stupid it was of me to come to this country without malaria pills."

"Don't beat yourself up over it. I don't have malaria pills, even though there's a pharmacy right down the street from my office. Trust me, if you had them, Joey wouldn't take them anyway. Neither would his followers let you give them to him. He's got this Xhosa woman, Namhla, who sees to him with a homemade remedy of garlic, olive oil, and beetroot. That's all he eats – that and yohimbe bark. He can still put away his beer though. Yeah, he drinks a lot.

"It's no good worrying over malaria pills; you can actually grow immune to it if you live through it. But there are a million things in the desert that could be killing Joey. We've discussed AIDS, syphilis, malaria, dysentery, poor diet…did I mention ink poisoning?"

I didn't answer.

"Yeah, he could have blood poisoning from printing dyes and inks; they use mostly newspaper for toilet tissue out there."

We drove another twenty minutes without speaking then pulled off down a dirt road; pebbles rumbled beneath the bakkie's tires. Bush drove a little further then shut the bakkie off. He yanked the blindfold from my eyes. I squinted and rubbed them, adjusting to the night. The buildings had all disappeared, replaced by hills and sparse foliage. Our path was obscured on both sides by thistle bushes. Bush blinked the headlights twice and turned on the interior lights.

"This may be the last time we meet, Secret Agent Luna."

"Then it's come to Jesus time," I said. "If you give a damn about him at all, tell me something that can help him."

Bush lit a *Stuyvesant* cigarette and exhaled it slowly; looking like Sammy Gravano, ready to turn Fed. "I think Joey miscalculated. Although the money is nothing to GM, they still don't seem willing to let the matter go. The homing device they gave you is sufficient evidence of that.

"If the cure works, it's a PR goldmine; if it doesn't, it's a tax write off. So what do they care? What more could they want? The mainframe? He really does plan to restore it."

I recalled my first conversation with Nelson last week…all his anger, his rage. "I'm beginning to get it now. Damn, it was so obvious! Nelson doesn't care about the money. It's pride! It's about saving face. This thing between him and Joey...it's personal."

"And Nelson knew you would lead him to Joey. Somehow, he knew Joey wouldn't hide from you or have you killed. Hell, he had you escorted right to him. It's a set-up, don't you see? You're nothing more than bait. You're like a fake rabbit on a rail used to guide racing dogs around the track. They're going to kill him. Soon, they'll be swarming this place like-"

Just then, there was a knock at the car window. Men were standing on each side of the car, armed with assault rifles. In the dark and with the dome light on, we didn't see them approach. Bush turned off the dome and headlights, opened his door, and motioned for me to get out.

"She's safe; I frisked her myself," he said to the man near his door.

The man nearest me waved a security wand up and down my body, while spot-checking me with his free hand. These men were so dark! I had never seen anyone this black before! In the darkness, the wooden stocks of the *AK-47s* slung over their shoulders were more visible than they were.

Bush reopened his driver's side door. "Well, give the man my best! Gotta run!"

"Sorry Bush, he wants to see you too," said his guard.

Bush blanched, becoming agitated. "Lindiwe I…I can't just leave the truck here in the…in the desert!"

"Yes, you can." said Lindiwe. "You have to. Sorry."

Bush jumped quickly into the bakkie, closing the door. Lindiwe smashed the driver's side window with the butt of his rifle, cocked it, and placed it at Bush's temple. Bush shrank down in his seat, cowering, arms raised. The man near me stepped back and placed the barrel of his *AK* in my stomach.

"Bush!" I screamed, raising my arms.

"It's okay! I'm just getting the keys. Everyone just…calm the fuck down!" Bush yelled frantically. He took the keys from the ignition, got out of the Land Rover, and nervously extended the keys toward Lindiwe.

"Forget the keys," said Lindiwe, taking the keys and tossing them back through the smashed window. "Don't worry Bush; who is around to steal it? And where would they go without petrol, brother? Don't get this lekker lady killed for nothing." Lindiwe laughed as he pointed Bush toward the front of the bakkie. The man next to me slowly lowered his rifle, neither laughing nor smiling.

We were herded together, patted down once more, and made to walk in front of the armed men. In which direction, I couldn't tell. No one spoke. Bush lit another cigarette, after which, Lindiwe took the lighter and chucked it into the roadside brush.

We made our first turn at about one hundred sixty-seven paces. From there, we walked a little further on through some thick brush until we suddenly stopped. I could hear voices and saw a huge bonfire in the distance. There was nothing else to see but pitch black.

"Welcome to Tulaniville," Bush said. "Welcome to hell on Earth."

***

04December2003: I had a skinny Black girl over today. She claimed to be "born again." She was young (maybe twenty), with snake-ashy skin. I've already forgotten her name. I met her at *Starbucks*. I finished the stale martini on my nightstand and then we fucked. She had a bush that looked like a *Brillo* pad. I thought about using her pubes to scrub the bottoms of my pots and pans. I haven't seen hair that kinky since *Buckwheat*.

She had absolutely no suck technique and wouldn't take it from behind – not even doggy. I found no redeeming qualities in her...other than her availability, and that she only cost a cup of coffee.

07December2003: I was in Birmingham last night, at this Chinese chick's condo. The whole thing was about as small as my living room but the neighborhood was nice. The chick's name was Eva. I met her at Dino's in Ferndale while I was having a martini with Francis. Yeah, I know...but Francis is like the pied piper. I try to avoid him but the world he lives in is too difficult to resist. I'm probably damned anyway. It's not like God can give me double eternity, can he? But I digress...

Eva is pushing forty – a separated mother of two who has no intention of divorcing her husband or his money. "Sometimes," she said, "I just need a good fucking." I liked her drunken honesty but her condo was freezing! Was this broad Chinese or an Eskimo?

Eva spent our first half an hour together on the phone with her neighbor, and then put *me* on the phone with her. I didn't know where that was going...but I ordered Chinese, and that's all I expected to get.

Eva's a hot looking chick with clothes on, but once we were in bed, I discovered she had absolutely no ass, and sagging, uneven tits that looked like her kids used them for slingshots. She was also difficult to kiss because she had these sharp little smoker's teeth and (worst of all) dieter's breath – the kind of breath that comes from fucking starving yourself to look like someone's idea of beautiful.

She was also on the rag so I settled for a blowjob, which turned out to be more of a bitejob. It was worse than virginal. I'm trying to think...yes! That was the worst blowjob I ever fucking had! She perforated my penis with her *Ginsu*-like teeth. I ended up having to jack myself off and then place her mouth back on my exploding cock.

To ad insult to injury (literally), she refused to swallow. Listening to her spit me out in the bathroom sink was about as sexy as watching a bat vomit. I'm better off with the fat girls; at least they aim to please. I left soon after that. Two hours later I was still horny.

13January2004: Meeting Francis tonight for a goodbye drink.

I have to go back to NYC and then get ready to move overseas. Leaving the country in April.

14January2004: Last night was...the most amazing sexual experience I've had since San Francisco. I just walked Lisa to my front door. I can even remember the broad's name!

I met her last night at Gracie's, while meeting with Francis. Beautiful blonde hair, dancer's legs, Black girl's ass...we fucked outside in the alley, then came back to my place and fucked most of the night. I REALLY needed that. All my cards lately had been ugly eights.

I can still smell her. Lisa Rosatti...again with the Italians. What fabulous fuck-machines!

17March2004: It's about 11 p.m. and I'm...fucking PISSED off! Francis has just ruined my night and I'm almost certain we'll never meet again. It's a testament to *Xanax* that I'm not spending the night in jail.

I had flown back from NYC just to spend St. Patrick's Day with him. He said he had a surprise for me. The surprise was his chick; Francis was getting married. He acted all weird around her, censoring the conversation. He didn't seem himself; at least I never saw this side of him. But everything was still cool, until he and I got in an argument over the Simpson verdict.

I said The Juice should have been presumed innocent. Francis thought he was obviously guilty.

"Where there's smoke, there's fire," he said. Was I drinking with a racist or *Smokey The Bear*?

"He's got a history of this kind of stuff," Francis said. "He got off before. Now it's twice? He should be put *under* the jail!"

"Everyone's done bad shit before; it's just not spilled all over the evening news! You smoked crack before; does that make you a drug addict?"

"No," he said quietly. But I guess underneath he was seething. His chick excused herself to the bathroom.

"Maybe you can kick my ass or maybe not," he said, "but if you ever talk about my past in front of my old lady again, you and me are gonna fight!"

"What past? We just got high two months ago."

"No, fuck you! You're wrong for that!"

At that moment, I realized I didn't really know Francis at all.

I didn't even know he had a girlfriend. Eight months he's been hiding this dame from me while fucking everything east of the sun. He had only let me so far into his life, a life he was about to share forever with someone else. He had kept me at a distance, like two guys on the same team of a bowling league. We met once a week, played some games, and then went our separate ways.

We weren't ever really pals; we were plastic men. Two plastic men, in a thousand plastic bars, in a plastic fucking world. I drained my martini, put on my coat and walked out.

"Fuck you!" Francis yelled at the back of my coat. "Fuck you!"

02April2004: I'm flying over New England now, headed for Amsterdam and then Cape Town. My phone just rang. Now that's great cellular service! I let it go to voicemail when I saw the number. It was Francis, probably calling me from his bachelor party in Vegas. Best of luck pal; The Sands is all yours.

When I'm not looking out the window, I'm reading *Meditations* by Marcus Aurelius – the Philosopher Emperor of Rome. He kept a written journal about himself most of his life. Probably history's very first blog. Maybe I should write one; teach people how to sin on a budget.

23May2004: I made a mistake by moving to Goodwood. I'm in the wrong time/space location. I should move downtown, right into the heart of Cape Town, but maybe that's just as bad. I was eating down there at a restaurant on Long Street once and a cockroach crawled onto my *Coke* can. They wanted to charge me when I asked for another one. "Was it in the *Coke*, or just on it?" the dumb bitch asked.

People downtown are just as insensitive as they are in Goodwood. There are still homeless children, sniffing glue out of bags. Cars still try to run you down as you cross the street. It's not like they want to deliberately, it's just...they don't care. They don't care if you suddenly drop dead in the street, as long as you're not blocking their lane.

Goodwood...there's nothing good about it. The parks are blighted fields of grass. The library is an imaginary beachfront where drunks pass out after a long day of rummaging through other people's trash. The sidewalks are a citywide connect-the-dots of discarded gum and dried phlegm. The days are a haze of heat and car horns, blowing outside of discordantly painted pastel stucco walls and sporadic razor wire. The stifling, noise-polluted days are followed by the more humid, more dangerous nights.

My lovers are loveless. A string of one-night stands and psychic vampires that would rather rob me as I sleep than stay with me in my palace of fleas, in my quiet solitude, during the mosquito hours.

"These people are all uncivilized," says Yvonne, my elderly Dutch neighbor. "They're not like us," she says, running her fingers through dyed brown hair while clutching her pink robe closed with the other hand, almost like a dare.

12June2004: It's about six o'clock. I'm at The Purple Turtle, waiting for the Rune Man to come. I met him here last night and since then, I've thought of little else. The Rune Man, whose real name I don't yet know, writes symbols in a leather-bound notebook and on *Popsicle* sticks. Sometimes he uses the sticks as templates, tracing them into the notebook. What does it all mean?

By the way, I'm smoking a lot of dagga (weed) lately because I'm completely out of *Xanax*. Why else would I be waiting for some nutcase who wears a tattered sports jacket, pissy pants and no shoes?

13June2004: I'm late to several meetings as I pen my account of last eve. The Rune Man never showed, but while waiting for him with the deejay, Lucky, I met the most beautiful woman ever born of man.

"Joey says he's got some Red Beard," Trevor told Lucky (Trevor looks like Bob Denver). Trevor and I were discussing dagga earlier and now Lucky and his crew were staring at me like I was lunch because Trevor said I had some good shit.

"No! That's not...what...I said!" My response came out slowly, like frozen honey, because I had been high for so long. "Benjamin One offered me a choice of two baggies...one small and one large... both for the same price. I took the bigger bag...and that has made all the difference." No one got the pun. The pun was lost on everyone.

"You like Frost? Robert Frost?" I asked Lucky.

"I like records. Old vinyl. You must send me back some vinyl from the States, okay?"

"Yebo," I said. I've been picking up some different phrases. Yebo is Swahili for yes. It may come from 'yes boss'.

"Sharp, sharp," Lucky answered.

"Have you seen the Rune Man?" I asked. "The crazy guy who writes on *Popsicle* sticks?"

"Rune Man," he laughed. "Is that what you call him?"

"Yeah. What else should I call him? I don't know his fucking name."

"His name's Bevan. He was formerly a doctor from the Eastern Cape."

"Bullshit! That nutty bastard? He's a homeless bum."

"Ne man. Some lost people chose to be lost. He'll most probably be here later."

"What about that other guy, the American reporter from last night?"

"Mr. Bush? He comes here...I would say...about every night. Just be patient, me broer." So I got high and waited, because Lucky was right: sooner or later, everyone came to The Purple Turtle.

6:30 p.m., and still no sign of the Rune Man. I had taken a few phone calls from team members being shaken down for dough by local politicos. "Pay them," I'd say, "and get a signed receipt. No receipt, no pay."

Meanwhile, I'm just sitting here, sipping at my *Castle* beer, writing on my laptop/flash drive, and watching all the people gather around Lucky. People didn't gravitate to him just for his dagga; both Benjamin One and Two had socks full of dagga, but even *they* orbited around Lucky. Lucky was just one of those people – a hub that connected people of different destinations together. He was like Amsterdam; no matter where you were flying to in Europe, you always passed through Amsterdam.

But why was he a hub? He's tall and of good posture, with good islander skin tone and a sharp nose – perhaps with a bloodline from New Zealand. He wears his hair in a short ponytail with waves of gray over black, like the foam on a wavy sea. Lucky is always clean-shaven and has all his teeth – a rarity here, as most of the young Coloureds and Blacks I interview have knocked out their four top-front teeth as a fashion statement, or in some form of tribal pride.

One married homeowner told me it makes for better kissing. I think she meant sucking. Her kissing was very good though. She also gave me an excellent hand job before going back to cleaning her fish for dinner. My pants and hands smelled like Hake fish for the rest of the day, which I spent fending off flies, dogs, and fleas.

I was still too high to stand up and suddenly realized I was in the middle of a conversation with a Xhosa man named...Voox? We were talking about the difference between the raunchy camaraderie here at The Purple Turtle, versus the baroque elegance of M Bar, located inside the Metropole – the hotel I just moved into (anything was better than Goodwood). I was trying to explain M Bar's overt symbolism of Heaven and Hell, achieved by designing a pristine white dining room adjacent to a bar with red lighting and faux-reptilian skin furniture, when Voox cut me off.

"They need to make a bar down here for the brothers. Somewhere that the brothers can feel comfortable, you know?"

He's right. This is their country, but there are very few places that cater to them. Xhosa bars are always immediately identifiable. They're located in places Whites wouldn't want to go to, and they ALWAYS have a *Coca-Cola* signboard hanging over the entrance.

In town, Xhosa people always have to compromise. To get service jobs, they have to wear nametags adopting Christian names like James and Brenda because Whites can't flip their tongues to click the Xhosa names. It's insane but Blacks never complain. They just play the game.

"You're right," I said to Voox, shaking his hand, which was like placing my hand in a vice. Voox was tall, bald, and built. He probably eats more in a day than I had since I landed here.

"How would you like a job, Voox?" I slurred.

"What kind of job?"

"Knocking the world on its fucking ass."

"Seriously, brother."

"Seriously? Driving me around through the townships, translating for me while I gather information."

"That kind of job is dangerous. Asking questions here can get you killed."

"I know that; that's why I'm hiring you."

"For how long? How much does it pay?"

"Well, Voox...I'm really thinking of scoring some ass right now. Talking business will fuck up my chi. But come to the Metropole in the morning and have them ring Mr. Bosco's room; that's me. I'm somewhere on the second floor. Uh, Voox...by morning, I mean twelve-ish."

Voox thanked me and left to catch his train back to Khayelitsha. Lucky and his entourage were long gone also. Half the town shuts down when the trains and taxis stop running at eight p.m.

I finished my beer and went inside to see who was left in the bar, which would only be those people who had a car or lived within walking distance. I passed Trevor inside the bar and noticed, sitting next to him, the unclaimed Coloured daughter of Sophia Loren.

She was dressed in all pink with a cream colored jacket. Even her eye shadow was pink. She raised her half-finished wine glass to me and said "Cheers." Trevor introduced us but I didn't catch the name. All I heard was Aerosmith singing "Pink".

I sat down next to her, staring at the purple table to keep from staring at her.

"You like women don't you?" she asked.

"Exclusively."

"I know; I've seen you around town before. Every time I see you, you're with a different woman. Do you always need so many?"

"Who told you that? It's a gross exaggeration. Actually, I don't need any."

She laughed softly and took a sip from her glass, maybe a chardonnay. "And why do you *want* so many?"

"Right now, I just want one. Hey, do you have a quarter?"

"A quarter? Ya, you need one?"

"Yeah, I want to call my mother and tell her I just met the girl of my dreams."

Pink clapped sarcastically at my clichéd pick-up line, but smiled as we talked a bit more about South African life for her and American life for me. But the undercurrent of our conversation was inaudible things said with our bodies that only the lonely could hear. Trevor was inexistent.

Pink led me downstairs to the main bar for the privilege of buying her multiple shots of *Jack* and *Frangelico.* Pink took a powder, but stayed gone so long, I wondered what she was powdering.

Achmed, a local moocher, sat down next to me, unconcerned that he had owed me ten rand for weeks now.

"How's it, me broer?" he asked.

"It's lekker, broer. Lekker."

"Brother, loan me some rand, neh?"

"You still owe me ten rand."

"Where's your girlfriend?"

"She went to the bathroom. She might be on the phone."

"She's definitely on something, brother!"

Fuck him. Pink didn't need drugs to be special. Some people come into a room and the temperature drops one below zero. Others walk in and it's summer in July. Pink is like that – a summery kind of chick. She wore summer on her face, in her hair, and on her pink shirt bearing number sixty-eight, covering petite nipples that she periodically rubbed for my benefit upon her return.

"Marry me," I said to her.

"You're full of kaak, Joey."

"Full of cock?"

Pink laughed, running her lithe fingers through my hair. "If you want to marry someone, you have to look at the person first. You have to be friends first, and you have to like the person for who she is. You do everything wrong. You look at the pussy first and that's all you see. Don't confuse love with lust."

"I know the difference."

"You don't know anything. You don't even know why you like foreign girls."

"Enlighten me."

"You like them because they can't fight you back. They can't leave you because they can't speak any English."

"That's not true! They speak English!"

"Yeah, they can say *green card*. You have to be careful; when women see you here, they just see a plane ticket to America."

"Thanks for spending all of my money, getting tipsy, and then ripping my fucking guts out."

"It's true what I'm telling you, Joey. Think about it. There are two million American and British tourists here. All I see you with are Dutch, Afrikaans, Coloured, and Xhosa. Ask yourself why."

"Well what's wrong with your English? Why not keep me all to yourself, spare all those foreigners needless suffering?"

"We'll see, Joey. We'll see."

Pink was soon drunk beyond all comprehension. Being so thin should have facilitated that cheaper and earlier, but I ended up spending over fifty rand on our drinks. As we talked, she leaned in so close to me I could feel the heat and whiskey escaping her pores and became intoxicated by it. We kissed with our tongues, and I swallowed her lips with eager aggression.

A dyke friend of hers came over to us at the bar and cock-blocked me by hugging Pink and talking to her in Afrikaans. Pink left for the ladies room again, shadowed by her dyke friend, but not before the dyke gave me some aggressive advice.

"You shouldn't be making out with her at the bar! She's not in any shape to be doing this with you!"

"What's up with this dyke cock-blocking me?" I asked Achmed. "Did you see that shit?"

"She's not a dyke!" said a burly skinhead next to Achmed.

"Yeah, she's not a dyke," repeated Achmed.

Something told me to be still and quiet. I looked around the bar and noticed it was ninety-nine percent men. The loud music had imperceptibly changed from soul to rock. A band was playing on stage behind me but it seemed all eyes were on me. There were whisperings in foreign tongues...they whispered to each other like circling vultures, communicating by caws and flight patterns... waiting.

I could see it as clear as a map now. The dyke's sexuality was immaterial. Pink's job was to get me drunk and jealous, while the dyke was bait to instigate me into a fight with the skinhead next to Achmed.

Suddenly, everyone here would be related to him somehow and have to jump in. I would be stomped and robbed inside the bar where there were no cameras, and then tossed into the street by bouncers who would say I was the cause.

Being drunk and insulting, I wouldn't be able to deny it. Within one hour, all my credit cards would be maxed out and there would be a dozen people walking around pretending to be me. This moocher Achmed, was he my friend? No...he was the friend of my enemy.

I cashed out at the bar, trying to sober up and think a way out of my inevitable demise, when Pink came back from the bathroom. Pink hugged me while the dyke passed me by and went over to plot with some blokes at the billiard table. I had fucked up bad, and was about to get fucked up...bad.

"Have some more drinks with me," Pink said.

"Yeah bro'. You must stay and drink some more," said Achmed.

"Oh, definitely!" I answered. "But let me go to the ATM and get like...a few hundred rand out, and I'll stay as long as Pink wants me to. But she has to promise to go home with me. Deal?"

"We'll see," Pink said smiling, and finished my drink for me.

Then Trevor and some other asshole came over to collect Pink for their next stop. If she left, it would be my American ass alone in a bar full of drunken Arians, drug addicts, and pseudo-Muslims. I tried inviting myself with Trevor but he said he would be meeting up with friends later and it would be inconvenient. I got the feeling he was more of Pink's pimp than her friend.

I wanted to kill her for keeping me there so long, for trapping me, but there was another part of me that wanted to protect her, guide her back to the virtue she pretended to have. But it wasn't to be; the night's itinerary consisted of Pink getting fucked, and me getting fucked over. We were both fresh meat in our own way, both to be devoured by birds of prey.

"I'll be back in just five minutes, Pink. Can't you wait for me?"

"I can't, Joey," she said, caressing my face. "I'll call you, okay? I'll call you."

"Well then, I'll walk you to the car. It's the gentlemanly thing to do, right?"

Pink smiled, seeming to know I was scrambling for a way out. "Right. That is how a man must treat a woman."

We all began the eternal walk toward the bar door. I held onto Pink's hand like it was a lifejacket, floating me to the surface from a ship that sank while I was sleeping. My body was numb. My heart was a drum. I barely acknowledged it when Achmed grabbed my arm.

"Hey brother, loan me ten rand." Achmed was trying deliberately to separate me from Pink and Trevor.

"I'll give you twenty rand...when I get back." I pried his hand from my arm and continued on with Pink.

A large man backed up into me from somewhere. "Hey! You must learn to watch where you're going!" he yelled. He was a menacing White man with a Nazi Iron Cross tattooed on his arm.

"Sorry", I said jovially, "I'll be right back and buy you your next round."

"Fook uff!" he said in heavy Afrikaans, deliberately trying to provoke me.

But I just kept holding onto Pink's hand and she kept holding onto mine. I slipped my surgical steel pocketknife into my free right hand. I could take at least one with me if they swarmed. That would be good enough.

If I were a betting man, I would say I would *never* have reached the door. Maybe management wanted to get a bit more rand out of me before the buzzards fed off me, or maybe I shook their bait and their hook so well, they didn't know how to respond. But somehow, we were suddenly all out on Long Street.

I closed the backdoor of Trevor's white sedan and said goodbye to Pink, kissing her once through the opened window. The car drove off and I knew I'd never see her again. I'll always believe I should have done something more. I heard footsteps in the street behind me, too many to count and coming steadily. I breathed the humid night air deeply, weighed the option of running, then opened my knife and turned to face the darkness.

It was Voox and two other big men..."I thought it would be better if I started work tonight," he said. "My brothers are looking for work too, but for night work, we charge extra."

"Sure," I said, trembling. "Yeah, night work should be extra."

Voox, Tulani and Mandla began to walk me back to the Metropole as the denizens of The Purple Turtle glared at us from across the street. Friends are like batteries; you sit them somewhere in a drawer and expect they'll perform well when you need them. But you never really know for sure...until you need them. Voox had come through for me good. Real good.

I thought about Pink as I stopped at some camera store and pissed in its doorway while my bodyguards shielded me from CCID cameras. I wondered who was pissing on Pink right now. We parted ways but her aura, her energy, was inescapable.

I walked back to the Metropole like a good company man, thinking if I were really a Spit Baby...if I were really like Old Joe...I would've bashed Trevor's head through his windshield and carried Pink off with me.

But that was last night when I thought those things, and today is another day in paradise. The sun came up red and changed to amber...and the creamy clouds were tinged with pink.

20June2004: Today is my birthday. No one here knows or fucking cares. I don't recognize where I am. It's morning. There's a Michelangelo relief to the left of me, comprising the wall of a bedroom Jacuzzi. I turn my head slowly toward my feet. There are Grecian statues out on a patio in front of a sunken swimming pool, and a beach on the horizon. I turn my head to the right... indentations in a satin pillow from a head that was recently there. Strands of red hair.

Sibyl? Calistoga? Celestine! I remember now. I met her at a V.I.P. club opening last night. She looked like Barbara Streisand

and the old guys were all over her. But she had chosen me, to take back to her Sea Point condo, down by the sea.

Celestine...the Dutch woman who owned that creepy looking restaurant on Wale Street: The Castle. Her husband/business partner had divested his interest as part of their divorce settlement; how amicable. Where was she now...the shower?

I had flashbacks of her playing the piano for me, and then some Gershwin recordings. Afterwards we came upstairs to her soft bed, candles and satin sheets. Her face was beautiful but her breath was old, and her breast wore the incision of a pre-nineties tumor removal. What butchers they were. Lumpectomy; they might as well have taken the whole damn thing.

I tried not to notice the scar; it was easy to do so as she rode me with such energy and youthful vigor that she found herself laughing, delighted in our secret sin, our shared knowledge at what a horny slut this proper Dutch businesswoman was. I must have come at some point; on the nightstand next to me, there's a used condom on a coaster. Well...happy freakin' birthday.

Celestine had gone to make us fresh orange juice, one of those things the elderly do to stay alive. It was sweet of her. Later, I showered in opulence beneath a gold-plated showerhead.

"No wonder Whites never left after the fall of Apartheid. This condo, this area, is beautiful," I said.

"Ya, this is the Western Cape," She said. "In the Eastern Cape, a lot of Whites were butchered by squatters and Zulus. Forced from land they had held for generations. We needed someone like Mandela as our President to teach us how to forgive, how to move on as a country."

"You mean the Amnesty hearings. The Truth Commission?"

"Yes, the Truth Commission. You are learning a lot in your short time here, yes?"

"Did we talk about how long I've been here?"

"We talked a lot last night, as I drank *Frangelico* and you drank scotch."

"Another *Frangelico* dame. And I did all the talking? Don't you hate a guy that won't shut up?"

"No! I especially love a handsome man with a big cock, who spends his birthday with such an old woman. Happy birthday, Joey."

"Thanks, doll. Don't mention it. And you're not that old. Old is for poor people. Not for people who live in palaces, own fancy restaurants, and drive Mercedes convertibles."

"That's nice of you to say, Joey. You have your international license right?"

"No. I keep putting it off 'til tomorrow. I have to get one from the Embassy, but what good will it do? You fuckers drive on the wrong side of the road anyway."

"Come drive me down the street to the beach and you can see how easy it is. And then maybe up to Stellenbosch, the wine country. I'll show you a good birthday. I'll show you a beautiful South Africa you've never seen."

"Sounds like a plan."

"Only...if you don't mind, can it just be the two of us?"

"What?"

"Your friend, Voox, is downstairs listening to music. He seems restless. I think he's ready for you to leave."

"Voox is here?"

"He wouldn't let you come without him. I thought he was going to spend the night in bed with us too," Celestine said, laughing.

"Yeah. I'll take care of it. It'll be a country day, with just us two. But I'll need to stop at home when we drop him off in town. I need a change of clothes."

"Don't worry, we'll just buy some new ones along the way. It's your birthday Joey. Remember it's your birthday."

The day with Celestine was great. She made me remember things I tried hard to forget. How beautiful life is, how wonderful it is to celebrate one's birthday, the smell of wine grapes (Joe used to make his own wine), and the beauty of the country. I even recalled how much fun it was to walk shoeless upon the beach.

Celestine showed me all the good things about South Africa, all the clean things; unfortunately...all the White things. But at the end of the day, I went back to my Black friends and my Black world. How old was I anyway? It didn't matter. I felt certain this would be my last year.

04July2004: Today we saw an animal on the train to Khayelitsha. She was feral-eyed and high, looking out the train windows as if she were caged. Pure ferocity. She seemed like some cornered cat. She was braless and brazen, with erect nipples pointing through a second-hand shirt. Her hair was like the rays of a reddish-black sun.

She was about thirty. She reeked of cheap liquor and cirrhosis. The old White man next to her brought her a *Coke*, which she drank quickly, like she was tossing back aspirin. Our eyes met for a moment. I looked into her but there was no reasoning; there was only the moment. She looked away and the moment passed.

"ILM," I said to Voox. "Do you know what that means? It's Arabic for knowledge. It's mentioned scores of times in the Koran."

"Yes. That's right," he said.

"I'm thinking of having it tattooed on my arm. *I-L-M*; just like that. So when I die, people will know I died searching for truth and knowledge, like the knight in *El Dorado.*"

"Why not have it tattooed in Arabic script?"

"Because no one who needs to see it will be able to pronounce it. If they can pronounce it, then maybe on a subconscious level, the meaning will seep in."

"It does not matter whether or not someone knows what it says."

"But it does, Voox. What good is a message for all mankind, if no one can understand it?"

17August2004: MOUSTEZARU...a name in a dream. What hellish dreams...holding Mother Mary's organs in my hands, all slimy and foul, as she lay there, unconscious and supine. I was looking for something in her splayed bowels. Looking for ova.

I was trying to save us both from future misery. I was in the past, in the locked door of Joe's office. I was looking for the correct tool with which to remove the evil, but the only available tools were sticks, rocks, and twigs.

Then I found the strainer spoon Joe had used to bang that pot of spaghetti down on my head. It was stainless steel and sterile. Mary lay there, insensate, while I removed myself from her loins. Then I dug further...looking for the thing that made her so evil, looking for the tumor that made her Moustezaru...the monster of my dreams.

14September2004: I can't stop thinking about Pink. In all this time, I only heard from her once. She called one day from a payphone and asked for money. I agreed to meet her but the phone went dead and I never heard from her again. I don't know what she means to me or why I care so much.

I'm spending less time working and more time with the Xhosa people in the townships. They have so much love, pride and integrity; it's hard to believe they could ever be thought of as inferior or uncivilized.

There is danger in the shack towns, but no more danger than anyplace else or any major city faced with economic adversity. High instances of poverty and disease, of crime and urban blight, should have been expected when the country declared itself a democracy ten years ago. Its borders were flooded with refugees from every direction. Still, they sojourn on, loving, laughing, and looting.

I read an interesting article in the paper today. It was by that American writer, Bush, whom I'd met once at The Purple Turtle. It was about a doctor who stumbles upon a cure for AIDS, while researching a genetic cure for obesity. When she advanced her theory, she was defamed and discredited. She subsequently died impoverished of an obesity related illness.

It reminded me of that guy...the Rune Man. Lucky said this guy actually worked in genetics. Two professionals...two lives destroyed. Boy, that must be a hectic line of work.

I always heard that AIDS began here, in the cradle of civilization. As the story goes, sometime around nineteen fifty, humans were unwittingly hunting infected bush monkeys and contracted the blood-born HIV pathogen. So if it started here, then maybe it can end here. How much would it cost, I wonder. I should contact that reporter. Maybe he can even help me find the Rune Man.

23September2004: I've noticed two small red lines on both sides of my tongue. It stings to drink lemonade. I need to watch what I eat...and whom I kiss.

In St. George's mall, I passed by a woman sitting on the ground and holding her baby. They do that here; they just plop down wherever they are, like they're on a beach or something. Next to her was a girl of about eleven, huffing glue from a used potato crisp bag.

There are cameras downtown everywhere. They see everything and do nothing. It's like GM, we involve ourselves in people's lives but we only record; we never act. We could be doing something humane, inspiring other big businesses to do the same. Instead, we're building a database of every man, woman and child, living or passing through this country, and selling that "guaranteed confidential" information to the highest bidder.

But how does any of this affect me? What do I care if their crook of a Deputy President, Jacob Zuma, loots the country seven ways from Sunday? Or should I care if the State prescribes a useless natural cure for AIDS, instead of making it a financial priority and a threat to national security? Why should I care about people who conspired to kill me at a bar before I had even unpacked my bags?

We're on our way to Mink's to meet with Bush. Maybe he'll have valid answers, and reasons for me to get involved that I can live with.

03October2004: A lime-green Volkswagen *Golf* just drove by my hotel window. There was a woman sitting in the back of it, profusely bleeding from her back and slumped over the front seat. She was Muslim. She had on one of those long things that cover everything up – a sari or burka.

Oh, here they call an SUV a bakkie, the hood of the car is the bonnet, and the glove compartment is...I forgot. But the trunk is called the boot. I can see that; I can see how the top of something is called a bonnet or hood, and the bottom of a thing is called the boot. These people are Einsteins! But I digress...

I called in sick several hours ago. I shut off my cell phone, disconnected the room phone, and pulled a chair up to the window facing Long Street. I've been sitting here ever since. I got up once to piss and once to let in Voox and Mandla – my brothers who seemed to have no analogous translation for the phrase "downtime."

"You should not stay inside all day," said Voox, "it's not good for you; not good for your head. You must come with us back to the townships."

"Where is Tulani?" I asked.

"He's sick, brother," said Mandla. "You know he has HIV. It's getting bad for him now. You should come see him; it's good for him."

"I swear to tomorrow, but please, not today. There are way too many ghosts in my head. I just need some downtime to think."

"Okay, Joey," said Voox. "We'll go, but you must just be good to yourself, okay brother? Stop blaming yourself for everything.

In Xhosa, we say: There is a ghost in each of us, and if you are kind to him, he'll stay quiet."

They left me soon after and I tried to be nice to my ghost, but there seemed to be more than one in me, and they were set one against the other.

My ghosts showed me things just outside my window...madness! The casualness of violence here, the cheapness of life, were perhaps the result of a people living with too many ghosts. I couldn't see those things if I sat in front of a window in America for a whole year. Across the street from me, a CCTV camera loomed like a Cyclops – watching but doing nothing.

There are too many electronic things here. Too many cars and too much compartmentalization led to a lack of personal responsibility...to cruelty and inhumanity. This used to be a village, then a town; now it's just another city blighted by poverty. No one sees the homeless anymore; they're just potential road kill. People drive like they're in a video game and get points for running them over.

Today, one of the usual alcoholic beggars (I'll have to check the database for his name) sat in the middle of Long Street, blocking traffic with his wheelchair in protest, because he was almost run down earlier. He remained in the street the rest of the day. Not even the police removed him.

At drinking time, some of his mates came and retrieved him. They didn't do it out of kindness; they did it because he was the one that got the monthly pension check. They did it because he was the one who garnered the most sympathy while begging outside of the local Seven-Eleven. Years ago, his legs had been cut off by a train that he was thrown in front of in lieu of debt repayment. Where were the police then? And now?

20October2004: I'm having a recurring dream that never ends. It's like a peep show that I moronically keep pumping dimes into. In the dream, I'm fighting with Joe. It starts with screeching monkeys hanging down from palm trees in an oasis. Then the screen widens, showing that the oasis is in the middle of a desert inhabited by the entire Xhosa nation. Joe is wearing armor of blue steel, and I'm naked.

We begin fighting and it hurts like hell. Joe is killing me. I want to run but it's like wrestling with a rottweiler; if you run, you die.

Meanwhile, the monkeys are screaming and the people are toi-toing. I'm disoriented and scared...then I wake up.

Voox and Mandla took me to a mosque in the Bo-Kaap district, earlier. They said it was the first established mosque in all of South Africa. Afterwards, we drove up to Signal Hill where they surprised me with a present. To refuse the gift would have been an insult to them but I didn't know what it was for.

"Thanks," I said. "That's very thoughtful. Is today a Muslim holiday?"

"No, but we thank God for everyday. The gift is for you, for being fair with us and for being our friend. For being our brother."

In the distance, there was a bonfire and we could hear drumming. Below us was Cape Town, all lit up like Las Vegas. I needed a drink.

The small box they gave me contained a sterling silver rope necklace with a medallion. Something was written on it in their language. I asked Voox what it meant and he said "Man that fell from the sky." An angel. They thought I was an angel. But I was the one that needed my life saved and was grateful they were around.

I thought of the irony of trying so hard and so long to get my family to love me with no results, while these strangers had made me their brother for doing almost nothing.

We sat on the hill away from others, discussing in detail what we only discussed broadly with Bush: where was the best place to make the camp, how would we select the infectees to bring, how many should there be, could Bush live up to his end and track down the Rune Man, and could I live up to my end and come through with the money.

"The inoculation has to work," I said. "There is speculation that two-thirds of all human life will perish before a natural immunity is developed. Subtracting those that will die of wars, famine and Avian Flu, mankind will be left with a post-plague population of... around thirteen percent."

I'm in the middle of something I don't really understand. I thought I started it but it's more like *it* started me. Now it's moving faster and everyone is looking to me for answers. I'm not even sure I know the questions. But I know the name of the place. In honor of Tulani, we will call it Tulaniville. I only hope there is still time to save him.

31October2004: Exchanged my BMW rental for a *Land Cruiser* (the engine light keeps coming on). Today is Halloween but they don't really celebrate that here. The closest thing to it is something they celebrate on November fifth called Guy Fucks Day or something like that. It's in honor of a British traitor that tried to blow up both the king and Parliament. They executed him and now he's burned in effigy as a celebration.

The irony is that the Boers who founded South Africa were once at war with England. So when they celebrate that day here, are they celebrating the fact that he tried to blow up the government, or are they celebrating the fact that he was found, tortured and executed? Before I came here, I thought *I* was a barbarian; there are mosquitoes here with bloodier hands than me.

I remember last Halloween...I had two installs. The first one was in Pontiac, where a woman threw up on the carpeting behind me then left it there and went to sleep. And on her kitchen table, there was a bucket full of meat waste and bones that her family saved, but they had no pets.

The next install was also in Pontiac and was equally disgusting. We installed a family whose television and DVD player were so infested with cockroaches (they like the warmth) we had to take them out on the porch and open them up. It looked like dark-brown waves of water pouring out. Awful. I never saw anything like it.

"Code everything," I told my guys. "I do NOT want to come back here."

But I ended up having to go back anyway...four times within the first two weeks. The family's sixteen-year-old daughter had a crush on me and kept unplugging our shit so I could drive back out there. She had a kid already and an awesome body, but she was still a minor. On the other hand, she was costing me bonus money and weekends off. Finally, I just bought her some McDonald's and fucked her. I never had to go back there again. Like I said...I have ghosts. Who in this world is any better? All have sinned.

I like to imagine God forgave me for my sins, then I died and went to Cape Town. There are parts of it so beautiful, they make me want to cry. Then there are other parts so fucked up, they make me think I got sent to hell by accident. Outward apathy, an unspoken caste system, flea-infested, high-crime public transportation that ends at dark, public defecation and urination, children living on the streets, nepotism and cronyism, basic utilities that work on prepaid cards at per minute rates, the prevalence of long-since curable diseases, and parasitic worms that fall from the cunts of menstruating women and girls...there are two Cape Towns; I have a tear in each eye for both.

Going back home would be just as bad as staying. Corruption is so sophisticated in America that it would take an army of me and an endless supply of money to change it. CIA, FBI...all they tell us are lies. GM has been tied into homeowner phone lines since the 1970s.

Lobbyists control every facet of our government. For twenty years now, automobiles have been privately manufactured that run on used vegetable oil. Willie Nelson *and* his wife drive one. It just doesn't make the front-page. The only news that makes page one is fear.

The first cars, ships and trains ran on steam. Even the first diesel engine was designed to run on vegetable oil but there was no money in it – no stocks to buy or sell and no wells to dig. No countries to invade. The economic system of the entire world would destabilize if we suddenly stopped using petroleum as fuel. None of us are blameless as countries, but we are all to blame as individuals for not controlling those we elect as our controllers. The Holy Bible says all have sinned. And God is watching.

CHAPTER 15

BUSH AND I were goaded further toward the huge bonfire. There was a lot of whispering, like the dull droning of a hive of bees but it was difficult to tell how many voices were there. I could see little points of light, little reflections in the night, flickering and blinking around the fire. As we came closer, I could see…oh my God! Those were eyes! There were hundreds of them. Thousands!

"How many?" I asked "How-"

"Almost two thousand," said Bush.

Others now joined Lindiwe and the silent man goading us. They shoved us forward until we had closed the distance between us and the whispering inhabitants of the informal settlement. We suddenly halted; someone huge was blocking our path. It was a tall, muscular, Black man the size of a building. He was shirtless, and his black skin glistened in the raging fire's glow. The settlers began chanting again and encircled us. There was no escape. They suddenly surged forward grabbing at us. I screamed!

"Stop!" someone said, and everything became silent.

"Let them come, Voox," the voice said again.

I was shaking and my heart was beating wildly, drowning out my ears. But when I heard that voice, relief washed over me because I knew that voice. It was Joey's.

Voox and the settlers parted en mass, clearing the way to the massive bonfire. Lying regally upon mats of animal skins beside the flames was, at long last, the object of my desire.

"Down here, Lisa," Joey said. "Come sit next to me."

I inched toward him and sat. His appearance had changed dramatically. Gone were the thousand dollar suits, replaced by only a tattered, dirty, white robe and a silver necklace that glistened red in the fire. He was thin and ashy-pale but his voice remained unaltered. "I've been expecting you, Lisa," he said, smiling. "I knew they'd send you. I'm glad it was you."

The grimace he managed for a smile gave him a skeletal look, and when the fire suddenly surged, it outlined in great detail all the bones of his head. I looked away and broke down sobbing. It was too late; I had come so far, too late.

"Now, that's not nice," he said softly. "You're crumbling the fragile house of my self-esteem."

"Sorry," I said, still unable to look at him. "I just wasn't prepared for this." I covered my forehead and eyes with one hand, trying to will myself back into control. I never lose control.

"Welcome her!" Joey bellowed. The masses began to run in place, chanting in Xhosa. Drums made from inverted food containers echoed in the night.

"They're toi-toing," said Joey, but I didn't look at him. I stared forward into the flames, listening to the thunderous sounds of the natives running in place and chanting.

Something began to take shape around the fire: two thick Y-shaped metal poles protruded from the ground on two sides of it. Suspended by these poles and running straight through the flames was a long bar with a makeshift crank on the end of it. They had built a man-sized roasting spit.

"I'm sure you have questions," Joey said, "if you can force yourself to look at me." He waved his arms up and down and the toi-toing settlers became quiet, each sitting down in the sandy earth as close to him as they could get. But the one Joey called Voox remained standing behind him, gripping a machete in one hand, while the other hand rested on the butt of a .45, tucked in the waistband of his camouflage fatigues.

The change in him physically seemed almost…impossible! I half-expected Sally Struthers to pop out of the crowd and pose next to him holding an empty rice bowl. Everyone here was in denial…I was sitting next to a dead man.

"What happened to you, Joey?" I asked. "What are you doing here?"

"My part to save the world. Doing whatever I can to tend to these…strange and bitter fruit trees."

"When did you become the world's savior? You're just…a guy from Detroit, sent here to collect statistical data. Now you've lost your damn mind! Look at you…you need help."

"You think because I had a salaried job, and paid taxes, and went to church, and bought a condo…you think that made me human? It made me plastic. THIS makes me human.

"What is GM doing to save the world? Last time I checked, they were the ones helping to fuck it up. To whom much is given, much is asked."

"What can you do that their own government can't do? Why not just donate your salary to research? Why do you need GM's?"

"As I said, to whom much is given, much is asked. As far as leaving it up to the SA government, they don't recognize the full magnitude of this plague, and have a surgeon general who suggests beetroot, garlic, and olive oil as a viable AIDS deterrent. As far as I can tell…it's not really useful for anything but diarrhea."

"So, support UNICEF! Why do YOU have to be here? Why do YOU need to get personally involved?"

"Why does it bother you so much that I care? Millions are dying."

"It doesn't bother me that you care, Joey. It bothers me that it's killing you. What are these people doing for you? Except watching you die? You need a doctor! We need to get out of here!"

"But the body will live on."

"Not in the next world. And not in this world if we don't get you OUT of here. You look like a corpse!"

"The body is not made up of one part but of many. I don't need to be the President of South Africa to help save South Africa. I don't need to be a global pharmaceutical conglomerate, or an info-database warehouse to help save the world. I admit, I'm just one of six billion parts, but does that make me any less important than the other parts? If I admit I am not the brain, the eyes, or the hand, but am the foot, would I not still be an important part of the body? Would my absence not be noticed?

"Robert Kennedy said, 'Few will have the greatness to bend history itself, but each of us can work to change a small portion of events.'"

My head was spinning. His soft voice and piercing eyes seeped lunatic logic into me like ether. I felt disoriented, tired, and helpless. He leaned toward me to speak, touching my hand. The stench was unbearable.

"Remember," he said, "the parts of the body that seem weakest are the most indispensable. And when one part suffers, all the parts suffer with it, even if they are collectively too selfish to conceive it. Mankind is as one body."

Joey reeked of decay, of rotting flesh. The smell overwhelmed me, making it difficult to breathe. I was hyperventilating and on the verge of passing out. I leaned into him desperately but it was like clutching air. I held a man who wasn't there...

I awoke next to the smell of curry sauce; I was back at the Metropole Hotel. It had all been a horrible dream. I sneezed, and a clammy, bony hand wiped my face with a dirty robe-sleeve. Slowly and fearfully I opened my eyes and saw that my nightmare was real.

Turning away, I struggled to sit up. I was lying on a pile of animal skins and Joey was lying next to me. I was in a small room made of corrugated steel walls and a flattened dirt floor. In the center of the room was a small, circular table with an oil lamp. Beneath the lamp was hot food. I recognized rice and smelled the curry.

"How long have I been here?" I asked.

"You passed out about seven hours ago. It's about eight on Sunday morning. That's your breakfast."

I hadn't eaten in a day and my stomach growled defiantly. I crawled over to the table and poured some *Castle Lager* into a metal cup. "Do you have any water?"

"Trust me," he said, "you don't want to drink the water here. I mean, look what happened to me." He laughed but I didn't look back at him. He sounded like Joey and that was enough. I thought if I didn't look, it wouldn't hurt.

Joey leaned back into a corner of the shack, out of the direct light. He stuck his fingers into his matted hair and scratched his scalp. "You know, sooner or later, you'll have to look at me. We've got a lot to talk about and time is...fleeting."

I scarfed down curry and rice as Joey talked.

"You want to know why I'm here? I'm here because someone has to be; someone has to care. The Xhosa people are dying at genocidal rates from a variety of causes, but the common denominator, the central reason for their plight, is the color of their skin. They're dying because they're Black."

In the curry was something that looked and tasted like meat. It was rich, gamey meat but I was too hungry, too scared to ask what it was. There was something there that looked like jelly but tasted like pickles; I even ate that.

"Why are they cut off from overwhelming global support?" Joey continued. "Tourists visit this country and recall it in much the same way children speak of visiting the zoo or the circus; with no regard for the hardships the animals – or in this case the people – endure."

"So, let's go back and tell the world about it," I said between swallows. "Tell them what you're doing about it. Give everyone a chance to help. But…you can't go back looking like you're sick and sounding like you're crazy. You should be over here eating too!"

"Lisa…that's what I had hoped you'd do for me. Go back and tell the world what you saw here, what we did. Tell them…Blacks are people, NOT guinea pigs! Tell them the world went mad first. I just tried to keep up."

I moved away from the table and lay flat on my back, still clutching the bottle of lager. The coolness of the dirt floor was like an ice bath. "I think it's safe to say…you're more than winning the madness race."

Joey began to laugh, but it was drowned in a succession of dry coughs.

"Um…is there any kind of plumbing here?"

He stretched out his arm, pointing to the wall of the shack beyond the table. I looked and saw a white bucket bearing the name *Kikkoman*. Loosely covering it was a cracked plastic toilet seat. On the floor next to it was a stack of newspapers.

"No. No, I have to move my bowels like really bad and I don't feel comfortable doing that in front of you…especially not in a soy sauce bucket!"

"Well…you can go to someone else's shack and use theirs. Do you have any idea how deep we had to auger before we hit the water table? It was about thirty meters; probably because of the drought."

"Joe!"

"Look at me, Lisa. Take a real good look at me, then put things in perspective."

I sat on the bucket, relieving both needs at once and trying to ignore the hollow sound of my waste. What the hell happened to the four star hotel? I broke down whimpering and crying. A Rosatti had lost control. I'd given up everything, maybe even my life and for what? I thought about home, cried for a bit, and then wiped myself with last week's sports section.

I moved back to my beer on the floor and lay down. Joey knocked on the wall and a man quickly opened the shack door. Sunlight came streaming in.

"Namhla," Joey said.

Soon, a tall, caramel-skinned, thick woman with long braids came into the shack. She replaced the white bucket with a similar one, sitting the fouled one outside the door. She knelt beside Joey and felt his forehead. They spoke in Xhosa and she laid him back down, wrapping him in animal skins. She picked up a small bowl from beside the bed, making him drink from it before kissing his forehead and leaving.

"What did she give you?" I asked.

"That beetroot shit I told you about. If I thought it would work, I wouldn't let them give it to me. But they'll be racked with guilt if they think I…expired, while they did nothing to prevent it. This shit tastes worse than death. Bring me some of that beer to wash it down."

I hesitated a moment, then went to him. Beyond the gauntness, the paleness and the stench, I could still see my Joey. I lay down next to him on his bed of skins and gave him beer from the metal cup. I felt guilty about not offering him the bottle. I didn't know what was wrong with him but…I knew I was afraid to catch it.

"How was South Africa, besides having to hunt for me?"

"It was…okay," I answered tentatively. "I think seeing people living in a cemetery is…unusual."

"What's so strange about that? They have no jobs, no way to pay rent, and they need a roof over their heads – a place to plant a flower and call home before they die. Twenty-five percent of the population is HIV positive and will all be dead inside of ten years; building shacks in cemeteries only expedites things."

"That doesn't justify it. No one would stand for that back home."

"What difference does it make what's accepted back home? This is South Africa; all that matters is what people accept here."

I emptied the bottle, and rolled it down to the end of the mat. Joey knocked on the wall again; no sooner had he knocked than a man appeared. They spoke in Xhosa. The man picked up the bottle and cleared the food off the table. He returned a moment later with another bottle of lager and handed it to Joey. They spoke again and he left.

"I found it…not to be what I expected," he said. "I was looking for the great Black Nation. The wise, benevolent, omnipotent, God-fearing proof that Blacks in America were the stolen descendants of kings and queens; a race of people who once comprised the totality of civilization on Earth; who brought the secret of fire and raised the pyramids…but I never found that.

"I found the Coloureds living better than the Blacks – in homes, not in shacks – and the Whites *still* living better than them all, while comprising under twenty percent of the country's total population. Yet, only nine percent of the population speaks English as their first language. So why are Whites still running it, even though Blacks have both freedom and political power? Because they make the trains run on time. Because they give value to the rand."

I was getting used to Joey again. After a few more drinks, I could look him dead in the eyes. Once again, I was falling in love with him, as if I had ever stopped. We treaded softly for a while, avoiding the land mines of his reality, and focusing on things that were light and easy. But we ran out of those things, and the doom of his reality exploded to the forefront. I was sitting with a ghost…I could see all the bones in his head when he smiled. And his eyes, his beautiful dark eyes, were now just empty spaces.

"Not what you were expecting either, was it? Me…this place."

"No," I answered looking down again.

"The things you loved about me are still there, unless you only loved what you saw on the outside. In which case, you never really loved me anyway."

"Don't get all mystical on me."

Joey rolled his head back and laughed. His silver necklace jangled on his visible collarbones. "It's amazing how we found each other again…how circular life is. Like at a certain point, you meet all the people you are ever going to meet. Then you just keep crossing paths with them, over and over again, like people in a supermarket."

Joey leaned in to kiss me and I let him, beer masking the scent of decay. He was the best kisser I'd ever known, not only because he had the softest lips, but also because he kissed me with his soul. I reached over to caress his thigh and he flinched in surprise. He grabbed my hand firmly and flopped it back on my lap.

"What is it? Is it…Pink?"

"What do you know about Pink?"

"I know that your blog says you dated her."

"I will not dignify that with an answer."

"Well, we both know what that means."

"Don't be deceived; I never dated Pink. I admired Pink."

"I thought it was love."

"Who ever loved me? I've never been with a woman who loved me."

"Oh, so you think I flew twenty-one hours just to drink beer and eat curry?"

"Look, we fucked once; that's all. That's not love. If you loved anything, you loved my potential; you loved everything you thought I could be to you. But that's *your* construction; that's not my path, not my destiny."

I didn't speak for a moment. I needed to process that he wasn't coming back with me…that I had wasted a year of my life on an illusion. "Is that how you sleep at night? After you shit on people? You use people only when you need them, when you want to bend them over and fuck them, then you go on about God and your purpose?"

Voox knocked and came in. Joey swatted a mosquito on his ear. Voox glared at me, dropped something on the mat next to Joey, and marched out.

Joey and I sat against the wall and faced the center of the room. I placed my hands on his arm and leaned my head on his shoulder. I needed so much to feel him now, to know he was human again. To know he was my man.

"Did you betray me?" he asked suddenly.

"Joey, I don't work for GM anymore; I gave that up for you. I gave up *everything* for you!"

"Who is Kleinhurst?" he asked. My heart suddenly froze.

***

01November2004: When I touched the thermostat, it dropped one degree. It's 6 a.m. here, and 68 degrees Fahrenheit (20 Celsius). I dreamt I was drowning...choking...on insecticide. I woke to a throat full of phlegm I had to hack out five times. My nose was bleeding. All I wanted was water. It tastes good today, the tap water.

The 1980s...Dead Or Alive...I can't get their gay music out of my head! The music acts back then were so gay. It was like...a requirement. Men wore more makeup than women, and real music died with John Lennon.

Even films back then were a wasteland. I remember using my paper route and Taco Bell money to see them. All I liked in the world were films. Now I recognize them for the colossal waste of time and brainspace they were. They had no morality. No real spirit or sense of character. All they had were shoulder pads and a wide circulation.

Hot in here, now. Fever. Water is good. I see things clearly now, in the quiet. In the first light. I see past the mirage. I see who am, who I was - the '80s itself, without a wide circulation.

12November2004: 8 a.m. and it's already humid. Still no wind; the heat is stifling, blurring the day like a smudged oil painting.

It was AIDS day a few days ago; people threw parties. The government will make any excuse for a holiday. The country is so poor but they always find reasons to give unpaid days off. People need chances to earn money, not more chances to spend it. There's nowhere the poor can go anyway; public transport stops at 3 p.m. on Sundays and holidays.

For several weeks now, I've given up all pleasures of the flesh. No more sex, drugs, cigarettes, dagga or *Xanax*...I've given up sin itself, but maybe it's too late. I'm starting to lose muscle density. Also, a rash that developed on my thigh (side effect of flea spray) has turned into a fungal growth and is spreading to my scrotum. The sores on my tongue are gone but my gums are separating from my teeth. I can fit a whole chicken in the sacs of my gums. I'm developing alopecia and increasingly have diarrhea. No sense in seeing a doctor. No sense in knowing the name of the disease if I'm going to die anyway.

Dr. Kelswitch is coming from Port Elizabeth in a few days, and we're still not sure about the site. We need to make damn sure there's water there. I've also got to write a DOS based virus with quadruple-hex encryption. I need to open a Swiss bank account, find the Rune Man, and figure out how to get selected infectees out to the site. After all that, I need to create an online blog.

17November2004: The meeting with Dr. Kelswitch took place on the promenade at Sea Point. Celestine jogged right past us and didn't recognize me; I've changed that much. I've also become increasingly sensitive to light.

The gulls and the sound of the sea, which assured our privacy, also romanticized our meeting. Liesel Kelswitch was more attractive in person than I had imagined.

"This is very cutting edge information," I said. "A breakthrough in a highly competitive field. How does it feel to know you can work for anyone, anywhere?"

"I don't want to work for anyone at all. I want to continue doing pure research."

"May I ask how you became interested in this field? When did you know this is what you wanted to do?"

She didn't answer for a minute, most likely trying to avoid bringing up the demise of her mother. "I'm sure you can probably guess that what happened to my mother was a big influence on what I'm doing now. I barely knew her; we only shared that final year together, when I was eighteen. It was the first time she had come to see me since a holiday visit when I was eleven."

"I'm sorry."

"My family initially shielded me from the media circus, but as I got older, I was told about her work and her...public crucifixion. Then in her final year, to watch her die like that, broken and humiliated, I felt I wanted to avenge her by continuing her research."

"Bush told me you never met your father until he introduced you, two days ago. How did that meeting go?"

"Everything is fine. Bevan kept Mother's notes in pristine order. So...once you are able to provide funding, we'll be able to begin testing within a matter of months."

"It'll have to be weeks. I expect the money soon. And my expiration not long after that."

"I can begin as soon as I verify my mother's original findings."

"I believe you will verify them. I believe this was all meant to be, and I am honored to have played even a small part."

"Joey...I just want to say thank you. Thank you for finding my father, for helping me clear my mother's name, and for bringing to an end this devastating plague. I wish you would let me help you. It can only be a few causes, and I'm sure we can at least prolong-"

"Prolong the inevitable? No thanks. And you don't owe me any thanks. You had the brains and strength to do this all along, Liesel. All I did was connect the dots and collect the money. Believe me... I'm the one that owes thanks to you, for giving me the opportunity to help."

Later, we flew by helicopter to the piece of desert land we called Tulaniville, in honor of our brother who had passed away two weeks ago; another victim of a grossly ignored but curable disease. We still needed at least one water well, maybe two. No water, no people. We needed to handle that even before the building materials.

After our day together, Kelswitch and I agreed to communicate only through Bush, for the security of the project. Voox brought me back to the Metropole, wrapped me in a blanket, and sat me in front of my window facing Long Street. I'll miss the hyper-hustle and bustle of this city.

Tonight is just as hot and humid as this morning. I want to walk down the street to The Purple Turtle and look for Pink but...I don't want her to see me this way. I look like I should be taking penicillin by the truckload. I'm using *Orajel* for my bleeding/ receding gums. It feels like someone is digging out my front teeth with stitching needles.

27December2004: When I think about how rich this country is...the land and its gold, the diamonds, and mineral deposits...even the streams carry everything needed to create a thousand dollar computer, but they are paid pennies on the dollar. When I think about how mercilessly they are crushed each time they try to rise up, and are then repaid with senseless death instead of pennies, then I want to pay Whites back measure for measure. I want to attack until blood runs like rivers.

But I could never kill enough to balance the scales; never make it right for those who have died or are dying. They are the living dead, waiting for the virus to switch on. So the best revenge is to find a cure, to keep this land Black, and to keep their population growing.

A generation may have to pass away, but as long as Blacks are still living and growing as a people, there is still a good chance they will reclaim their land - legally, from inside the system - because as long as they can survive this genocide, they are the overwhelming 8-2 majority.

I heard a news story once: in India, a farmer's chicken was discovered dead with no apparent cause. Hundreds of thousands of birds were culled to stave off public panic and infection. It feels like the same situation here with the Blacks: identification, isolation, and decimation.

The only difference is the Blacks don't have to be killed all at once. Those in power can just do nothing and let them die off when the virus no longer has use for them as individuals and mutates to AIDS. That way, they can live with themselves but avoid the national insurrection that followed the fall of apartheid.

28December2004: I've packed everything I brought from America back in my suitcase, except for my GM laptop, which is degaussing right now on the nightstand. Everything is prepared for the last entry - tomorrow's entry.

I picked up a crinkled napkin from the desk and wrote a line from a Pope poem on it - a cryptic clue to throw them off the trail before I disappear. Make it seem like suicide. If your enemy is bigger than you, confuse and elude him.

120 Days of Sodom - that's all I'm taking with me. A manuscript lost during the French Revolution. It was found and published over a hundred years later. But this *new* Sodom, this corrupt entity, has only to wait ONE DAY before their story is published.

I'm not afraid of dying anymore. I have earnestly repented and have lived sinless for months. There will be one last sin before I leave this world: theft by extortion. A sin I'll gladly pay for, as it is but one thief taking from another.

GM, Halliburton, and Exxon will not willingly give to definitively cure AIDS, so I'll take. To live without caring is...is a disgrace. If I die now, at least my life had some meaning, some purpose. People here won't soon forget the name Joey Bosco. The curse of generations, a family history of drinking, whoremongering, godlessness, and violence, will all be undone through me.

GM will do a benevolent thing, not at the behest of a messianic lunatic, but because they know it's the right thing to do. Otherwise, I may forget my manners and expose them as an illegal corporate monopoly. One protected by Congress, funded by unethical information peddling, and used by the Department of Defense for covert projects, up to and including the destabilization of entire governments.

I'm tapped into your mainframe, my love, my whore of Babylon. The money will be deposited within 24 hours, or I'll make public the biggest secrets the world has ever known. It'll make the Warren Commission look like a Dr. Seuss book. So either way, I'll see heaven.

CHAPTER 16

TELL ME how you know Kleinhurst," Joey said, tossing a U.S. passport into my lap.

I recognized the name from conversations with Bach and with Nelson, and from Martin's hotel room receipt. But when I opened the passport and examined his photo, I realized...I had been set up all along.

It was the face of the clean-shaven man who sat next to me on my flight back from New York. The same one who had checked Martin out at the Metropole and hijacked my investigation with Bach. He had chased me like Bush said, like a rabbit on a rail, straight to Joey.

"Weren't you going to tell me about Dieter Kleinhurst?"

"Joey, I have no idea what you're talking about. And I don't appreciate your tone!" I threw the passport back in his lap indignantly and leapt to my feet.

"Sit down!" he screeched. I sat down as two men burst into the room. Joey waved them away. He seemed a frightening figure now, in the eerie glow of the oil lamp. Noon's light shot at him crossways from a patchwork of holes and flaws in the shack. "The man works for the same company as you, entered the country the same day as you, and sleeps in the same hotel as you! How can you say you don't know him?"

I didn't answer. He slapped me across the forehead, knocking me backwards, and threw the passport into my face. "Look at it! Do you know what's at stake here? How many are coming? How many are there?"

I was in shock; only my third grade teacher had ever put his hands on me, and Dad had hospitalized him for it. But Dad wasn't here now, and I was being slapped around by the man I had come to rescue; the man I loved. A switch had been flipped.

"Well? Do you know this motherfucker or not?"

"Joey, listen to me. I was set up! I never met Kleinhurst and had no idea he was here. The only time I've ever seen him was on a flight back to Michigan from New York. I didn't know who it was then; I just never made the connection. I'm not you!"

He lay back down on his mat with some effort, exhaling loudly in a series of dry coughs. He smiled and raised his hand toward me. I flinched and moved to block his blow, but he ran his fingers through my hair, caressing my scalp. "I'm sorry," he said, "I overreacted."

Joey called for Voox who came in with some other men. They put dark glasses on him, picked up his cot, and carried him outside to the center of camp. It was hot and dry outside; I remembered Bush welcoming me to hell on Earth. Now I saw Joey looking like a demon…pale skin, dark glasses, and a filthy white robe covering a collection of bones, bones I remembered as packed with pure muscle. But the people around him reached out to touch him like he was a god, shaking tree branches at him and wands of horsehair. Were they blind, or was I part of a cult of death worshipers?

He motioned for me to sit down next to him and they erected a tent around us. Then he spoke to Voox in Xhosa. Voox commanded the crowd, which parted, murmuring, as a naked and bloodied White man was dragged in front of Joey and forced to kneel. His face and genitals were swollen and leaking blood. I had seen my share of beatings growing up, but even I had to look away.

"Lisa?" said the man hoarsely. "Tell him…tell him who I work for. This is his last chance."

It was Kleinhurst and there was nothing I could say to save him. It was ironic that this man who didn't seem to notice me on the plane was now trying to act like we were coworkers. I turned to Joey. "Joey, I swear on my grandmother's grave, I don't know him other than what I've told you. Do you believe me?"

Joey gazed at me emotionlessly behind his glasses and unsmiling face. He turned toward the half-dead Kleinhurst and questioned him. "How many of you are here? Tell me the truth and you'll be immediately released."

"You're crazy, Joe! You're losing your mind. Think back…I'm a technical auditor for GM, you know that!"

"Yes, I remember you. And your cover. And what you really are."

"The company wants to help! No one has charged you with

anything and…and…they paid the ransom yesterday. It should have cleared this morning. Is your bank here or…?"

"You think you can wiggle your way out of this, Kleinhurst? I already know they paid. But since they paid…why are you here? Doesn't make sense, does it?"

"No! Please…call Nelson. Let me explain. I'm just here for the antivirus program for the mainframe! I'm here for the equipment."

"And the small arms found on you? The sniper rifle? The Russian Mafia contact numbers in your cell phone?"

"I was set up! You can't believe them over me! How long have we worked together, Joe? I swear to you, I was only sent for the mainframe antivirus! Ask Lisa!"

"Don't put me in this, you asshole! You used me! All of you did!"

Joey looked down at the ground, shaking his head, and writing words in the sand with his finger. "You've…really put me in a bind here, Kleinhurst. Seriously, had you come tomorrow or maybe just… eight hours from now, I would have spared you."

"Please! Whatever you want! More money?"

"But since your sadistic efficiency has brought you here, it seems fated that you should die here. Efficiently."

"No! I don't even know where I am! Your men picked me up on the main road! Tell me what you want to know! What was the question? We just want to get the mainframe back up! That's the truth! If people are trying to kill you, I don't know anything about it!"

"That's *your* truth. *My* truth is that you work for GM but also take orders from whomever they tell you to, such as the CIA and the State Department. You speak five languages, lying efficiently in all of them, and you tour the world auditing and retrieving company equipment… as a cover. But all that was until you took this assignment; your *final* assignment."

"No!"

"Now you're a key figure in an ongoing global charade...a plot to conceal the existence of genetic disease controls so pharmaceutical conglomerates and medical professionals can continue fleecing the sick like sheep."

"Wait! I know things! I've got dirt on Nelson! On everyone! Even on the Vice President of this country! He's on our payroll! They're coming for you soon! But I have information that can get them to spare you! Do you want it? It's yours!"

"No, Kleinhurst. No one should own information." Joey spoke in Xhosa to Voox who immediately had Kleinhurst dragged to the site of the bonfire/braii pit. As he was dragged, the crowd spat at him and stoned him. He was chained to one of the poles of the spit where he begged for his life, terrified he would be cooked alive.

Again, Voox ushered his men back and forth. The crowd of riotous settlers parted for yet another bloodied man being dragged to Joey's feet. I recognized this man immediately.

"Martin!" I screamed, as his tortured body was forced to its knees.

"Martin?" said Joey. "I'm afraid there's no Martin here. This is Wendile Mfaketah, a multiple-murderer whose prison sentence at Polsmoor was commuted personally by Deputy President Zuma. This was done in exchange for a rather large political donation from GM.

"Wendile, I know you're on GM's payroll, but…do you have any other contacts here? Do you know when the SAPS are coming? Who is your contact with them? Do they know where we are?"

Martin said nothing and just hung his head low; either resigned to his fate, or making his peace with God.

"SPEAK!" Joey shouted. Voox struck Martin in the back of his head with the butt of his .45.

"Speak now or I'll have your balls cut off, cooked, and force-fed back to you! You were hired to drive Ms. Rosatti so you could get close enough to assassinate me. Who was your contact?"

"I don't know anything," Martin said, finally looking up. I noticed then that all of his teeth were missing. His mouth looked like one large, gaping wound. "I was kidnapped in town, at gunpoint yesterday, by your men."

"Don't you miss your wife?"

"It was Kleinhurst. My contact was Kleinhurst."

"And the others? Who else is here?"

"I don't know. I don't know anything. I am not afraid to die, broer! My uncle raped me when I was ten. I was part of a gang and killing people by the time I was twelve. I spent sixteen years in Polsmoor and I'm only thirty-five! So I'm already dead, broer! So if I knew anything else, I would tell you!"

Joey sighed, and dusted the sand from his fingers. "I was so close to heaven. Okay, Voox, give me the gun."

While two men kept Mfaketah kneeling, Voox stepped between him and Joey and put a bullet in his forehead. The settlers began tugging and ripping at his body even before it fell backwards into the dust. Others began cupping the blood that poured like a fountain from what was left of the back of his head.

"Voox, I said give *me* the gun!"

"Yes, Joey, but you pay me to protect you."

"What did I need protection from? The man was bound!"

"Sin. You needed protection from sin. That was between me and God, nothing to do with you."

"These men are not God's children. They're assassins! Think how many lives continue because of their deaths. It's no sin in my heaven to kill such men."

Joey gestured to me and I helped him to his feet. "Now give me the gun," he said to Voox. Joey walked toward Kleinhurst. The crowd parted for him and became silent again.

"Okay! It's true! It's all true!" said Kleinhurst. "You said you would spare me if I told you everything!" Kleinhurst fought desperately to free himself from the chains and from the settlers shoving his face into the blood-speckled sand and charred matter. Joey stopped just behind him, pressing the gun into the back of Kleinhurst's head.

"Please! You'll never be safe! They'll hunt you down! I was sent by GM!"

"I know. So was I."

"But I've told you everything!"

"Kleinhurst, do you know…what a Spit Baby is?"

"Spit Baby? No. No, I don't know."

"It's this."

The gun recoiled too hard, hard for Joey's weakened state. He fell down into the ashes of last night's fire, dropping the gun and clutching his wrist. Settlers scrambled to cup Kleinhurst's spurting blood, then began to remove his chains.

"No!" Joey said. "Not him. Leave him there with me. Cook the other one, but this one stays with me. Until the end."

That's all I heard before I passed out for the second time.

I woke again to the smell of…fried chicken. It was dark now;

no light seeped through the walls. Joey was sleeping next to me, breathing raspy and labored. The lamp on the table had burned out so it was dark inside the shack also. My eyes soon adjusted enough to make out the white bucket across the room. I tried getting up but the pain in my neck was intense. I must have fallen wrong.

Flashbacks of Martin and Kleinhurst and the horrible manner in which they died came back to me like a slow motion film. I sat up straight against the wall and listened to Joey breathing. Outside, I heard chanting. I imagined them around the bonfire, eating. Eating things I didn't want to imagine.

I always had a high tolerance for pain, but this was *severe* pain. I'd fallen off my bike one summer when I was about ten and broke my nose. I went around all day like that. Mom finally took me to the doctor at about three in the morning, when I could no longer sleep because I was choking on my back and couldn't breathe through my nose.

There was a knock at the door and someone came in. The figure walked softly to the table and relit the lamp. It was Bush.

"Bush! Get me out of here! Please!" I whispered.

"Don't worry kid, this will all blow over. If the man wanted you dead, you'd be dead. Voox is securing the perimeter with his men, and making sure we don't have unsuspected surprises. We're having important visitors tonight. Dr. Kelswitch is coming with her staff and the Rune Man; they're going to inoculate everyone here."

"Joey told me he's not taking the shot. He doesn't want to know what's wrong with him. He wants to die."

"I don't know if he necessarily wants to die. It's like those people who won't jump from a burning building. It's not that they want to die, it's just that they're afraid to jump."

"But *he's* the one that's burning the building."

"No, that's GM. They've had this building on a slow burn since nineteen fifty-four."

"What's that they're cooking out there? Is it…is it…chicken or something?"

"You know what it is. Did you happen to see any damn chickens out there? It's rats, and it's Martin. Kleinhurst's corpse is still sitting out there, chained to the spit and gathering flies."

I doubled over on the floor, vomiting. Joey woke up.

"What is it?" he asked. "Bush?"

"Yeah, it's me."

"Is Kelswitch here yet?"

"No. Voox is out there checking around. Everyone else is eating."

"What time is it?"

"I'd say about nine. I don't know; you're the only one here with a watch."

Joey held up his hand to check the time and yelled out in pain. Four men burst into his room. "It's all right," he said. "I must have sprained my wrist earlier."

He called for Namhla, who came and cleaned the floor where I was sick. She said something animated to me in Xhosa, pointed at the bucket across the room and left back out. The breeze from the briefly opened door passed over Joey before reaching me, making me want to vomit again. It was the smell of carnage and unwashed sickness.

His soiled white robe had come loose while he was sleeping, revealing skin that was a collection of ulcers, bites, and excoriations upon dried, wrinkled, sagging leather. He called for a bottle of lager, tidied himself up, and dismissed everyone but me from his shack. He stared at me, glassy-eyed like some deep-sea creature, and silently smiled. I knew then that Joey would never harm me.

"And how is the spy who loved me?" Joey asked.

"Dirty. Disgusted. Afraid."

"What have you to fear? You're not my prisoner. No one forced you to come here. And you'll be leaving soon enough."

"When is that?"

"It's almost over," Joey said, closing his eyes and looking down. He moved over to me slowly, bones popping like hot grease in a skillet, and pulled me back next to him on the skins. Outside, there was a great exclamation of excitement and a man came in to tell Joey that helicopters were coming.

"Just be cool for a few more hours, Lisa," Joey said, "It won't be like today. Things got out of hand. You don't know what's at stake here. I had to make sure no one else was coming. I needed time. You'll see; I'm trying to help. And disgust? You should have been disgusted long ago, working for GM. Didn't you ever care where all that information went? Didn't it matter to you that you were being used?"

"Six months, Joey! I only worked for them six months! And I only worked for them at all to find you! I…I love you."

Joey looked down next to the mat and began scribbling in the dirt with his finger. He was withdrawing from me again. Withdrawing from emotions and from physicality. "I'm only interested in the 'no-matter-what' kind of love. Can you love me…no matter what?"

"Yes! I do that already, Joey. I have since we met. You and I share a special bond. Don't you feel it? Don't give up yet. Please don't."

"Ever wonder why your relationships don't work, Lisa? It's because you don't want them to. You don't want the confines of a successful relationship; being a housewife scares the piss out of you. Can you see yourself…in a minivan?"

"That's not fair."

"We're not talking about fair, we're talking about life. Be honest; the only reason you love me is because you can't have me. The moment I say 'I love you', your desire and respect for me would begin to deteriorate. It's the result of having a father who was never around. You perpetuate the cycle by falling for men who can't possibly stick around."

I kept shaking my head "no", but inside of me, the things he said resonated. I accepted the absurdity of Secret Agent Luna in a minivan. Maybe my world could go on without him, but it wouldn't be the same world. It might even be a better one. Knowing that made me love him even more.

"This is where I'm supposed to be, Lisa. I've been heading to this desert all my life. I've traveled pole to pole…seen everything, good and bad. I've been to places time has forgotten and others places that don't have names. But Tulaniville is where God intended me to be. When I'm done here, I'm going home. My first and only home." Joey erupted in a spasm of dry coughs and quieted them with the bottle of lager.

"They're out there, you know," he continued. "They're out there… somewhere in the dark. Maybe in Cape Town, maybe flying over us now. Eventually, they'll come. Think about what's at risk: we're conducting illegal human trials on genetic alteration. Conclusive results will take years. There's no way to keep Kelswitch safe – to keep these people safe – unless absolutely no outsiders know about it.

"Killing those scum bought us time. With the influence that pharmaceutical giants hold over this continent, they could hijack the experiment, blacklist it, or have everyone involved with it blown off the map. And GM could ensure the media never reported it."

"But Joey, killing is wrong. I've been running from that world my whole life. I thought you were different. Remember 'vengeance is mine sayeth the Lord'?"

"In this place, I am God's vengeance."

At the end of the lager bottle, Joey mumbled for me to pass him the bucket. He propped himself up on his forearm, held the bucket angled with one hand and urinated into it with the other, wincing from his bad wrist.

He called for another bottle but this time he couldn't hold it up. He was weakening dramatically. Placing his head in my lap, I poured lager into him. I could hear it work its way down into his stomach. It was like pouring beer into an empty glass.

"I'm in love with you, Joey," I said.

"You're not in love, you're just…brainwashed. I seduced you with my suffering. There's nothing special about me. I'm the same as you; I fear the same things you fear."

"Then fear death. Let Kelswitch help you."

"Perfect love casteth out fear," he said with finality, turning on his side and closing his eyes.

When the helicopters finally came, it sounded like the end of the world. They flew low to the ground – three surplus *Hueys* bearing United Nations insignia. Two were filled with medical equipment; the last was filled with clothing and camping supplies.

By now, Joey had almost no immune system and drinking didn't help. He weaved seamlessly in and out of reality. Sometimes his closed eyes rolled side to side, sometimes he coughed up blood and phlegm, and sometimes he just lay still. It was sad; after all his work and planning, he was too ill to watch the inoculation of his own people.

Kelswitch was a burly woman, short and full-figured, but beautiful, with a look of extreme intelligence. Voox brought her inside the shack to see Joey, whom she awakened by patting his hand.

"Hey…Liesel Kelswitch. My hero," Joey said wanly. "How's the Rune Man?"

"He's fine. He's out there working with the people; treating minor ailments. I think he's found his calling. How are you, Mr. Bosco? How are you feeling?" She knelt beside him, checking his pulse and temperature.

"Hey…look at me. Tell me what's on your mind. Tell me quickly!"

"It's the test pool," she said. "There's a problem with the number of Tulaniville people actually eligible for genetic testing. Our inoculation is based on inhibiting gene A-5 – the Killswitch gene – from triggering genetic alterations in T-cells hijacked by the HTLV-III retrovirus. But if any T-cells were altered *prior* to inoculation, the retrovirus within them will continue to mutate, ultimately causing the immunicological disorder know as AIDS.

"This results in accelerated corruption of cell-mediated immune response manifested by increased susceptibility to opportunistic infections. And to certain rare cancers, especially Kaposi's sarcoma."

"Now, try all that in English."

"At this stage in our research, we can only expect to positively cure those infectees whose T-cells have been invaded but not mutated – people who are HIV positive but don't have AIDS. Succinctly, in anyone we inoculate who has been exposed to the virus for more than thirty-six months, we have less than a thirty precent chance of preventing AIDS. It's a sliding scale that drops even further from that point upwards in exposure time."

Joey shook his head sorrowfully and signaled for us to help prop him up against the wall. He was sweating profusely. Bush told me that in this time of year, the temperature in the flatlands could be in excess of one hundred degrees Fahrenheit, even at night. He tried to speak but instead, coughed up globs of phlegm and red-green bile.

"Africa is the root of all mankind," he muttered hoarsely. "If the root can't be saved, what chance has the tree?"

"I'm so sorry, Joey," said Kelswitch. "We've triple checked and re-verified everything. The Killswitch gene is like an egg timer controlling pituitary responses. That's why it was of interest to my mother in her search to cure obesity.

"The Killswitch gene controls the pituitary gland that in turn controls hormone secretion. Changes in hormone secretion are viewed as a threat by the retrovirus because it results in decreased sexual activity, meaning decreased chances of retrovirus replication. The retrovirus, then having no further use for its host, mutates to AIDS, destroying its immune system like pirates scuttling a plundered ship."

Joey drank more lager, regurgitating it all back up. He was thinking, and for the first time, I saw him afraid. "Inoculate them all!"

"But higher incidents of mortality will skew my results! The scientific community won't take them seriously! I might as well have given them the damn beetroot and garlic!"

Joey began hyperventilating. "These are NOT your test subjects! I just gave you ninety-five million dollars! You can start a million test groups!"

Joey turned to his side and began to dry heave. I brushed by Kelswitch and put the bucket beneath him. A group of men rushed in and Voox sent them away. Kelswitch was beginning to sweat.

"I gave you…enough…to start another test group…after I'm gone. Lisa, sit me up."

Voox and I moved to prop Joey up against the shack wall.

"You can start over clean," he said. "First with the theory, then with primates. Wasn't that our plan?"

Kelswitch nodded in agreement.

"Liesel…you're younger than me. There are things your mother found out about the greed and cruelty of people…that I don't want you to know. This test group is secret; I told you that. It can never be published unless the results, either way, are conclusive! If it doesn't work, life goes on for you. In fact, they'll all try to hire you, just to keep you busy on something else.

And if it does work, you'll be saving millions of lives, but costing the conglomerates billions of dollars. If you go public now, they'll kill you before you ever finish testing. And if they are feeling merciful and let you live, you'll be stripped of your license and imprisoned for over seventeen hundred counts of conducting unsanctioned human genetic tests. Plus, they'll have to find some way of involving medicine with your cure…or kill everyone involved before positive results are confirmed."

"Yes," Kelswitch said. "I'm sorry, I just expected my mother's notes to be more advanced."

"Your mother never had time. But you have all the time now, and all the money. In exchange for that, you WILL inoculate everyone! And you WILL keep your mouth shut! Now make me believe you understand that."

"I'm sorry, Joe, you're right. I was just thinking selfishly. We both want the same thing, to save as many lives here as possible. We'll inoculate them all. If everything goes as expected, we can publish the results in about two years. If not, you've left us more than enough to keep trying until we get it right. You have my word on that."

"No, I have Voox's word on that. You get what I'm telling you?"

Kelswitch turned back above her shoulder to see the stiff mountain of a man standing over her, eyes like coal…and no discernable heartbeat.

"Don't worry," Joey said, "life will find a way."

"Joey, you're burning up," I said. His face looked like someone had poured a pitcher of water on it. "Maybe it's time for you to be alone now. You need some rest," I said, looking at Voox and Kelswitch. They began to leave out.

"Voox…(cough)," Joey called out. "Prepare the camp for migration. Distribute the petrol. Make sure everyone is inoculated, brother. It's after midnight. Almost time."

"I'll take care of it."

"You've got four million dollars, Voox. See to anything they need for as long as you can. Use some money to begin voting drives in the townships. Make the government notice them. "

"They'll notice us. I swear to you, brother."

"Then…coordinate the…township assignments with… Kelswitch…" Joey became nauseous and lay back down. Kelswitch came back to his bedside.

"I don't give a damn what you did," she said, "or what anyone else thinks of you. You're a good man, Joey. God won't forget that. If you need anything to help with the pain, let me know." She kissed Joey on his forehead. She and Voox hugged him gently goodbye and then they left, leaving us alone together.

"I'm…faking my own death…just...between us. Getting out

(cough)," he whispered to me as I toweled off his face. "See you at Gracie's. We'll dance all night."

His breathing became labored and thick. Suddenly he was vomiting everywhere but the bucket. I tried wiping it up but only made more of a mess. Joey was right; I wasn't housewife material and never would be. I wasn't Namhla. We lay together in the stink of the shack, on the skins of animals, and in the lurid glow of the oil lamp. When his breathing became too labored, I turned him on his left side, facing me.

He reached up with effort and touched my face, outlining my mouth with his ice-cold finger. His hand dropped limply.

"No!" I hugged him fiercely.

"Hush…it's okay. Just…let me..."

Joey was unconscious again. There was a bustle of activity outside now, like a wasp hive disturbed by a child and preparing for war. Joey came to about half an hour later; babbling incoherently and telling me not touch him. Soaking wet, he crawled out of bed and onto the bucket across the room. He stayed there a while, straining his runny guts out. He wiped himself with the latest edition of the *Vukani* and crawled back toward the bed. He made it as far as the table before passing out again. I called for Namhla.

It was during the hours between late and early. Back home, it was time to wake up for work, but here it was the club closing hours, the fuck-some-stranger hours, and the music was over. I moved his sweaty arm from around my waist and sat up. I stretched my neck, which still felt stiff, and tried to stand up. Suddenly, the shack shook as the helicopters departed into the late night sky. There was no turning back now. Joey Bosco was going to die.

"Stop fucking snoring! And don't touch me!" he yelled hoarsely.

I cradled him in my arms; he was stiff and cold. Part of me felt trapped, which wasn't really fair to say because I wanted to be here, but I didn't really know this Joey. I knew a beautiful man, full of life, with a voice as sweet as temptation – not a talking corpse with a Christ complex.

Bush knocked quietly, came in and sat at the table. He looked at me with pity and shook his head. "The problem with the civilized world," he said, "is they think they're above the diseases that affect the uncivilized. Fines should be handed out to people still dumb enough to have unprotected sex and *everyone* should assume their partner is HIV positive. Otherwise, STDs will continue to adapt and mutate. One day, we'll wake up and have to bury a quarter of the world. Another quarter will die from the resulting contamination of land and water."

"What's going on outside?" I asked.

"They're all packing up to leave, migrating to other informal settlements. Every shack is being doused with petrol. When Joey dies, this place will be blown up like the World Trade Center."

"Why?"

"Didn't you hear him? It's Plan B time; the joint has been compromised. He wants the whole place razed to the ground and the settlers dispersed anonymously into townships. The Tulaniville experiment must be allowed to run its course. Hey! That's a great title for my book: *The Tulaniville Experiment*. It grabs you, doesn't it?"

"Where are they going to go?"

"I haven't seen the list. That's between Voox and Kelswitch. Believe me, the less you know about it, the better."

"Can they find housing that quickly without drawing attention?"

"That's what the fire's for. It's a pretext for the migration. The government will work on the housing while the proper forms are filed and they'll have to live in tents for a while. But they'll be taken care of discreetly for the rest of their lives, if the test doesn't work. If it works, we'll see how long it takes almost two thousand people to run through four million dollars.

"But Voox is in charge of that. As far as I'm concerned, they can do whatever the hell they want with it. I made a deal for fifty grand and the man paid me. He's dying now, so my book's coming to an end, and I'll be leaving. The thing is…I was kind of hoping you'd come with me."

I didn't answer him. I looked down at Joey, stroking his wet, matted head. "This is all too weird. It's all too strange and risky. It's like a cult! I don't see how any of this will work."

"Are you kidding? The man's plan was brilliant! For the past week, certain members of Tulaniville were taken to live at various informal settlements. They set fire to them all. He sent only men with family here, to ensure their loyalty and prompt return. Now, a fire here will be no different than a fire anywhere else.

"It'll be a breeze for the victims of an informal settlement fire – the latest in a rash of them – to take their place in line with all the others squatters who have been promised durable housing, electricity, and indoor plumbing, since the ANC was voted into government ten years ago.

"Right now, there's about one toilet for every twenty shacks in most camps. You know what the lucky few do to get electricity? They modify appliances for use with stolen car batteries."

"You really have gotten to know this place. Are you staying in the country?"

"Hell no! I'm literally running back home. This revolution was a writer's wet dream! I see a Pulitzer! I see *Oprah!* And if it brings GM down in the process, then so be it. You know…it wouldn't hurt to have someone from the inside to corroborate what Joey said. They've paid the ransom, so he won't give me any hard proof. You know anyone with guilt pangs about the global theft of information and the destabilization of third world governments? You could be my *Deep Throat*."

"Is that all you want from me? To be your *Deep Throat*?"

"It's a start," Bush said, blushing. "I know you'll leave with me anyway."

"Why is that?"

"Easy," he said smiling, "I've got the only truck." Then his face became very serious. "When he dies…we go."

Bush got up, walked over to the mats, and leaned over Joey's sleeping face. "Show me a hero," he said, "and I'll write you a tragedy." He shook his head and walked quietly to the shack door. He looked back once more at me and then walked out, closing the door behind him.

The night air that had crept through the opened door caused a coughing quake in Joey that sounded like laughing. He turned beet red like he was choking, so I slapped his back as he spat out dark phlegm into the bucket I leaned next to him.

"I'm…hot," he said weakly.

I opened up his soiled robe enough to sponge off his chest and neck. His body was beyond grotesque; beyond anything remotely human. He smiled at me with filmy, yellowed teeth and cracked lips. "Chinch bugs," he said. "Bed bugs; they're like fleas. Get you yet?"

I fought back the tears and continued sponging him to bring down his temperature.

"How do I look?" he asked.

I didn't answer.

"Look there…my legs," he said, pulling up his robe. "Rat bites. Squatter camp rats…not like rats back home. They're so big, you can put a leash on them and walk them. They're in every refugee village and squatter camp on the continent. They come in the dark…to the young and the dying. They flatten themselves like paper and shimmy through cracks and under doors, drawn to the rotting scent of cuts and wounded skin.

"You'd feel it if a regular rat bit you, so these rats have evolved not to bite. They eat like flies. They vomit out enzyme-laden saliva that breaks down scabs, allowing them to suck blood-juices right out of the wound while you're sleeping. You'd never know it until you've got blood poisoning or rabies or some other kind of infection. Happens all the time."

"Disgusting." I said.

"Why? They're just like Global Media – parasites who take and give nothing back. You just lack perspective. But I have faith in you. So…I'm leaving you the last million dollars. Use it as seed money to establish a grassroots organization. Expose political collusion and civil rights violations by GM. Your job…Secret Agent Luna…is to expose and destroy them."

"How the hell am I supposed to do that?"

"Contact the online news agencies that have been reporting on the blog. Respond to the citizens who have posted comments on the page. Use petitions, marches, and sit-ins to provoke national debate. Bring public pressure and media exposure to bear upon politicians who sold off our civil liberties for more terms in office and offshore accounts.

"Find out the truth…bribe government insiders. Expose illegal wiretapping: it's illegal to eavesdrop on American soil without a court order but GM does it everyday – you know that! They piggyback data collection equipment onto household phone lines to download TV viewing information, as well as live conversations – conversations that are crosschecked for key words, and passed onto the CIA. In exchange, the State Department influences governments worldwide to grant GM data collection contracts.

"There's more dirt than that. It's a mountain of dirt. GM is a white-collar mafia. They've done things that would make La Cosa Nostra blush. A world where they're left unchecked would be...Orwellian. A world without a future."

"Then why don't you stay and help us fight them?"

"Because I gave my word that if they paid, I wouldn't reveal what I know. I also said I'd restore the mainframe here, but when they find Kleinhurst's body, they'll know why I didn't.

"Now, I gave them my word, and the only two things I'm taking from this world with me are my faith and my word. But you and Bush are free to find out more, and free to reveal what you already know. People are ready for the truth. They can handle it. Are you with me?"

"Okay. I'm with you. But it's going to be hard."

"Do it *because* it's hard, Lisa. That means you're doing the right thing. And don't ever forget...it'll be dangerous. Your only protection is the attention of the world press. Voox has a Swiss account number for you. Don't transfer directly to your bank account back home. Withdraw it a little at a time as needed. Keep off their radar."

Joey had begun sweating profusely, so much so that blotches of the affliction ravaging him became visible through his putrid white robe. His burial shroud. His glossy, black eyes rolled back and forth in his reclining head. He bolted upright suddenly and called for the bucket...but it was too late. He soiled his mats and robe with the foulest smelling shit to ever come from anything living. I covered my nose and mouth to keep from vomiting and called for Namhla.

"Old blood and bile," Joey said. "All the evil coming out of me... all my sins. Almost done."

He was cramping and beginning to heave again, so Namhla leaned him over a fresh bucket but they were dry heaves. After a minute, she laid him back against the wall and sat the bucket back beside him. "Sorry," he said. "People who want to live in the desert...shouldn't have intestines. They knot up at will, and rot from the inside out."

After about two hours, another helicopter – I guess the last one – could be heard starting up outside. The shack rumbled, then Kelswitch and the Rune Man came to pay final respects to their benefactor. Kelswitch offered Joey a morphine drip but he cursed it and refused her, calling her *Mother Mary*.

She placed her hand on his distended stomach. "It's kwashiorkor now," she said. "He needs a saline/protein drip, at least."

"No doctors!" Joey gurgled.

Kelswitch and the Rune Man touched him, prayed over him in Afrikaans, said tearful goodbyes to us, and left. I went to the door to see if the helicopters had all gone; they had. The sound was deafening. Part of me wanted to jump on with them but when the courage came, they were already specks in the sky. God had sent Joey one last flying chariot and he refused to take it, but awaited Death's slow carriage with eager anticipation.

Joey became delirious from pain, and anxiety. He called for the bucket again, and threw up rivers of blood. After a while he asked me for more lager. He seemed calmer now, and more lucid, almost like the Joey I used to know. I tried sitting next to him while avoiding his fetid robe, which he refused to give to Namhla when she cleaned him off earlier and took the soiled animal skins. I sat somewhere near his head and stroked it, fingering what was left of his spots of hair. He looked like the victim of a really bad haircut.

"Joey, you look like the victim of a psychotic barber."

"*Sweeney Todd,*" Joey said, laughing.

We both laughed. It seemed like that night on his bed…way back in Royal Oak. My eyes began to tear-up. I kissed his head.

"Watch that…get lice."

"Lice? Are you just now telling me you have LICE?"

"What are lice, really? We're lice. It's all in how you look at it; how you look at the world. There's something about South Africa that changes people who come here. You'll never leave the same, no matter how you were before you got here. You'll think of things differently. The experience *itself* is what changes you."

"And what if someone absolutely can't be changed?"

"Then they'll hate it here because they can't be."

"Well…you've definitely changed."

"You know, I've never seen a lion here."

"Never?" I asked, stroking his sweaty brow with a cold wet towel.

"Nope. Not one. I've never even seen…a giraffe."

I rubbed his swollen stomach while trying to think of something else to say, like keeping him talking might keep him alive. "I think

I quit smoking. Actually, I haven't smoked since I got here. I never really liked it anyway, smelling like smoke. I hate it when it gets in my hair and all over my clothes. I think if I were to smell someone smoking now, it would nauseate me. I don't know how I could ever have smoked for so many years."

"People…who...give up sin…hate to see others…sinning," he said, panting.

I could tell he was ready to hurl again, so I sat him up over the bucket. After a minute or so, the bloodbath came. Joey wretched so hard that he pissed himself.

I laid him back down, wiping his mouth. He was soaking wet and clammy. He gripped my hand faintly and was...crying. "Hey…listen to this! America was…founded on freedom of religion. Then…they killed off all the witches…and the Indians…for not worshipping God."

He began to cackle loudly and insanely, making an effort to crawl off the mats and to the door of the shack. I called for help. Men came and gently laid him back down. I sent them for Namhla.

"Are we…near Thorn...Apple...Valley?" he asked.

"No. Why?"

"Eastern Market…pig trucks…stink so bad…in summer. Smells like…pig's ass…in here."

He began to dry-cough again, so hard it made his eyes tear. Namhla stopped cleaning him and left out crying. Now he seemed afraid, like he wanted to change his mind. He twisted his face inward looking for reason, for peace, and found only death.

Joey began spitting at "ghosts" in the shack and mumbling unintelligibly. His breathing was terribly labored. He opened his eyes wide and shouted, "Close the door!"

"It is closed, Joey."

"And stop shaking…don't…shake the bed."

"What bed? You don't have a bed! You need a doctor. Let us get you out of here, baby."

"No! No…doctors. Fuck him…he had it coming anyway..."

I went to the door and called for more covers, more skins. Namhla quickly brought more skins and heaped them on him, this time not bothering to clean him. She kissed his unconscious lips, touched my shoulder and left out.

Joey came to again, spitting, cursing, and foaming at the mouth. The hollow shrillness of his screaming pierced the night. Just outside the shack's door, Namhla chanted prayers in Xhosa, while crying and tossing dust in her hair.

"Joey," I whispered, "are you awake? I'm not going to let you die on me. You hear me?"

He breathed slowly and rattled for a while, as if he'd swallowed a dog's chew toy or a baby rattle. His pulse was faint. I held his face and whispered in his ear. "Is there…is there anyone I should contact back home?"

"No. Dead to them…long time ago. My fault." He struggled to say something more but it was unintelligible, gurgled through an eruption of phlegm and blood.

I cried hard now. I held his hand to my heart, but he kept pulling it away to wipe my tears. His eyes rolled around to the back of his head and his breathing became quick and shallow.

"Lisa (cough)…why are you crying?"

"I'm not crying."

"Tears…are coming out of your eyes…but you're not crying?"

"Uh huh."

"What…is it then?"

"Nothing. Just water coming out of my eyes."

"Listen…listen. I want you to know…I know you love me."

"Of course I do! I have since I met you. I always will!"

His cracked lips smiled, splitting them even more.

"Do you, Joey? Do you love me?"

Still smiling, his eyes fought to focus on me. "Yes…I…love you…this much!" With all the strength he had left in the world, he threw his arms around my neck and pulled me onto him.

"This much…" he whispered again; then he stopped panting. His chest no longer moved beneath me. I felt the tension in his arms give way as they fell from my neck. Joseph Bosco Junior collapsed back onto the mat of animal skins. Dead.

CHAPTER 17

ABOUT TWENTY men stayed behind as the rest of the seventeen hundred marched somberly toward the main road. Bush and I veered off with a can of petrol toward Martin's Land Rover. Voox had already given me a sealed envelope bearing the number to a million dollar Swiss bank account, and now stood at the center of camp barking orders. Those who remained tipped over the remaining barrels of petrol, making streams in the sand visible by the light of the bonfire.

Then they congregated in the center camp and lit torches in the bonfire, heedless of Kleinhurst's manacled, rotting corpse. They chanted and toi-toied, while I prayed they had done some kind of headcount. I looked back while Bush filled the car, and though I could no longer see the men, I saw several small fires at different ends of the camp.

Bush was driving and I was looking back out the rear window, regretting that we hadn't taken Joey's corpse with us, but accepting that it was final decree, and that I had been outnumbered seventeen hundred to one.

"There are small fires everywhere," I said to Bush, who was peeling out of the brush and back onto the road toward town.

"Better shield your eyes," he said. "Like I told you, it's hell on Earth."

Moments later, Tulaniville had gone up with a big WHUMP! The roofs had actually shot into the air. No one could have survived it. Some shacks blazed together and some exploded one at a time. After the last shack ignited, the entire settlement became a gigantic fireball. The effect caused the Land Rover to vibrate, cracking the rear window. And through it, I could see the firefly-like torches of the great Tulaniville migration snaking slowly in the opposite direction. There would be no evidence that Joey or the Tulaniville experiment ever existed. They had put two full barrels of petrol in his shack.

Surely he had been incinerated. One day, I promised myself, I'd come back and make sure.

Bush was driving in pitch black at speeds above one hundred thirty kilometers per hour. The stereo's clock said it was 3:12 a.m.

"Can you slow down some?" I asked.

"Sorry, I want the next flight out of town. They're gonna blame people for this shit and I don't want to be around for it."

We'd driven hours without a word passing between us before Bush summoned the courage to say something. "Lisa…come back to the States with me."

I didn't answer but it was all I wanted to do, really. I wanted to go home…get away from all the unpleasant things I discovered but didn't fully understand, from mysteries, from the smell of things burning, and from the burning desert, where even angels die.

"What are you going to do with the money?" I asked.

"What I said I would. I can't print the story in my paper here; perhaps even the American press won't touch it. But if I make it into a book and call it fiction, I can evade censorship and litigation. I can get all the truth in under the radar and expose the entire hypocrisy. You could help me you know. We could help each other." Bush looked over at me but I pointed him back to the road. "What are you going to do with your money?"

"Disappear for a while. Come after GM in my own time, in my own way."

"Disappear? What about the people that love you? What about…if I love you?"

"I'd go on," I said. "Maybe we'll see each other again; I don't know. Maybe I'll come to one of your book signings and we'll get coffee afterwards. The world will still go on. You'll meet plenty of whores and tequila. My heart died in the desert."

It was bright and early Monday morning, February 7th, when we neared the city. We both had our passports with us and agreed it would be best to get on the N-2 and head straight for the airport. The odds were fair that GM and both sides of the law would be looking for us in town. I remembered Joey saying that when they came, they would make my death look like an accident. Life was cheap here; the whole country was accident-prone.

I turned toward my window so Bush couldn't see my cry. Rosattis never lose control. I looked out on Voortrekker Road as we drove. We passed the Maitland Cemetery and I glanced over in the direction Bush was looking and saw the shacks of those who lived there among the graves. I imagined them all on fire.

Bush paid for parking at the airport to avoid suspicion and turned off the engine.

"This is our last chance," he said. "I have contacts on national television programmes; we can burn GM from here. A coward dies a thousand deaths!"

"Sorry, Bush. I'm really not at my best now, and maybe not for a long time. I just…I just want to go home."

Bush charged our tickets on his *Visa* card and since we both had our passports, the only question we had to answer was where was our luggage. "Stolen," Bush said. "Right from in front of the hotel. We're *never* coming back here."

There was a little over an hour to wait before we could board our flight so we sat near the airport entrance, seeing who was coming and going. Soon, I fell asleep, and when Bush woke me to board the plane, there was an unanswered question in my head…some unanswered question…what was the question?

We sat in first-class and I had déjà vu. Then I had a martini.

I slept for about nine hours. When I woke up, we were landing in Amsterdam. Bush was still staring at me.

"Sorry," I said. "I didn't sleep at all last night."

"I know. No one did."

I tried to untangle my thoughts and my hair, but my awareness of what was going on was disjointed and superficial. I felt very tense and unsafe. The air in first-class…what was wrong with it? I was so used to the smell of death that filtered air was making me nauseous.

I had seen dead men before, but I never saw anyone rot to death. And breathing the temperature controlled fakeness of this artificial air made me fight to keep from vomiting.

It was just a few hours ago that the man I loved rotted to death in my arms. I sat with him in the heavy darkness, holding that hollow man in my arms…and waiting for him to die. But I had forgotten to ask him a question first. What was it?

"Bush," I said, "I always meant to ask something; the blog's title, what is *Head167*?"

Bush was smiling at me and then suddenly his smile was gone, as if that overwhelming question had violently shaken his memory. He could smell it now too…the squalor…the stench of death. He turned toward the window as the plane landed with two bouncing thuds and a gradual slowing.

Bush kept looking toward the window, and seemed to be wiping his eyes. He didn't turn my way again until it was time to deplane; then I could see he had been crying. He smiled that know-it-all smile of his and undid both of our safety belts. As we stood, he hugged me tightly and said: "Head's dead, Lisa. Head's dead."

END

Printed in the United States
71780LV00002B/103-132